Til Dust Do Us Part

CATIE O'NEILL

CAMO PUBLISHING

For more information, please contact catieoneillauthor@gmail.com

First paperback edition October 2025

Book by Catie O'Neill

Map by Catie O'Neill in Inkarnate

Copy/Line Edited by Juicy Details Romance Editing

Proofread/Formatted by Hope E. Davis

Cover Design by Catie O'Neill

ISBN 979-8-9913858-8-6 (paperback)

ISBN 979-8-9913858-9-3 (ebook)

https://catie1024.wixsite.com/catieoneillauthor

To my mother:
who always told me I must've
been a witch in a past life.
The bitch wanted out.

Author Note Before You Proceed:

Enter at your own risk

This book is darker than my previous books and contains the following:

- Graphic violence (including against children)
- Child loss/graphic death of a child on page
- Sexism/misogyny
- Death/Suicide
- Explicit sexual content
- Foul and sexual language
- Instances of homophobic behavior (not main characters)
- Depiction of discrimination, prejudice and oppression

The Enclave
Witch's Way
Leighis Mansion

Dracht
an Market

Chapter One

Unknown Narrator

They say that nobody is the villain in their own story, but that simply is not true. I *know* I'm the villain. Maybe I've always known it. But now...I merely don't care. I ponder this each morning as I sit on the cliff overlooking Dracht to watch the sunrise. Not many know this, but if you wake up early enough, there are no winds. The overgrown stalks do not sway, the rodents do not scurry, and the trees around me do not bend. It's as if the entire planet is asleep. The truth is not far off. The life force of magical beings has not yet awakened. This close to the full moon, when our powers are the strongest, all the other witches and warlocks are still asleep. They've stayed up too late making mischief to wake up the winds before dawn. But I sit, and I watch, and I plan. I will make them pay.

Hours from now, the most powerful of them will wake within the large chateaus directly below me. Now that I've returned, I'm surprised to find most of them still occupied. They'll scurry around, going about their days, oblivious to the wrath they're about to endure—that they brought upon themselves. These legacy families may have passed down the business of running the estate, but I'm sure the truth of their indiscretions was passed through the generations as well. Apples never fall far from the tree. People don't change. Not even those with wealth and power. Some of them are the worst of all.

The involvement of the middle-class magic users—comfortable in their smaller villas—in the wretched past of Dracht was unclear, but it was one of the reasons I had decided to investigate before my rampage. The humans mostly lived on the east side of town, along the bay and the furthest away from my observation cliff. They didn't know any better and followed orders out of fear. I'll do my best to keep them away from my path of destruction as long as they stay out of my way.

For as long as any of its current residents have been alive, the small hamlet of Dracht was like any other town: quiet, beautiful, and teeming with magic wielders. But that's not what I remember. Unlike the witch trials of other towns, the Dracht Purge was buried in human history. I doubt that I'm the only one who remembers. The stories have been passed down through the legacy families, I'm sure. Each one that remains was part of the great witch hunt, on either end of the violence. Many lost a relative or two, though nobody knows this pain more than me.

From my covert surveillance, the magical beings in Dracht are now welcomed for their talents by those who don't have them. They have also developed a close working relationship with the authorities and infiltrated the local government. Fear has given way to curiosity, greed, and lust...among other things.

Well before the humans came to accept magic, the townsfolk sought out the healers of the Leighis family, though they hid their visits from other humans. But none alive cared to remember their own persecution of witches all those years ago. The witches know the truth, however, for it was the Triumvirate who ordered the Dracht Watch to hunt down witches for sport. All because of a prophecy.

Chapter Two

It's said that when Dracht was first built, the wealthiest magical citizens chose to reside in the westernmost section. Tucked underneath the sparkling cliffs, it was a stunning location for watching the sunset.

"We're almost there, Miss Leighis. Another ten minutes or so," my driver Roth shouted through the coach window between us. "The roads are more crowded than I expected. The return of a Leighis family member is quite the celebration. It's been ages since we had a talented healer among us."

"Perhaps if you hadn't announced my arrival as we entered, we would've been able to pass through easier?"

He peeked through the window at me. "Sorry about that. Leighis Chateau has been abandoned since your Aunt Astrid disappeared—except for Mrs. Yates of course—but this is the most exciting thing that's happened in...well...decades. We thought you'd return long before your twenty-fifth year."

We were travelling at a snail's pace, now that humans, witches, and warlocks had surrounded the vehicle to catch a glimpse. Loud whispers filtered in through the closed windows.

"I wonder if she looks like Astrid."

"Do you think she has her aunt's healing abilities?"

"Her father passed away when she was a child and her mother just passed too. Poor dear is all alone."

"What took her so long to take up her duty as heir?"

How quickly the residents had forgotten about the persecution of Astrid, but the legacy of her healing skills had remained. Though I had no idea how they knew, they were right. Both of my parents were dead, and I was utterly alone. Except for Ranai. I buried my fingers into her soft, thick, midnight fur. It was rare for witches to have large familiars. Having a wolf was an honor.

As the sole heir to the Leighis estate, it was my duty to take over as head of the household, but times had been different when Astrid left. It didn't used to be safe for witches, but from what I had been hearing through the magical grapevine, it was the perfect refuge for magical beings now.

I sighed when we finally stopped. Other coaches had dwindled when we left the crowded streets of the main part of town. I slid the curtain aside to take in the chateau looming in front of me, nestled among a grove of trees that separated it from the previous house. The sun peeked through the only clouds in the sky, shining down on the manor like divine intervention. Like the trip was exactly what fate wanted, that fickle bitch. It was too early for the leaves to change color, but I could taste autumn in the crispness of the air. The birds squawked cheerfully as they fluttered about hunting for bugs. It was their last hurrah before they flew south in a few months.

Unlike the typical clapboard and wooden shingle homes in the area, Leighis Chateau was built from brick, which withstood fire much better. I had inherited that genetic gift as well. Roth opened the door and held out his hand to help me step down. I slid my fingers across the gold-plated moon phase design on the outside of my carriage, then turned my attention to the home. Ivy slithered up the outer façade and clung to the brick like a snake squeezing the life out of a mouse. Stone sills protruded from under each window, and the closest to the door housed a dusty-brown owl. It tilted its head at me before flicking its pointed ears and closing its eyes, unperturbed.

Stopping at the base of the stepped walkway, I closed my eyes to enjoy the nutty aroma from the nearby coffee shop. It had opened the year before in the wealthy area of town, and according to my driver, was quite the novelty. Albeit an expensive and rare one, since it had to be imported from Europe, then transported from Boston to Dracht Bay. After all my years of brewing my own tea and coffee, now we had a shop! How close would the morning market and herbal shops be? Roth caught up to me with my luggage. He avoided getting too close to my wolf, Ranai, but she simply assessed him.

"Everything alright, Miss?"

"Yes, thank you. Just taking in my new home."

He nodded and continued up the stairs. Before he could knock, the door swung open, and a petite and gray-haired woman filled the doorway with her stern aura.

"Put her things upstairs, third room on the left," she said curtly, shrewd eyes following him all the way up the curved staircase. She smiled and gave me a polite nod. "I trust your travels went to plan?"

"They did. Thank you, Mrs. Yates. It was a lengthy trip, though. If you don't mind, I'm going to take a bath and get some rest."

Mrs. Yates was the only member of staff from my great-aunt's time. Her husband had died many years ago, but she kept his last name to honor him and had never remarried. Her official title was housekeeper, but she ran the entire household. From our letter exchange, it sounded like the current staff was made up of herself, a lady's maid named Libby, a butler named William, and Roth.

"Tea and sandwiches will be ready in thirty minutes. I've prepared a room for you, upstairs and the third on the left, as I told the driver. There are other options if it is not to your liking, but it does have a private bath."

"Thank you, Mrs. Yates," I said, hugging her awkwardly. After

I released her, she patted Ranai on the head cautiously. The wolf's tail rarely wagged, but she nudged the housekeeper's hand.

The large, crystal chandelier in the foyer reflected the warm, magical glow all around. The maroon runner led through the center of the entryway, then split off in multiple directions. Staircases swept up both sides. A fire roared underneath the arch they formed, a door on either side. The room was warm and smelled vaguely of baking bread. This home was old, but the housekeeper's magic prevented it from smelling musty.

Paintings lined the walls up the staircases, but each was covered with an old sheet. I was tempted to peek behind one of them to take in the images of my ancestors. Most legacy chateaus were adorned with paintings of the entire lineage. Generational resemblances were common in witch and warlock families, even more so in families like mine where the men were not graced with magical arts. The witch genes were strong in the Leighis line.

The rest of the staff were lined up, but I was so tired that I didn't catch their names. I had already met the driver, but the maid and butler stood tall with their hands clasped in front of them. I nodded politely as I stifled a yawn. Mrs. Yates dismissed them, and I ascended to my room, fingers tracing every delicately carved vine and leaf along the railing.

Libby was unlatching my luggage as I entered the room. She started when my lupine friend entered beside me, her fingers freezing. Her eyes remained glued to the large wolf, while her lips pinched into a tight line. The window was cracked open, letting the end-of-summer air fill the room. Ranai curled up underneath it, grateful for the fresh air.

"Her size is intimidating, but she's friendly to those who are kind to me. Or those who have food." Ranai eyed me, then rested her large head on her paws with a sigh.

"I'll put your dresses and shoes in the wardrobe and undergarments in the dresser while you bathe. Mrs. Yates said you prefer to do the warming yourself, but I've filled the tub. Should I lay out a clean dress for you, Miss?"

"Yes, thank you. Lay out the crimson dress please."

"Of course, Miss," she said, with a curtsy.

As a family of fire wielders, much of the house had been built or modified accordingly, so there was a firepit below the large, clawfoot tub. Calling forth the powers that Hecate blessed me with, I willed it to light and smiled when she answered my call. Simple elemental powers like this didn't cost much, but darker spells that weren't a witch or warlock's specialty were a different story. The price for many of them was steep.

Dropping my dress and undergarments inside the door, I sank down into the large tub and let the hot water replenish my energy and soothe my achy, travel-worn body as the scent of camellia enveloped me. Just as I drifted off, Libby knocked and entered.

"Miss, there is someone important here to see you. Mrs. Yates requests your presence to greet our guest. She asked me to inform you that he is someone she suggests you get acquainted with. He is also *very* handsome." She averted her eyes with a giggle, collected my discarded clothing, and then left the room without my answer.

"So much for relaxing," I whispered to the walls.

Dressed to impress in my finest ankle-length gown, I descended the stairs with Ranai close to my side. Though they were in fashion, I was never one for a hefty skirt. By the third step, William announced my guest, whose back was turned to me as he stood with Mrs. Yates at the bottom.

"Miss Leighis. Chief Constable Michael Sheehan from the Dracht Watch is here to welcome you to town."

A broad-shouldered man in a dark-blue uniform turned to face me. The brass buttons were polished and straining to keep the front closed over his muscular physique. I wondered what he looked like underneath it. He eyed me up and down before removing his black bowler cap and tucking it under his arm, revealing light brown hair that just reached his ears, not a single piece out of place.

When our eyes met, a rejuvenating burst of energy flowed into me. He hurried to the bottom of the staircase to take my hand before I descended the last two. The feeling caught me off guard and I slipped, but his sturdy arms steadied me before I pitched forward. It was as if his energy was feeding directly into me. Like it was making me stronger.

He was a good half of a foot taller than me with a clean-shaven face and midnight-blue eyes, which made his blush stand out as he held my gaze. I guessed he was in his mid-to-late thirties, but he was—as my maid had said—very handsome. The air crackled with the intensity between us until he noticed Ranai, but he didn't back away. Instead, he reached his flat palm out for her to sniff. The little traitor wagged her tail and licked it.

With a smile, he took his hand back from her and held the other out to me. "It's lovely to meet you, Miss Leighis, my name is Constable Sheehan, or Michael if you please."

I gave him my hand and he bent to kiss it. "The pleasure is all mine, Michael, and please call me Anna. Have you come to introduce yourself and welcome me to Dracht, or is there something I can do for you?"

He grinned but raised an eyebrow. Had he been taken aback by my abruptness? That wasn't the way I wanted to start my time here. The Dracht Watch was the human police force, and the chief constable was the highest-ranking member. He was not someone I wanted to offend. He was someone Mrs. Yates had insisted I get close to, and I valued her opinion.

"I'm sorry. My trip here today has been taxing, and I seem to have lost my manners. Would you join me in the sitting room for refreshments?" A small voice in the back of my head didn't want this very attractive man to leave. It seemed Ranai wasn't the only little traitor.

"That's very kind of you, Miss. I'm sure you're exhausted, and I don't want to keep you. I need to get back to work, myself. I just wanted to welcome you to town and to convey on behalf of all the residents how happy we are that you're here. We hope you take up your aunt's legacy as a healer. Unless, of course, your magical talents lay elsewhere. Either way, we are happy to have such a lovely young lady among us, and we are thrilled another legacy family heir has returned." His mouth opened as if to say more, but he snapped it closed.

"Thank you, Constable. I would be happy to help. It's why I am here, in fact. Please, should anyone need me, send them my way." I gave him a warm smile, and his shoulders relaxed.

"I won't take up any more of your time, Miss Leighis. I'm looking forward to seeing you around town." He nodded and returned his hat to his head. Before exiting, he turned back. "Would you care to join me for dinner one evening if you aren't too busy?"

"I would be honored, though perhaps give me some time to settle in?"

"Of course." He nodded once more as William closed the door behind him.

After he left, I let my smile fade and shook my head as Mrs. Yates approached me. "How quickly they forget how they treated Aunt Astrid," I whispered.

"Humans are selfish, my dear. I'm sure you've learned that many times in your young life." Mrs. Yates raised her eyebrows and suppressed a smile. She did enjoy keeping a stony façade. Her emotions were so hard to read. "I wouldn't blame the young man. He has only been chief constable for five years. I doubt he has any knowledge of what it was like then. Besides, he is attractive and kind. You would do well to be seen in town with someone of his station. He will be a valuable friend. Even if he is only human."

I glared at the housekeeper, but then sighed in defeat. He was incredibly attractive and very respectful. Getting closer to him wouldn't be so bad. "I'm not here to find a husband, Mrs. Yates. But maybe you're right."

"It certainly wouldn't hurt your cause. All in due time, dear. Supper is ready. Eat quickly, and we can go into town so you can stock up, meet the shop owners, and collect the dresses you ordered."

After supper, Mrs. Yates left raw mince and a bowl of water for Ranai, who reluctantly stayed behind. Many humans believed our familiars needed to be at our sides for us to keep our magical strength, but it didn't work like that. As long as we were both alive and our connection wasn't magically severed, we could communicate and feel each other through a bond that felt like a string tied to my heart. I could speak to her through our minds, and I could see through her eyes, but she couldn't convey words back. Being apart didn't reduce my other magical abilities either. Her presence did make the humans uneasy though, so she was sitting this one out.

Mrs. Yates and I climbed into the coach for the short trip to Witch's Way. The smell of baking pastries, steaming aromatic teas, and incense seeped through the windows. I leaned back into the cushioned seat and breathed deeply.

"I know we're here to pick up my dresses and stop for healing supplies, but a few treats wouldn't hurt, right?"

"As you wish, Miss. But please, make it quick. You're not the only one who's tired."

I had enough tea supplies at home so I didn't need to stop there. I knocked on the roof to alert my driver to stop outside the bakery instead. A sign hung on two chains, identifying it as "Flur's Fancies." A chime signaled my entry and an elderly woman wearing an apron turned and gave me a smile.

"Ah, you must be the lovely Miss Leighis. Welcome, my dear. Are you looking for anything in particular? Would you like a sample?"

The smells of breads, pastries, cookies, and who knows what else battled for dominance while my eyes scanned the beautifully decorated delicacies in the glass cases lining the small shop.

"I'm afraid you have so many wonderful choices that I cannot decide. Surprise me with whatever you recommend, whatever this will get me," I said, sliding a large bill across the front counter.

"First order is on the house as a welcome, love. I'll put together a box of all my favorites, but make sure to come back and tell me what you think!"

"That's not necessary, but it is a kind offer."

Peering over the display cases at me, she spoke in a low voice as she carefully selected items to place in the box. "Your aunt was a friend of my late mother's. It was a horrible thing that they did to her."

"Indeed, it was. I'm afraid I never got to meet her. Did your mother keep in touch with her after?"

"My mother died thirty years ago. But I grew up hearing all about the Leighis legacy. It's an honor to witness it in the flesh."

Though I was drooling, the anticipation of the surprise kept me from looking as she filled the box with delectable goodies. "Oh, we're going to be fast friends. I'll be here so often that you'll be sick of me."

She chuckled and handed me the box tied in purple twine. "Welcome to Dracht, Miss Leighis. I'm Flur, and I'm looking forward to that."

Since Ranai wasn't in the carriage, I was able to leave my box of goodies on the seat while we made our way to the next stop. The dressmaker was across the cobblestone path from the magical supply store, so I handed Mrs. Yates a few bills to pick up my order while I went to peruse ingredients.

"Magickal Arts and Hearts" was painted on the outside of the store, and the large windows gave you more than a glimpse of the wonders inside. There was no chime as I opened this door, but a very angry customer was berating the store owner.

"The two of you should be ashamed of yourselves. It's one thing to have this kind of relationship behind closed doors, but to be out in public and running a store together—It's disgraceful! You dishonor the reputable warlocks of Dracht," the man shouted, knocking over a display of filled jars.

I narrowed my eyes at the man in the well-tailored suit and peeked back outside. There was an extravagant carriage parked right there, accented in golden swirls. Keeping the door open with one hand, I lit a fireball in the other and tossed it at the back of the carriage. The horses began to whinny and fuss as I crossed the threshold of the store, closing the door behind me.

"Pardon me, sir, but is that your carriage outside?"

He spun on me, his eyes angry. "Yes, not that it's any of your business."

"Oh, I'm sure it's not, I just thought you ought to know it's on fire."

His eyes lit with fear, and he rushed to put out the blaze.

"It's safe now. You can come out." I said, raising my voice. A tabby cat appeared from wherever it had been hiding and began smothering my ankles. A man with short, red hair and a goatee popped his head up from behind the front counter.

Lighting a tiny fireball and tossing it back and forth between my palms playfully, I said, "Serves him right."

He looked concerned for a moment, but then what I had done sank in, and he dusted himself off. "Thank you for that."

"You're welcome. And if I'm correct in what he was angry about, you have nothing to fear from me."

He greeted me with a glowing smile and a cheerful, sing-song voice. "Oh, my Cota must like you! He usually avoids all of our customers! Caltain! We have a guest you're going to want to meet!" He yelled to the back room before hurrying out from behind the counter to get a closer look at me.

"My word! Is that Astrid's niece?" A second man emerged from the supply room carrying a box of items that he quickly dropped. He was taller and skinnier but had just as much pep in his step. "Alder, don't be rude, let her come sit!"

"I'm not. She saved me and our store from a menace. She's an angel."

I couldn't help but laugh as they both fussed over me. Alder peeked into the teapot to find it had cooled.

"I can handle that," I said, reaching out for it. He happily handed it to me, and I heated it up between my palms.

As he poured, I grabbed the broom from the corner and swept up the remnants of the glass jars, carefully avoiding the liquids.

"Don't bother, dear. I can take care of that," Alder said, swirling a hand in a circular motion and spinning the air in a whirlwind. It gathered up the glass as well as the liquids, and dropped it into a bucket before dissipating.

"Impressive," I said, raising my eyebrows.

"I know," he said with a wink. "Only fair to show you my tricks after you saved us."

Caltain handed me a cup of the steaming tea as we pulled up three chairs against their counter to chat.

"It's lovely to meet you both, Alder and Caltain was it? I take it you already know who I am."

"Oh, of course dear. You're welcome to peruse, but we've already made up a few boxes of supplies for you. It's been ages since we had anyone with healer affinities grace our store. I'm afraid we were very young when your aunt left, so we didn't know her well, but we're so honored to have you," Caltain said, squeezing my hand.

"It was a shame what the humans did to her. They can be quite despicable. Not as despicable as some of our own, as you saw today, but the humans don't visit our shop," Alder said as he patted Caltain's hand lovingly.

Abruptly changing the subject, Caltain asked. "Are you married, dear? Seeing anyone?"

"Never married. No children. Not seeing anyone. It hasn't been a priority."

"Oh, I'm not asking to judge, my dear," Caltain added. "Trust me, there is no judgment here for the personal life you choose to lead. We heard Constable Sheehan visited you today."

"He did, indeed." I smirked, anticipating where their meddling was going.

"And what did he want?" Alder asked with raised eyebrows, sipping at his tea.

"To welcome me to the town."

"He didn't ask you out on a date?" Caltain questioned.

"He may have asked me to dinner."

"And...did you accept?"

I couldn't help but laugh at their prodding. "I did, after I get settled in."

"Well, you'd better come back and tell us all about it!" Caltain said.

"He is such a handsome fellow. And much higher class than the other humans in my opinion," Alder added.

After more tea and gossip, I took a peek at what they had boxed up for me. Cork to make my potions hold longer, dried witch grass to increase the power of any mixture, angelica root, ginseng, and dried clementine peel for healing and immune boost, arrowroot to cure poison, eucalyptus oil to ward off illness, and dried marigold flowers, which were a powerful antifungal and antiseptic. They had hit all the essentials, but I grabbed a few extra quartz crystals, cooking herbs, and tea leaves for good measure. I tried to hand them a few coins, and Caltain pushed them back as Alder shook his head. "It's on us, gorgeous. Come back any time you'd like to chat!"

Fortunately for the townsfolk, I was up early the next day, preparing tinctures, ointments, and potions from the supplies I had collected. The calls began two hours after sunup, all on recommendation from the constable. The Leighis secret to a good ointment was double boiling the ingredients in a base of oil, which most witches weren't patient enough for. Within two days, I had aided twelve residents of Dracht, an even mix of human and witch.

Most were looking for remedies for minor ailments, although one was looking to speed up the process of healing his broken arm, and one was hoping to mend her broken heart. The minor remedies were simple, as was the broken bone. Just rub on a salve or ointment or take a tincture. On a handful, I had to put my hands to the affected area and funnel my powers into them to aid the healing. My fingers tingled and my heart warmed each time, but I had never healed this many in such a short period.

The broken heart was another matter, though I did not turn the girl away. I provided her with a memory-wiping potion in the guise of a sleeping tincture mixed with chicory, geranium, and echinacea powders. The girl was none the wiser.

Every magic had a cost, and the cost was my energy. I was exhausted at the end of each day. I spent my free time in between visitors or late at night on my latest personal project—a potion that all witches knew of, but none had perfected. I was determined to be the first.

1 tsp. of ambergris oil for love, sex, and lust

2 tbsp. ground bloodroot to draw a male lover

3 chili flakes, 1 oz. of coconut flakes, and a crumble of dark chocolate to turn up the flames of desire

A pinch of cardamom to draw love

1 chopped sardine for seduction

1 mouthful of my spit
    Infuse with a copper rod to open the channel to
attract a mate

I closed my eyes and gripped the glass bottle between my palms, winging a spell on the spot.

"My flames beckon forth my heart's delight. To find my true love, I call upon Hecate tonight."

I could feel the mixture heating up, so much that it almost burned my palms, which were used to enduring my fire magic. Yanking my hands back, the glass bottle dissolved before my eyes, the toxic mixture spilling out onto the work table. Grabbing the pitcher of water I always had by my side, I poured it over the remnants before it ate through my countertop. With a sigh, I noted the results.

Love potion 1: failure.

After thoroughly wiping down the countertop, I put away the failed ingredients before there was a knock at the front door. I was greeted by a young boy holding out a note. I tipped him with a few coins, and his face lit up like the sun.

"Thank you, Miss!" he said before running off to his next delivery.

I flicked the note open. It was from Constable Sheehan.

"Odd place for a first date," Mrs. Yates said, peering around me to read it and startling the wits out of me.

Once I calmed my racing heart, I answered. "He requests my presence immediately at the morgue. This should be interesting."

<h1 style="text-align:center">Chapter Three</h1>

<h2 style="text-align:center">Michael</h2>

Two days after Miss Anna Leighis arrived in Dracht, a young man's body washed up by the bay. He was unrecognizable because most of his skin had been burned away or sliced off, judging by the knife marks covering his body. There had been no missing person cases filed, so he was likely from out of town. I did my best to keep what had happened between myself and the coroner, Conor, who was a good friend.

My next step was obvious; I had to call the Triumvirate. I sent a messenger to call for Anna Leighis first, to see if she could inspect the body to determine cause of death.

That's why I told myself I had invited her, though part of me knew I only wanted to see her again, and she had yet to reach out regarding my dinner invitation. I couldn't get her out of my mind, but I didn't want to look desperate. Though I'd never been chased out of a witch or warlock's home, it was clear how they felt about humans—I was below them. But Anna hadn't made me feel like that. She had been kind. And she was stunning. I couldn't resist asking her out.

A mere thirty minutes later, the Triumvirate arrived, before I had even sent for them. They shook off the remnants of the torrential rain from their umbrellas and their moss-colored, hooded cloaks. Each had a golden amulet with a strange eye dangling around their necks, and all three had their familiars with them, which always unnerved me. Miss Leighis came through shortly behind them, squeezing the moisture from her hair, despite the short walk from her coach to the door. It was as if the weather had known it needed to foreshadow the bad news.

"Gentlemen, I'm grateful you were able to come so quickly. And Miss Leighis, have you been properly introduced to Dracht's Triumvirate?"

She accepted my help in removing her cloak before she responded. The ebony material was soft in my fingers, and I imagined running them through her ebony waves instead. She smelled like citrus today. I inhaled her scent so deeply that orange hit my tongue. Her long, dark hair had a shine I had never seen. I swore her green eyes could see right into my soul. "I have not had the pleasure yet, though I am familiar with them from my late father's journal entries. I'm afraid I've been too tied up aiding the town residents to get out much these last two days. It is an honor to make your acquaintance." She curtsied charmingly and smiled at each of the men in turn.

Though I had been working closely with the Triumvirate since taking up this post, the magic wielders in Dracht didn't trust me enough to divulge how their magic worked, so I feared that she could read what I was thinking.

"Then allow me to make the introductions. Mr. Elias Hornsby has been the leader of the Triumvirate for 20 years now." I gestured to the portly, balding man whom I had come to know quite well. He was an effective leader, but not a very personable man. My father was the constable when Elias was elected and they had become fast friends, my father also not being a personable man. Elias had been instrumental in getting me the role when my father passed. His falcon, Bas, was perched on his shoulder. His beady, yellow eyes followed me as I walked, like I would be his next meal when the time was right. I wondered how he held the bird on his shoulder without wincing in pain from the talons.

She smiled at him and curtsied again, but did not offer him her hand as she had to me a few days ago. He did not seem surprised by this in the least—perhaps it was some kind of magical etiquette I was not aware of. I did not recall any witch or warlock offering their hand to shake.

"This is Mr. Aiden Bates." I nodded to the middle-aged man of the group. He hadn't begun to lose his hair, but it was peppered with gray and was not as lean as when he started ten years ago. He had always been my favorite of the three. He didn't seem as astute as Elias, but he was much kinder. His familiar, Rex the salamander, rested on his shoulder. The gray and yellow-spotted creature had his face angled towards the warlock's ear, as if he was sharing a secret. Again, she did not offer her hand to him. I would have to ask her why that was. Something told me she'd be much more forthright with me than any other magical being I had met. She had already been kinder than most.

Finally, I pointed to the youngest of the group. He was also the tallest, a few inches taller than me, and the most rugged. To be fair, it didn't take much to beat out the other two in that regard. I probably had thirty pounds of muscle on him, though. His fox Sion stayed close to his ankles, tail happily swishing back and forth. "Lastly, the newest addition, Mr. Killian Tine-Radharc."

Something in me stirred as the two of them sized each other up, their cheeks pinking slightly. I was disgusted to think it might be jealousy. I wasn't married, but I certainly wasn't lonely. Being the constable of Dracht had its perks. Most ladies found a man in uniform quite attractive. I had never experienced jealousy. He approached as if to take her hand, but her glare stopped him without a word.

Elias cut in. "I understand you are a healer and a descendant of Astrid Leighis. I never had the pleasure of meeting her person-ally, but I had become the newest member of The Triumvirate before she left. Her talents are famous in this town, as are the tales of her beauty. My father was very disappointed when she left town. Tell me child, exactly how much have you learned of us from your father's stories?"

Her lips pinched, and she scrunched her nose. Was she afraid to answer? She crossed her arms and began. "The Triumvirate has been around for centuries. Three warlocks are designated to speak on behalf of all witches and warlocks in Dracht. Each time a warlock steps down or passes on, a new warlock is elected. Somehow, it works out to be every twenty years, almost on the dot." She paused again and looked to me, then back to Elias, as if for approval.

Aiden, the kind one, tried to assuage her. "It's alright, Ms. Leighis. We have worked with Constable Sheehan for a few years and his father before him. There isn't much he doesn't know about us at this point. We trust him and do not mind him learning whatever else is left."

That was news to me. They were secretive around me, quieting when I entered any room the three of them were in.

She took a deep breath and unwound her crossed arms. Despite the tranquil façade, I thought I spotted a hint of anger in her expression. "Only seers can be elected to the Triumvirate, and once you complete your induction ceremony, your seer talents are heightened. Instead of daydreaming visions of possible futures, you can see things simply by touching people, witches, or even corpses."

Well, that explained the lack of physical contact between her and the group. How much did they know of me from shaking my hand? It should have disturbed me more, but I had nothing to hide. I had assumed that their input on cases came from the visions, but this skill of theirs was news to me. The cold sneer on Elias's face suggested pride at having kept this hidden from me all these years. So why let her tell me now? And why was she so angry?

"Tell me, sir, what do you know of my Aunt Astrid's disappearance?"

Ahh. Perhaps that was it.

"Not much, I'm afraid. My mother said the human residents of Dracht turned on her. She never told me the details. One day, she was just gone without a trace. Would you be willing to share what actually happened?" Elias fiddled with his amulet as he questioned her.

"I don't have much more to add. She felt persecuted, but she never told us why. None of our family has heard from her since." Anna said. She folded in on herself, her shoulders sinking. For a moment, she almost looked weak, which contrasted with how she had previously presented herself. The room remained silent for a few moments.

The dead air was interrupted when the coroner's assistant entered. She looked to be in her early twenties and had long, wavy, blond hair. She peeked over at Killian—who smiled at her—and set down the tray she was holding, cheeks flushing.

"Fresh water for you all to drink. Let me know if you need anything else," she said quietly, eyes never leaving the youngest warlock.

"Thanks, sweetheart," he said, winking. She giggled, then scurried out of the room.

Elias pulled us back to the task at hand. "Constable Sheehan, perhaps you can get to the point, now that we have all been properly acquainted."

Anna opened her mouth, but she abandoned the thought quickly and smiled up at me.

"Well gentlemen, and lady, I have an unfortunate case I could use your assistance with. Although, I was surprised you beat my messenger," I said.

As I led them into the room where the coroner had examined the corpse, Mr. Bates whispered to Elias. "So far, it is just as I told you. This isn't going to be the last." Elias nodded, and they solemnly followed me to the body. Anna joined me on the opposite side of the table, peering back at the three warlocks.

"Hell to Hecate. A little warning would've been nice, Constable," Anna said, pinching her nose at the stench of the mutilated, rotting corpse. Killian gagged.

"I apologize, Miss. This isn't for women's eyes. If you'd like to leave, I wouldn't be offended. I can explain after," I said.

"I'm not a child, Constable. I can handle the sight, but the smell I could do without. Who is this, and what happened to him?"

That had been my response upon first entering the room too. The taste of decaying flesh was hard to avoid in the unventilated room. It was going to be hell to wash the sticky stench out of my uniform.

"I'm not sure. He washed up at the bay mutilated. His eyeballs were removed. I'm assuming he's a human from out of town, as there have been no missing person cases filed with the watch."

Without touching the body, Aiden spoke in a somber tone. "He's a warlock. He's the youngest member of the house Nathair. One of the legacy families."

"Who would want him dead?" Miss Leighis asked.

"I have no idea," Aiden responded.

"Do we have an estimated time of death, Constable?" Anna asked.

"Accounting for the burns and water damage to the body, he couldn't narrow it down as much as we had hoped. We found him two days ago. Judging by the state of the body, Conor believes he died two days before that."

She pinched her nose and edged closer. Careful not to touch the body, she scanned it. "Has the body been handled or moved since it was picked up?"

"The coroner and I carried him in ourselves. The coroner hasn't moved or flipped him, only spun the wheeled table around as he made his standard incisions and such. Nobody else has handled him."

"Cause of death?" Elias questioned.

"It's hard to tell whether it was the stab wounds or the burns, but there are also signs of lung failure. We're not sure which did him in. I was hoping Miss Leighis's powers would help us glean that information."

She picked up the victim's hand and turned it to look at his wrist. Closing her eyes, she slid her fingers up his forearm before gently placing his arm back down. She nodded and backed away from the corpse. "The burn and water damage were both after his death. It feels like dark magic to me." She spun to look at me and the three members of the Triumvirate. "Are you going to touch the body and see what you can glean, or are you just going to stand there dumbfounded? This is why the three of you are here, is it not?"

Without pause, Killian answered. He looked much younger than me and perhaps a year or two older than Anna. He didn't show the worry lines I had accrued from my time on the job, even though I was only thirty-five.

"We can't, Miss Leighis. Our powers allow us to gain their sight memories. With the eyeballs gone, our skill is useless."

I didn't miss the glare that Elias gave him. He didn't want either Anna or me privy to this information. Perhaps both of us.

Reluctantly, Elias chimed in. "Whoever perpetrated this murder had knowledge of that, which makes this more disturbing. My guess is that they also have fire magic, which is uncommon, but not rare."

"Constable, do you gentlemen maintain a register of all magic wielders in town?" Anna asked. "I have a suspicion that this witch or warlock wouldn't be stupid enough to do something like this in their own town."

I nodded, but Elias chimed in before I could.

"The registry is still kept—which is public knowledge—despite the current relationship between our kind and the constabulary."

"Then it is most likely an out-of-towner, probably a warlock, trying to frame someone here," Anna suggested.

Bates cut in this time. "That's quite a leap, Miss Leighis. Women's intuition can only go so far."

"Slightly further when it's a witch's intuition, but you are right sir. It is only speculation. In my opinion, it's quite a risk to take. Have you ever had any similar cases, Constable?"

"No, Miss, nothing close," I answered.

She turned to Killian. "And you Mister...Tine-Radharc was it? Do you have anything of value to add?"

"Only that I agree with you. I think it's likely either an outsider or someone new to town who may not be on the registry yet. But... I also think they must have ties to one of the legacy families to have knowledge of how the Triumvirate works. I think we should look at a list of the legacies. See who no longer has family here, or who may have descendants nearby. And you can call me Killian, Miss."

She flicked her eyes up and down, assessing, and nodded. "Very well thought out, Killian. You three may have some hope after all."

Elias glared, but he masked it with a smile.

Anna's head dropped and she pinched the bridge of her nose. "I don't understand. Who could do such a thing?" she whispered under her breath.

Placing my hand on her upper back, I rubbed it gently. "A vile monster. Inhuman. A purely evil being. That's the only answer." She leaned into me slightly, and I never wanted her warmth to fade away. I wrapped my arm around her and held her as she rested her head against my shoulder.

"We'd like to take the body to handle the arrangements. Is that suitable, Constable, or does the coroner still need him?" Elias asked.

"I'll double-check with him in the morning and have him make arrangements to deliver him to your enclave."

"Thank you, Constable. Do keep us posted."

"Yes, sir."

"Oh, and Constable, please make sure that list makes it to all four of us. Keep us informed should you receive any updates, or if similar cases pop up. I'm afraid we must be getting back to the enclave. Good day, Miss Leighis."

She nodded to all three of the men as they left us alone with the body. I led her out into the lobby to escape the smell. Reluctantly, I removed my arm, and she turned to face me.

"Why do you dislike them so much?"

"The Triumvirate. Three men. Warlocks. No witches. Ever."

"And?"

"It's a bit outdated, don't you think?"

"There are no women in the Dracht Watch, either. It's a man's duty to protect women, is it not?"

"I need no protection," she spat at me.

Most of the women I had courted in Dracht enjoyed being protected. But her fierceness made me want her even more. It was refreshing. I held up my hands placatingly. "I meant no offense. Forgive me, it's clear you can protect yourself. But that doesn't mean you should have to. Thank you for coming today, though. I appreciate it immensely."

"Why did you ask me here, Constable? Normally, it's only the Triumvirate that assists with these situations, is it not?"

"I thought this case could use a woman's intuition." I winked at her. "In all honesty, sometimes I don't trust them to share everything with me. For some reason, I trust you, and I knew you'd be more help. I also wanted to see you again."

She smiled and squeezed my hand, her soft skin such a contradiction to my calloused hands. "Well, for what it's worth, I'm glad to see you again too. And I'm glad you called me. I'm happy to help with any cases."

"Would you like me to escort you home?"

"No, thank you. My coach is right outside."

My face must've shown my disappointment, but it was short-lived.

"I would like to take you up on that dinner you offered.

Perhaps next Friday night, after your shift? Send me a messenger with the time and place."

I tucked a strand of hair behind her ear and placed a chaste kiss on her knuckles. "That sounds wonderful. Perhaps you can wear that red dress again?"

"Of course, Constable. See you next Friday."

When the door closed behind her, my heart sank as all the warmth and joy left the room. My gut told me this woman was going to be trouble, but my heart told me I didn't care.

Chapter Four

Just as Bates had foreseen, the young warlock had been brutalized and robbed of his eyeballs. Granted, I had only witnessed a handful of crimes in my short time in the Triumvirate, but this was by far the most gruesome. Aiden's prophetic warning did nothing to prepare me for the sight. My disgust was evident based on the way Miss Leighis had stared at me. I had expected her to be the most put off of the group, but she surprised us all by holding firm. I was almost disappointed that we had to leave her, but she unnerved me.

A tiny tug had drawn me to her, and I had felt an overwhelming sense of recognition. Like I knew her but couldn't recall from where. She was the most beautiful woman I had ever seen. Perhaps it was our lunar-heightened powers calling to each other since the full moon had just passed.

In the three days it took the constable to get us that list, three more bodies showed up. Each had a varying cause of death or type of mutilation, but all of them had one thing in common—no eyeballs. Things were starting to look grim.

The constable called us and Miss Leighis back to the coroner's office. The bloated and discolored bodies lay sprawled around the back room. There had been three days of torrential rain, and humans and magical folk alike were staying off the streets to remain home. Dry and warm. Or so we had thought. The rain had finally let up, but the dark sky kept the coming autumn at the forefront of everyone's mind.

Entering the morgue, the magically-brightened oil lamps highlighted each body cut open on their respective tables. The sizzling and occasional crackling of the lamps was the only sound filling the silence. The chill from outside had permeated the space, causing me to shiver. The three corpses didn't help.

"None of the bodies have been identified, nor have any missing person cases been filed. The coroner has determined they all died approximately one week ago, the same time as our first victim."

"The full moon. No surprise there," I whispered.

Constable Sheehan eyed me and then continued. "There is not a significant population of residents experiencing homelessness, but I paid a visit to the shelter anyway. By their last count, nobody is missing."

"I can identify them. Two witches and one warlock, not humans. One from a legacy family, the other two middle-class. Winifred Kanniff, Ralph Harrison, and Jacob Garlick. I don't understand, Constable. Other than their magic, I can't think of any connection between our four victims. Have you been digging into it?" Aiden Bates asked.

"They're not going to talk to him. We'll send Killian," Elias added.

"I'd like to join him, if that's alright. I'd really like to know why their families haven't reported them missing. Sometimes these things require a woman's touch," Anna added.

I was thrilled that she wanted to come with me. It was most likely because she wanted to help on the case, but I was hoping she was intrigued by me. "I think that's a wise idea, Miss Leighis," I said, with a grin and a puffed-up chest.

"I don't think it's necessary," Elias argued.

Aiden tilted his head to the side and pursed his lips. "All of the families are very secretive. Killian's powers and Miss Leighis' insight might be exactly what we need."

I had met the families in passing a time or two, but Aiden knew more about them than I did. Although most magical families were private, I found it odd that he knew that about these particular families.

"I think it's too dangerous, Anna, maybe..." the constable began, but trailed off when Anna turned her furious green eyes on him. My eyebrows lifted so high they hurt. There was no way in hell I'd be talking to her like that.

"Looks like it's three to two, gentlemen. Should we get started, Killian? My coach is outside. I'll make sure to have you back to your enclave before your bedtime," she mocked, rushing out of the coroner's office before Elias or Michael could change the plans.

I shrugged at Elias and followed her out, climbing into her coach after giving her driver directions to our first stop. The only legacy family was the closest, so the Harrisons would be our first target. The clouds parted to let the first rays of sunshine all week peek through. Anna sat in the forward-facing seat against the far window. I took up the rear-facing seat against the other window, leaving her as much room as possible, but not trying to hide my glances.

"You're very brave, speaking to the leader of the Triumvirate like that."

"Why? Should I be afraid of him?" she asked, dropping the curtain she had been holding aside and turning to me.

"I didn't mean it like that."

"Then what did you mean?"

"I just—I mean—Most people are intimidated by him."

"Including you, I noticed."

"He's wise, powerful, and my boss. I trust him and believe in him. It's respect that he's earned. It's not fear."

"If you say so," she said.

Her coach was much larger than I was used to, with thicker

and more comfortable cushions. The inside was lined in a luxurious, light-blue fabric and adorned with decorative buttons. As we rode, I ran my fingers along the seat in appreciation before doing the same to the thick curtain.

"Am I making you nervous, Killian?"

I dropped the curtain and turned back to her. "It's very difficult to make me nervous, but you feel familiar, and I can't pinpoint why."

"You look too young to have met my Aunt Astrid. I've been told that I resemble her when she was younger."

"I'm twenty-eight," I said, not sure why I felt the need to give her that information. I had to be older than her, but it wasn't polite to ask young women their age. "You really never met her?"

"She was driven out of Dracht years before I was born. She kept in touch with my mother through letters, but the letters stopped a few years ago."

"I'm sorry. Perhaps she's been moving or travelling. What does your mother think?"

"She died last month. That's why I decided to return. My father died when I was a toddler, and I only knew him through his journal, and now, with mother gone...I was holding out hope that Aunt Astrid might return, or that I'd feel closer to her somehow living in our legacy home. We lived in a very small village, and it was lonely. Dracht feels...less depressing and isolated, I guess. I'm sorry, I'm rambling. I don't know why I'm telling you all of this. You're so easy to talk to."

Sliding closer to her, I tapped my fingers on her knee in consolation, the soft fabric of her skirts comforting. It was too thick to feel her warmth, but it was more appropriate to touch the fabric of her skirts than the bare skin of her arm. Especially now that she knew of our powers. I didn't want her to think I was trying to read her.

"I'm always happy to listen. I lost my parents when I was very young. I don't get to commiserate often. I know exactly what you mean, though. I was grateful the Triumvirate found me first.

They housed me, educated me, and raised me. I don't know where I would've been without them, but I still feel alone. I grew up among people much older than me. Things have changed since Elias and Aiden started the school for orphaned boys when I was eighteen."

She pinched her eyebrows, as if deep in thought. "I'm so sorry to hear that. It was fortunate they found you. I doubt Elias would like it, but you're welcome to pay me a visit when you're lonely. We can commiserate about being orphans anytime you like."

The coach clunked to a stop. I lurched forward, my hand gripping her knee as I tried to brace myself.

"I'm so sorry. I lost my balance," I said, staring into her sparkling, green eyes.

"It's fine, Killian," she said, with a sweet smile.

My heart beat so loudly I feared she might hear it, but being this close to her did something to me. I craved it. I was going to soak in every second of her warmth.

"You can take your hand back now. We have a family to interview."

Our day was short. All three families turned us away at the door. The butlers refused us entry, even when we stated the reason for our visit. They assured us they would notify the head of household of the death, but none admitted to knowing a member of the family was missing. Their behavior suggested otherwise.

"I can't believe none of them let us in. All I needed was a handshake from anyone inside those homes. And nothing," I said, shaking my head in defeat.

"They have to be hiding something. I wonder if it would have gone differently if I had gone alone. Perhaps I should come back with Michael."

Hearing her on a first name basis with the constable aggravated me. She unbalanced me. She was fearless and smart. I envisioned tucking her hair behind her ears and kissing her deeply. I wanted nothing more than to make it reality.

"Where can we drop you off, Killian?"

"The enclave please. If your driver is local, I'm sure he'll know where it is."

She leaned over me to inform the driver of our destination. Her delicious aroma enveloped me, and warmth radiated off of her.

We pulled up to the massive stone structure built partially into the carved-out cliff on the northern side of Dracht. In the moonlight, the opal-colored stone shimmered, and her jaw dropped. The hallway systems throughout were vast, but the warlock-built rock structure that jutted out of it was the most stunning feat of architecture I had ever seen. My jaw had dropped the first time I saw it too.

"This is where you live? Hell to Hecate, I thought my aunt's house was massive."

"It gets a bit drafty, but it comes with its privileges," I joked. "I'd invite you in, but Elias gets..."

"Understood. Good evening, Killian. I'm sorry the day was a waste."

"Time is never wasted in good company. Good evening, Anna," I said, tipping my head at her and exiting. Somehow, I knew the draft would feel colder tonight. Perhaps, I should take her up on her offer and pay her a visit. But not tonight. I needed to play it cool, because something told me that my life was about to heat up.

Chapter Five

Unknown Narrator

—◆—

I've grown fond of my spot on the cliffs, my seat now worn into the tall grasses. The morning sun warms my skin and fills what's left of my soul. It's the perfect place to sit and reflect on what I'm becoming. It also helps me plan my next steps. To track everyone's daily movements. Their morning routines, the paths their coaches take. Where they eat, who they meet with. None of them are careful.

The Triumvirate and the constabulary are aware of my actions, and have persuaded Anna Leighis to join their investigation, as if that will help. They have no clue who they're up against, what my motivation is, or where to begin. Despite the pileup of bodies, they haven't warned anybody to watch their steps. Not a single one of the insects darting below me takes caution. It's pathetic.

It makes me sick to see how close humans, witches and warlocks have become, but I can see through that façade. Just like in my time, both sides keep up appearances, but the warlocks move against the humans in the dark. Plotting. Planning. Conspiring to become more and more powerful. Keeping secrets —even from those closest to them—and telling lies. As of yet, they haven't seen me coming. And I doubt they ever will.

Chapter Six

Michael

Before knocking on the door of the Leighis Chateau, I wiped my sweaty palms on my pants and straightened my vest to ensure the buttons lined up perfectly. I only had one nice outfit, and I rarely got to wear it. It was stuffy, but it was surely necessary for a date with the impressive Miss Anna Leighis. The weather had warmed uncharacteristically this week, and the bright sun almost blinded me and only made the sweating worse. The door swung open, and the butler stood inside with an expressionless Mrs. Yates behind him.

"Do come in, Constable. Anna should be down any moment. Would you like to have a seat or wait here?" the housekeeper asked.

"I'll wait here," I said, removing my brown bowler hat and tucking it underneath my arm. The foyer was much cooler than outside, and the herbal-scented air eased my clammy hands. "How are you this evening, Mrs. Yates?"

"I'm quite well, sir. Thank you for asking."

"Well, you clean up nicely," a honeyed voice called from up the stairs. I turned to see Anna striding down the staircase in the red dress I had requested. Half of her hair was pinned up, and the other half cascaded down her upper back in silky waves. She wore a light layer of makeup, which only made her emerald eyes stand out more. But she still looked like the same, fierce Anna I was already fond of. "Although, I'm partial to your uniform. It highlights your toned physique, and girls do love the authority that comes with it."

I took her hand, helping her down the last few stairs. "You look absolutely stunning. That red matches your ferocity." Her wolf wagged her tail as I looked in her direction. "You look beautiful too, you magnificent creature." She nudged her face into my hands as I scratched behind her ears and kissed the top of her head. She smelled clean instead of smelling like dog, which shocked me. Her fur was soft and I could imagine taking a nice cozy nap snuggled up with her, like she was a blanket.

"She doesn't usually like humans. Seems she's a good judge of character, ay? Her name is Ranai."

"Is she mixed with domesticated dog? She's so calm."

"She's full gray wolf. It's her connection to me that gives her that demeanor. She's very obedient, unless I'm in danger."

"Be a good girl, and I'll have your mom home in a few hours, okay?" I said, kissing her on the head one more time. She let out a whine as I turned my attention to Anna, holding out my elbow. "Shall we, Miss Leighis?"

I helped Anna into the coach and took the seat next to her. The one I had rented only had one bench seat for two.

"I'm afraid I don't know much about familiars. Can you communicate with each other?"

"I can speak telepathically when we are close enough, but she can't speak back. I can also see through her eyes when she wants me to."

"So how does she communicate back?"

"She will acknowledge with a nod or headshake if I can see her face. Her eyes are pretty expressive, too. It's hard to explain, but sometimes it's like I can feel what she's thinking. I've had her since I was thirteen."

"Over half your life. I'm not surprised you're in sync. In my career, I've learned to read people's mannerisms and body language, and that sounds similar."

"Exactly!" she said, with an enthusiastic smile.

"And they're real animals? I've heard so many rumors."

"They are. But they're also spirits that were once witches or warlocks that have a connection to you, though I'm not sure anyone ever finds out who."

"That's fascinating."

Changing the subject, she asked, "Where are we headed, Constable?"

"There's a tavern right near the outdoor market. Is that alright?"

"It sounds lovely. Would you mind if we stopped by the market after? I've never been to the one on the eastern side of town, only the shops at Witch's Way in the west. I've been meaning to pick up some cooking provisions. Is it open at night?"

"It is, but doesn't your staff handle that for you? There aren't many women of your status at the market."

"My staff doesn't know what I'm in the mood to cook. I'm perfectly capable of purchasing what I want myself. Leighis family tradition. It's why we only employ a housekeeper, driver, butler, and lady's maid."

"I have no doubt, it's just not something you see every day. Especially in a fancy dress. You're going to get a lot of looks."

"Let them look," she said defiantly.

Her expensive dress would certainly stand out, but then again, she did everywhere she went. Human women often wore multi-layered, rounded skirts and poofy sleeves, but Anna—like the other witches—tended to wear less cumbersome dresses that bared more skin. "It can get a bit seedy at night, but if you're sure, I'll be happy to take you."

Wrapping both of her arms around mine, she said, "I'm sure I'll be perfectly safe with you. If not, I always have my fire." Her eyes swirled with red and a hint of mischief.

Fire was rare, and very powerful. No wonder she wasn't afraid to talk back to the Triumvirate.

"Have you always been fond of animals? Most humans are terrified of Ranai."

"We always had dogs when I was younger, but I'm not allowed to have one where I live now. I pay for my mother's apartment, too. Maybe one day, I'll have enough saved up to get myself something bigger so I can get a pet. For now, it's enough for just me."

The cart rolled to a soft stop outside of the tavern and I helped Anna down, taking in her floral perfume.

"Rustic. Charming. I love it. It smells heavenly!" she exclaimed, about to launch herself up the stairs without me.

"When was the last time you ate?"

"I've snacked, but I haven't had a full meal since I arrived."

It had been about two weeks since she made it to Dracht. "You poor thing! Well, let's get you inside and get you a hearty stew. Mrs. Osta bakes her own bread fresh each day and it's to die for in her flavorful broth."

I was grateful that I had planned an early dinner because the tavern was barren, except for two tables of patrons. The crowd got rowdier at the normal dinner time. Mrs. Osta ran out from behind the bar as we walked towards my usual table and threw her arms around my neck. "Michael! Look at you all dressed up! It's so nice to see you out of uniform for once."

Anna's eyes scanned the woman, her shoulders sinking slightly and her lips pursed. Was that jealousy? I hadn't wanted her to know I lived above the tavern yet, especially when she lived in a monstrous chateau, but her jealousy over nothing might be worse. "Mr. and Mrs. Osta own the tavern and the inn upstairs. I rent my room from them. Mrs. Osta, this is my date, Miss Anna Leighis."

Mrs. Osta's eyebrows shot up in surprise. "Leighis. Like *the* Leighis family? Miss, it's an honor to have you in our establishment. Your family is legendary, but you helped heal my friend with a lingering cough a few days ago. She's doing so much better. I'm so happy we have you in Dracht. And my, my, are you stunning!"

Anna relaxed and smiled, allowing Mrs. Osta to embrace her too. "Pearl is your friend? She's a lovely woman."

"That's her! What can I get for you both?"

Anna turned toward me for a recommendation.

"A honey mead and a beef stew for each of us and a loaf of your famous bread to share, please," I requested.

Anna's grin assured me I had made good decisions.

"Coming right up, sweetheart. Have a seat," she said, ushering us to our table.

While we waited for the food to come, I wasn't sure what to say. Anna smiled warmly at me and, fortunately, started the conversation.

"Do you have family in Dracht, Constable?"

"My mother lives close by, even closer to the markets than here. My father died two years ago. I visit my mother as often as possible, typically on the weekends. My father was the previous constable, so she's used to this life." I checked my hair with my fingertips, making sure every piece was where it was meant to be.

"I'm sorry to hear about your father. It's sweet that you're following in his footsteps. I'm sure he'd be very proud of you."

I looked down at my cloth napkin and fiddled with the loose string hanging off the corner hem. "I'm not sure it's the life he wanted for me. He made sure I had the best education he could afford, I studied law for a few years. But he couldn't keep me away. I signed up for the Dracht Watch when I was twenty-three. He did his best to keep me out of trouble and to scare me away, and by the time he died it had almost worked."

"Then why did you become constable?"

"Elias convinced me. He said there weren't many humans that impressed him, but I had what it took. Warlocks, witches, and humans alike all trust me, and I have an excellent reputation for honesty."

"Well, that makes me feel better about letting you in on the little secret of my powers," she said in a sultry tone. She rested her elbows on the wooden table marred with scratches, one side of her lips tipped up teasingly.

"Your secret is safe with me, Anna."

"Have you taken many dates here?"

Huffing a laugh, I felt it safest to answer with a simple, "No."

"It has such a warm and cozy ambiance, don't you think?"

Looking around and taking in the tavern for what felt like the first time, I answered, "I guess. I've never really noticed."

She smiled at me as she readjusted in her seat.

Mrs. Osta dropped off two cups of mead, eyes flicking between us with a smile. "I'll be back out shortly with your stew and bread. Don't mind me."

"I heard you and Killian didn't have any luck interviewing the victims' families."

"They wouldn't even let us near the door. I think his powers frighten them. I was going to ask if you would escort me instead."

"I wish I had known earlier. I paid each of them a visit shortly after you did. It was certainly Killian who was their problem."

"How did it go?" she asked in a whisper, noticing that Mrs. Osta was on her way out with our food.

We thanked her for the meal. The herbaceous scent made my mouth water, and Anna licked her lips in anticipation. She looked to me, and I nodded for her to dig in. Ripping a small piece of bread off, she dipped it in the broth and popped it in her mouth. I followed suit.

I scooped up some stew, a piece of meat, carrot, and potato all making it on my spoon. The meat had been cooked a long time, given how easily it fell apart in my mouth. The carrot and potato each popped as I bit into them, and the broth warmed my chest and heart as I swallowed. The crust of the bread cracked as I bit into the crispiness, and the inside melted in my mouth, having absorbed the delicious broth. After Mrs. Osta was out of earshot,

I began my tale as Anna shoveled spoonful after spoonful of the hearty meal into her mouth.

"Aiden told us only one victim was from a legacy family. Although that appears to be true, I did some digging. All four families mentioned being afraid that Astrid had cursed them. That this was her revenge for whatever happened that drove her out of town."

"A curse?"

I shrugged and took a hefty bite of the warm stew. "Two of the families believe her to be dead. She left forty years ago, and from what I've gathered, she was probably thirty. I know witches live long lives, but they think it's a curse from beyond the grave."

She sighed and slowed her pace, ripping off a dainty piece of bread and dipping it into the luxurious broth. "Not that I was hoping my aunt was a murderer, but I really want her to still be alive. Why were they afraid of Killian?"

"From what I could gather, all four of the victims had been working with the Triumvirate on something recently. The families didn't know what, but they are fearful that was why they died. They were worried about retribution, which was why they didn't report them missing. After they were identified by Elias and Aiden, I looked into their records. They were all mixed up in some nefarious nighttime activities and had each been picked up by my men over the last few months. Black market purchases, possession of illegal goods, that sort of thing. So far, that's all I've been able to find."

"That doesn't add up. My father's journals said the legacy families drove Astrid out of town. So why would the other two think it was her?"

"Ah, the most interesting part. I dug into the town archives. The two middle-class families have fallen on hard times in the past few decades and used to be far wealthier. Over time, their power has become more diluted as well. They each used to live in a chateau but were forced into the less wealthy area when faced with insolvency. Both chateaus now sit abandoned. It seems our middle triumvirate member wasn't aware of that."

"Hecate help us." She pinched the bridge of her nose and took a deep breath before ripping off another piece of bread. Dipping it into the broth, she stared up at the ceiling, deep in thought. "So, the only two links are their potential involvement in my aunt being driven out of town and their work for the Triumvirate. If my aunt is dead, it's almost like somebody is trying to set it up to look like her."

"That's the same conclusion I came to. It's either that, or someone else seeking vengeance for your aunt."

"Or, perhaps, someone who was driven out like my aunt? What should we do now?"

"Well, I think it's fair to say we can't trust the Triumvirate with this information. I think it's best you and I investigate further and only fill them in on the important stuff. We still need them, and I don't want to hurt relations. We also need to find out what they're hiding. Why are the families so scared of them? Think you're up for the task?"

"I won't get anywhere with Elias, and I doubt Aiden will be of any help, but I think I can help with Killian."

My dinner almost came back up, and I clenched my teeth to hold it in. The way he looked at her made me want to punch him square in the nose. "I have no doubt about that," I muttered.

"What was that?" she asked.

"With the way he looks at you, I'm sure that will be your best option."

I hadn't noticed that my hand was gripping my spoon so tightly that it had started to bend until she placed her soft, warm palm around it. "I'm on a date with you right now, am I not? Not Killian."

Shifting in my seat to correct my posture, I let go of the spoon and took her hand in mine, leaning down to place a gentle kiss on it. "You're right. And it is the best plan. Just know that I don't like it. I don't like him. I don't trust him."

"Well, so far, I do. Trust him, that is. I fear his blind loyalty to the Triumvirate, though. Did you know he's an orphan who was raised by them?"

"I did. My father led the case on his parents' murders. Suspected witchcraft. The Triumvirate had my father arrest a human who was put to death. Proof was never found."

She raised her eyebrows and fiddled with a piece of potato, dragging it back and forth with her spoon before scooping it up and popping it in her mouth. A tiny moan escaped her, and I had to readjust yet again. "I'm sorry. It's been ages since I ate a real, hot meal. This really is delicious."

Mrs. Osta interrupted us briefly to take our empty bowls. I handed her a few coins, including a little extra for excellent service, as always.

"Thank you for dinner, Constable."

"Please, Michael. And you're very welcome."

"I wouldn't have minded paying, or splitting, you know."

"That's no way to make a good first impression on a lady of your station, now, is it?"

"I guess not. Perhaps, I can make it up to you by cooking you dinner instead? Tomorrow after we investigate? Assuming the market has everything I need, of course."

"I'd like that very much."

She finished off the last few sips of her mead with a satisfied smack of her lips. Lips I had stared at all night and wished were on me right now. I debated inviting her up to my rooms, but I feared she'd run for the hills when she saw my meager accommodations. Not to mention, she might use her fire on me for being so forward on a first date. All in good time. "What do you say we head over to the market before all the good stuff is gone?"

She sat back and patted her belly. "That sounds like a wonderful idea, I need to walk some of this off."

Holding out my elbow, she wrapped an arm around mine and we waved goodbye to my landlady, who was glowing with joy. I asked my driver to meet us at the market since it was close enough to walk to. We were silent as we strolled, taking in the last of the early autumn warmth. As we turned the corner, the market came into view.

It was a grid that included a number of alleys, with different vendors lining each side. Some had carts and some had permanent wooden structures where they displayed their wares. The aromas of baked goods, fresh fish, produce, and flowers warred for dominance in the tight quarters. Displays were set up with clothing, jewelry, weapons, and more. Whatever your heart desired, you could probably find here, if you were human. There were no magical supplies sold in Eastern Dracht. This place was bustling first thing in the morning, but closer to dusk, it was perfect for shopping and a stroll.

"Wow! It's huge! In Western Dracht, we only have a row of shops. I didn't expect there to be so many vendors here!" I guessed for new eyes it would be impressive, but I had grown up here and took it for granted.

Many of the merchants and shoppers glanced at her, brows pinched in confusion, likely wondering why a wealthy witch was here herself, but not one commented. With a glowing grin, Anna inspected the wares in almost every stall and made small talk with each proprietor. Smartly, she didn't mention who she was, though a few recognized her after having visited for medical services. I made a mental note of a particular necklace she had inspected thoroughly, but I would have to save up for a few weeks to surprise her with it. It would be worth it.

Fortunately, with the sun almost set, the air was a more suitable temperature for walking. The light blue sky was now streaked with thin whisps of pink. When we reached the section of the market that sold produce and proteins, she was in her element. She asked questions about freshness and farming practices and amused me when she asked about how happy the animals were that had been butchered.

"You are well educated on produce. Have you always had such a passion for it?"

"My mother was human, but her green thumb was magical. We had a garden for as long as I could remember. There's something grounding about having your fingers in soil, and something so satisfying about starting a plant from a seed and watching it blossom into food over time. It's an excellent lesson on patience," she said with a grin. Holding up some type of gourd, she continued. "I'll dry some of the seeds out from this lovely specimen, among others, to start my garden next year. I grow my own herbs as well."

I couldn't help but smile back at her. She was fierce, but she was also nurturing. Sometimes her two halves contradicted, but she really was magical.

A short while later, we had two bags full of fresh vegetables, herbs, fish, meat, fruit, and even some duck breast. I couldn't wait to discover what she was going to put together for me.

The ride back took about twenty minutes, but we sat in silence with her head tucked against my shoulder. It was comfortable, and it felt right. Every now and then, I'd kiss the top of her head and she would snuggle into me a bit more, and my heart squeezed. I walked her up the three steps with her small hand in mine and we stopped outside the door. I placed the two bags of groceries on the porch to say goodbye.

"Tonight was a pleasure, Anna. I'm looking forward to dinner tomorrow. I'll stop by around noon to pick you up for our investigations?"

"That sounds wonderful, Michael."

My gut told me I should plant a chaste kiss on her cheek, but my heart took over. I pressed my lips to hers and she didn't pull back. Instead, she wrapped her arms around my neck and held me against her, her tongue gently swiping my lips.

Without a second thought, I opened for her, and our tongues tangled together. I dug the fingers of one hand into her hair as my other gripped her hip and pressed her back to the front door. The skin of my neck heated as the intensity of our kissing increased, but I didn't mind.

Reluctantly pulling my lips from hers, I trailed kisses down her neck as she slid her palms down my chest and let out a satisfied groan. The door swung inward, and we collapsed into the house, and I landed on top of her. Mrs. Yates stood above us, her eyebrows raised, and shook her head while we both reddened with embarrassment. Ranai let out a low howl as if mocking us, then came over to lick my face before either of us could get to our feet.

I helped Anna up and planted another kiss on her cheek, removing my hat to tip my head at Mrs. Yates. "I guess I'd better be going. I'll see you tomorrow afternoon?"

"I'm looking forward to it," she said, as Mrs. Yates snagged the bags of groceries and brought them inside.

"Good evening, Mrs. Yates."

"Good evening, Constable. I'm glad we'll be seeing more of you," she said as the butler held the door.

Nodding, I walked back towards the coach, adjusting my pants for the second consecutive day.

Chapter Seven

Although dating had been the last thing on my mind when I arrived here, I was glad that I had listened to Mrs. Yates. Michael was authoritative, intelligent, and an all-around good man. Moreso than any of the warlocks I had ever met. I couldn't fault him for his flawed views on the traditional gender roles. Those beliefs of his were already starting to crack. As I got ready for him to pick me up, butterflies were fluttering around inside my stomach. I had never thought I'd see the day when I was excited to see a man, rather than annoyed.

I was starting to realize why humans and witches were kept apart. Witches may never look at another warlock again if they knew what human men were like. And to think, most magical folk thought humans were beneath them. Because my mother was human, I hadn't shared that sentiment. Maybe they weren't as wealthy or powerful as us, but Michael was proving how beautiful their hearts were. Everyone at the market had been lovely, too. Nothing seedy like my handsome constable had anticipated.

The morning was a beautiful one, so I hit the human market again. Alone this time, so I could prepare a nice thank you lunch for my staff. They stared, but they all smiled or nodded in greeting. The first vendor I approached was the fishmonger. The catch was fresh, from the look of it. The fish had a light odor of fresh, salty water. The eyes were clear and bright, and the gills were a brilliant red. "Ah, you have excellent taste, Miss. We just pulled those flounder this morning! If you're interested, I can fillet it for you."

"Thank you, sir. I'll take you up on that. One whole fish please."

He filleted the fish with precision as I watched in awe. He looked up every so often and caught me eyeing him. "If you don't mind, Miss, would it be alright if I asked you a question?"

"Of course," I answered with a curious smile.

"Normally one of your...wealth sends their people to the market. I have friends who have come to you for healing services, and it sounds like you are unconventional for a witch. Why are you so much kinder to humans than the rest? None of them come shopping here."

I beamed. "My mother was human. You're no different than us aside from magic. The others let the power get to their head. The first sign is being too good to do their own shopping."

He snorted, then appeared mortified. "I'm so sorry, Miss. I just didn't expect you to be so honest. You caught me by surprise, is all."

"It's alright, a little honesty makes this world a better place, don't you think?"

"Of course, Miss. Here is your flounder, that's ten cents."

I passed him three half dimes instead. "For the extra work and lovely chat. See you soon."

"Thank you, Miss."

After cooking my staff—and myself—a delightful early lunch of battered and crisped flounder, I bathed in preparation for a full afternoon of working on the investigation and to get the strong smell of cooked fish off of me. I put on my favorite velvet dress. It was form-fitting, with a high neckline, but my favorite part was the portion of the bodice that had been replaced with a floral lace that showed off a generous amount of cleavage. The comfortable material was perfect for the summer-to-fall transition, and the soft fabric was like a cheerful hug. As I had a few hours until Michael would arrive, I decided to visit Witch's Way.

Witch's Way was fully illuminated in a cloud-free sky as I arrived at Magickal Arts and Hearts. I found Alder in the otherwise empty shop.

He greeted me with a big smile. "Well, good morning, sunshine! What can I do for you?" Alder was fiddling with a few ingredients, measuring them out before he placed them in one of the many potion bottles in front of him. The shop air was fresh and fragrant, almost spicy as it hit my tongue.

"I just came to visit. I'm killing time until I see Constable Sheehan later today."

"Is that so?" he asked with a teasing look. "Well, you're welcome to stay as long as you like. I'm working on healing potions, perhaps you can figure out what I'm doing wrong."

"What's the problem?"

"This one is meant to calm nausea. Unfortunately, it's having the opposite effect."

I crossed the store and parsed through the ingredients with my fingers, scanning the recipe he had scribbled down on a piece of parchment. "The ingredients look right, you're not using too much mandrake root, sometimes that can do it. Any chance you're allergic to any of it?"

"Not separately."

My lips pinched. The only other time I'd seen this mixture have the reverse effect was when... "You don't have any dark magic in you when you take it, do you?"

He pulled back as if he had been slapped, his face full of terror. "Dear goddess, I sure hope not. Not to my knowledge, anyway."

"Perhaps the combination of mandrake root and cinnamon is irritating your insides. It could just be a bad reaction. Swap out the mandrake for ground ginger. It's hard to come by, but will be less corrosive."

"Thank you! I think I have some at home, Caltain loves cooking with it. Perhaps I should work on some burn salves instead. I've become a master at those," he said with an eyeroll. "Have a seat, tell me how it's going with the handsome constable."

He sorted through some ingredients and laid out a few potion bottles. Switching between his knife and spoon, he concocted his salve while I caught him up on my love life.

After I had returned home, it didn't take long before there was a knock on the door. William opened it to reveal a very sullen-looking Constable on the other side.

"Good afternoon, Mrs. Yates. Ah! Anna," he said, spotting me after nodding to my housekeeper. "I'm afraid I have bad news. Another victim. The Triumvirate has been sent word—they'll meet us at the morgue." His face broke into a huge smile as Ranai rushed down the stairs, jumping up to lick his face. "I missed you too, sweet girl. You behave while we're out, okay?" He pulled a dried piece of meat from his pocket and handed it to her, which she accepted before bounding back up the stairs to eat it in secret.

"Bribery for her affections, huh?"

"All females are happier when their tummies are full of delicious food."

Through a bemused grin, I said, "Very true. How was your evening? Did you sleep well?"

"Same as always. Why?"

"I was just making small talk, I guess. Shall we?"

I took his arm and felt my body fill with energy, exactly like the first time we'd met. I didn't know what it was, but he made me feel strong enough to burn the whole world down with a single flame. Since we would be returning here for a meal later, we took my coach. Peering out the window, I took in the withering flowers that lined the cobblestone streets. The telltale sounds of summer—children playing outside—had faded, and the town was eerily quiet.

We arrived at the morgue, and the warlocks' coach was outside. Entering the main door, we overheard whispering coming from the back room where the bodies were examined. I grabbed Michael's forearm to stop him before he could open the door, holding my finger up to my lips. Together, we leaned closer.

There were only two voices chittering back and forth, but it was easy to tell who was who between Aiden and Elias. I wasn't sure if Killian was silent, or if he wasn't in the room. My magical and feminine instincts told me it was the latter.

"What are we supposed to do?" the middle-aged man asked, his voice pitched higher with worry.

"We have to find more willing to help us. We've only lost six. We still have nineteen left. Warn the rest. Make sure they know they're in danger," the older, hoarser voice whispered.

"Whoever this is knows about us. Why else would they keep removing the eyeballs? They're targeting us. Who else knows our plan? Who could be plotting against us?"

"Don't be ridiculous. Nobody knows the plan. We haven't let Killian in on it yet. This has to be a coincidence, but we need to be cautious. Miss Leighis seems fond of Killian, so we can have him keep an eye on her for us. The whole town thinks it's her dead aunt. Maybe we can reframe it so they suspect her involvement too? It'll keep both of them out of our way while we recruit the rest of the people we need. We'll have to move up the timeline before we lose any more."

The whispering faded out as the rear entrance door slammed shut, startling us. "Anna's coach has arrived. She and the constable should be coming in any minute."

Killian. He must've been outside keeping an eye out for us. We were out of time to avoid suspicion. There was only one way to make up for it. I pulled Michael in for a kiss as I shoved through the door, feigning shock that we weren't alone. "My goodness, I'm so sorry! I didn't realize you gentlemen were already here," I said, using my fingers to put my hair back in place.

"You missed our large coach outside, did you?" Killian asked. His eyes were a deep, chocolate brown that looked almost black as he analyzed me.

"I apologize, gentlemen. I think we were a little too...distract-ed," Michael added, straightening his uniform tie.

"Perhaps we should get to business then, so you two can get... back to business?" Aiden commented.

Michael slipped into work mode, which was one of the reasons I liked him so much. "As you've already noticed, we have another body. This one wasn't as badly damaged as the others. The eyes are gone again, but this time, we found bite marks."

"It's not unusual for animals to pick at the dead. It's one of the main reasons for burial," Elias said, matter-of-factly.

"And that would be my assumption if the bite marks looked animal-made. They look human. It's hard to tell with the decomposition. Look, here. The teeth puncture deeper than human canines would. Could it be a werewolf or a vampire?" Michael asked.

"Don't be silly, there's no such thing as werewolves or vampires," I added.

"Two hundred years ago, there was no such thing as witches, either," he snarked.

"There was, we just hid ourselves better," I said sweetly, fluttering my eyelashes at him. "Trust me, if there were werewolves or vampires, the witches would know."

"Then it only leaves human, witch, or warlock. Are there any bizarre rituals that involve biting?" he asked, looking to me.

Killian apathetically moved closer to the body and ran two fingers over the bite. Murmuring, he said, "Occasionally, on rowdy holidays like Beltane, lovemaking can turn aggressive, but it's a beautiful, sensual, and personal thing. It rarely ends in death. This wasn't lovemaking, this was torture."

"Whoever it was, they didn't spend as much time mutilating this one. Perhaps they were almost caught? Where was this body found?" Elias asked.

"In the woods along the southern edge of Dracht," Michael said.

"On the human side, or the magical side?" Elias questioned further.

"Right on the border."

"They're getting sloppy," Aiden added.

"Or it's getting less personal. Perhaps they've lost their motivation. This close to the new moon, their power is weaker." Killian sounded detached. Shaking his head, it was as if he suddenly realized he wasn't alone in the room.

My eyes narrowed. *What the hell was that about?*

"We need to dig deeper, Elias. I need you three to press the magic users. I'll focus on the humans. I'm tempted to implement a curfew," Michael added.

"I think that would be wise. Issue your order, and we'll make sure the magical community complies. Thank you for keeping us informed, Michael. I don't know if I've told you this, but I'm ecstatic you decided to fill your father's shoes. We're always grateful for your cooperation."

"Thank you, Elias. The feeling is mutual. Enjoy your evening."

"Good evening," Aiden said, nodding to both of us.

Killian lingered, arms crossed and leaning back against the

coroner's table, eyes flipping between myself and Michael. Eventually, after a long, awkward pause, he pushed off. "Good evening, Anna. Constable."

We both nodded as he followed his elders out of the morgue.

When we were in the safety of my coach, Michael turned to me with cherry red cheeks, a vein in his forehead starting to throb. "What the hell could they be planning that they need twenty-five people? And to not let Killian in on it? At least neither Elias nor Aiden is the killer. We need to figure out what they're doing, especially now that they have Killian trailing you like you're the problem? Are they mad?"

I couldn't help but relish in his protectiveness, but I also felt bad that he was so concerned. Lighting a ball of fire in one of my palms, I said, "It could still be either of them, and they may be hiding it from the other. We can't rule anyone out yet. But we're going to be fine. Killian is not a concern. None of them are. They forget who I am. The line of powerful witches I come from. With you by my side, they don't stand a fucking chance. We investigate, and we take them down."

"If they try to turn the town against you, we're going to be up against a lot. They've spent the last sixty years building a reputation for protecting this community, and they've infiltrated almost every part of town. The police force, the government, you name it."

"Well, I guess we'll have to make sure the town doesn't buy it. I'll throw a party for Mabon at the chateau. We'll invite warlocks, witches, and humans alike. Make sure we build more unity than they do. They may be nice to everyone, but they're not letting both sides intermingle. Let's change that. We'll have it end in time for the curfew, of course," I added with a cheeky wink.

"I don't think any of the humans know anything about Mabon. It's not something the magical community shares with humans. I don't know what it is."

"Don't worry, all you'll have to do is help spread the invites. I'll have some made up for you. There is plenty of time to plan."

He pushed back into his seat, and his shoulders sank. "From the outside, it looks like humans are happily coexisting with witches and warlocks as equals. The Triumvirate has been cooperating with the Dracht Watch. But many people are suspicious. My father feared the warlocks were trying to take over the government, with the intention of driving out humans entirely. My mother used to joke that he needed to give up on these conspiracies. Perhaps if he had, he'd still be alive."

I turned to face him, my jaw dropping in shock. The three warlocks could see what he saw. Access his visual memories. I, myself, could get an excellent read of whether someone was telling the truth. It was a rare power for a witch, and one I kept hidden. But interestingly, I couldn't sense any of that when I was around Michael. "You've been keeping this from me? How do you keep it from them?"

"I have no idea. I didn't know they could read people like that, but I guess it doesn't work on me. I didn't intend to keep anything from you, but until today, I hadn't pieced it all together. The humans I've been speaking with over the last few weeks have been growing concerned." Michael spoke quietly with his arms crossed as he scanned the room. "It's harder to get magic wielders to talk to me, but they're running scared. The Triumvirate has been taking more and more power, and nobody seems to be standing up to them. People linked to them are disappearing or showing up dead. If I hadn't witnessed how concerned they are about the bodies, I would've assumed it was them."

"I still think it's them," I said. "You heard them talking about *their plan* and Killian not being in on it. Perhaps they knew we were listening and wanted to throw us off. What else could it be?"

"Maybe Killian discovered their actual plan," he said, turning to meet my gaze.

"And he's murdering the warlocks involved as his way of stopping them?" I asked, leaning closer and running my fingers up his chest, hoping others would think we were flirting and not discussing treason.

Michael shook his head but then looked down at me with a serious expression. "Killian is no murderer. I don't like him, but I would never suspect him. I can't say the same about the other two. There's something...creepy about Elias lately. I didn't feel that way when I first took over as chief constable. Whatever it is, we have to stop them. We need to focus on discovering their plan under the guise of the investigation."

He was right. The magical leaders' secret plan seemed even more menacing than a vigilante murderer. "Are you okay?" I asked, cupping his cheek in my palm.

"Of course. Why wouldn't I be?" He wrapped an arm around my waist and pulled me flush against his chest.

"I don't know, all of the dead bodies turning up? I know it's your job, but you're seeing all of this firsthand. It doesn't affect you emotionally?"

"No. It's simply part of my job." His face remained flat, not a hint of worry or sadness creeping in.

"What about your father, did it affect him?" I searched his eyes for any hint of emotion. Remorse, regret, sadness. Nothing.

"We never talked about that aspect of the job." His tone remained even.

Though I knew hiding emotions was typical for men, it didn't make it easy to get to know them. But I wasn't getting anywhere, so I dropped it.

Arriving back at the chateau, the constable's stomach grumbled loudly. "I'm starving. Anything I can do to help?"

"I'd love it if you kept me company, since you work so hard every day. Come, have a seat and chat with me. My Aunt Astrid set up this kitchen perfectly for entertaining, but that's not that surprising for a witch."

Many coven meetings and celebrations focused on cooking and group feasts. The worktable surrounded by stools was the perfect centerpiece of the large kitchen and something I had never seen in another home. The marbled top was smooth and didn't show a single nick or scratch, despite there being no cutting boards in the house when I first arrived. Most of it was covered in empty and filled bottles, herbs, spices, produce, magical ingredients, and other random items.

I selected a fancy bottle from the rack built into the side and poured us each a finger's worth.

"What's this?" Michael asked, as I handed him one.

"Absinthe, have you ever tried it?"

"I've heard of it. I'm not usually a drinker, due to my job."

"I won't take offense if you don't drink it. Will it bother you if I drink?"

"Not at all, I don't have anything against it. It's a little sad to drink by myself after work. But I'll happily drink with you." He gave it a swirl as he sniffed it, then tossed it back. "Mmm, tastes like licorice!"

"Whoa there, you may not want to drink that so fast. It's awfully strong." Absinthe was something you sipped and not chugged.

"I'm sure I can handle it."

Raising my eyebrows at him mockingly, I said, "We'll see about that."

Mrs. Yates came up from the cellar with the duck breast from the market and placed the paper-wrapped parcel on the kitchen island, smiling at Michael. "I hope you two enjoy your evening, Constable Sheehan. If you need anything, Miss Leighis knows how to call for me."

"Good evening, Mrs. Yates."

After sharpening my knife on the whetstone, I scored the skin of both duck breasts and sprinkled a generous bit of salt on top. Lighting a fire under the pan with my right hand, I poured in a dash of olive oil and let it heat up before dropping them skin side down, a loud sizzling indicating the pan was the correct temperature. I plucked the bunch of grapes out of the chaotic mess on the worktable and began slicing them in half.

"That smells divine. I don't think I've ever had duck. It's a bit out of my price range," he said, causing me to pinch my lips in guilt.

"I'm sorry, I didn't think..."

He leapt up from the stool, almost losing his balance, and gripped the table to keep himself upright. He looked at me in shock and I couldn't help but laugh. "I think you were right about the absinthe." He sat down and paused. "Don't feel guilty because you can afford things I can't. I'm not disappointed with my life. I do well for a human, and I know that this meal is going to be one of the best in my life."

"You do more than well, and not just for a human. Money corrupts people. Your humility only adds to your attractiveness, Constable. But it does bring me great pleasure to spoil you." Halting my cooking for a moment, I rounded the worktable to kiss him, feeling his lips part into a smile against me.

"And I, you."

I refilled his glass of absinthe and pointed an accusatory finger at him. "Sip this time, yes?"

"Yes, Ma'am," he said, taking a tiny swallow from it.

I flipped the duck breasts and dropped the halved grapes into the pan, letting them cook down a bit. The brown bits of flavor stuck to the pan until I added a dash of wine to deglaze it. The smell had my mouth watering, and I wished I were a timewalker so I could jump ahead to eating.

Michael slid my black, leather recipe book adorned with brass runes and a latch etched with the face of a wolf towards him and started flipping through it. I smirked at his curiosity as I turned back to finish my task.

"You keep your culinary and witchcraft recipes in the same book?"

"They're not such different things. Cooking is a magic of its own. It alters your emotions, invoking all of your senses. They bring me the same amount of joy."

"You've used your fire in front of me a few times now, the whole town knows of your healing abilities, and you mentioned being able to read people's honesty. Do you have any other powers?"

"Other than cooking?" I asked, peeking at him again. He had a toothy grin and lust in his eyes. "I'm afraid not. Just the boring trifecta."

"I don't think it's boring. I think it's amazing. You're amazing."

"You're not so bad yourself, Constable." I placed a duck breast on each plate, spooning a heaping mound of glazed grapes over top.

"Please, Michael."

"What if I prefer constable?" He sat up straighter.

"I would say to hold off calling me that again until after we've eaten. It would be a shame to let this gorgeous meal turn cold before we get to enjoy it."

"It's a good thing it's done then. I'm not a patient woman." I placed a plate in front of him, then picked up my knife and fork to cut into the crispy, browned skin. "You're supposed to let it rest for a few minutes, but I've never had the self-control for that," I said, staring into his eyes.

"Me neither." He speared a single grape half before slicing off a piece of duck to go with it and slowly placed it into his mouth, maintaining eye contact. A pleasured groan escaped him as the flavor electrified his tastebuds. "When I was younger, witchcraft scared the hell out of me. I had no idea what I was missing. This might be my favorite of your magic," he said, pointing the empty fork at me before taking another sip from his glass.

"I think you'll change your mind in about half an hour."

He spat his absinthe across the worktable in shock before rapidly picking up the pace on his meal.

I slid a bottle of purple liquid over to him. "This will remedy any effects you're having from the absinthe. I wouldn't want you to feel coerced into anything tonight."

"Trust me, Anna, alcohol or no alcohol, there's nothing I've wanted more in my life. I've thought about it since the moment I met you."

I rested my forearms on the table, allowing him the perfect view down the lace window of my dress. "I guess I'd better hurry up and eat then. I think we're both ready for dessert."

He took a tiny mouthful of the purple potion, and we inhaled the rest of our meal. Once my last bite was down, he slid off his stool and stalked towards me, caging me against the worktable. He pressed his warm, soft lips to mine. Our hands explored each other's bodies as the kiss grew more passionate, the sweet taste of the grapes fueling our tongues. Bunching up the skirt of my dress, he slid my drawers down in one swift motion before lifting me by my waist and depositing me on the table.

His tongue glided up the column of my neck, then gently nibbled at my ear as he slid one finger into the warm, wet crease between my thighs. Removing it, he licked my wetness off his fingers and groaned. "Damn your sorcery, woman, you're just as delicious as your cooking," he said, in a deep, gravelly tone.

"I think you've earned yourself a feast, *Constable,*" I said, taunting him.

He took the bait, making a show of sliding his head under the layers of skirts. His tongue met my tingling bundle of nerves with lightning speed, like a man starved. My hands immediately went behind me to stabilize my bucking body as his tongue wrung pleasure from me. His rough hands gripped my thighs, ensuring my safety as he buried his tongue deep inside me. My release was building, but he slowed and gently circled in languid movements.

"Don't slow down, I was so close."

He chuckled, his voice muffled between my thighs. "I've been waiting too long for this. I'm going to draw it out all night, Mo Chridhe."

My heart. My own clenched at his words. I had never experienced true love before, and I wasn't sure I wanted to start. But could I deny it? Was that the constant squeeze inside my chest?

But then why did my body feel such a pull towards Killian? I couldn't process it, so there was only one thing left to do.

"Bedroom," I whispered, yanking the skirts up to grip his hair and tug him away from me to look into his eyes. His own shone with lust, his gentlemanly side melting away. I repeated myself. "Bedroom. Now."

"Yes, ma'am," he said, scooping me up by my rear end. I wrapped my legs around his waist and directed him up the stairs to my bedroom. He flung the door open and startled Ranai, who jumped into attack mode until she realized who was with me. Letting out an approving howl, she left us in privacy. Dropping me to the floor, he made quick work of removing my dress before scooping me back up.

He laid me down gently on my back and unbuttoned his shirt, his gaze roaming my whole body. I sat up and began to untie the rear laces of my corset as we stared each other down. The heat building between us felt stronger than my own powers, and it warmed the room. As he exposed the well-defined muscles of his chest and abdomen, I was pleasantly surprised to find him covered in a smattering of hair.

"I had planned to tell you earlier," I said, in a sultry tone. "But I didn't want to seem too forward. I think we're past that now."

His hand moved to the ties of his trousers.

"I made a contraceptive tonic with cohosh and pennyroyal leaves. I drank it this morning, and it lasts for one full day. I wasn't sure if you were familiar with this particular magical brew," I said, flinging my corset to the floor. My entire body was on display, and his eyes flicked between my eyes, my bare breasts, and between my thighs.

His warm smile warred with his sensual movements as he dropped his pants and undergarments to the floor, exposing his impressive body to me for the first time. "That wasn't necessary, Mo Chridhe. Children are a gift, and I couldn't ask for a more impressive woman to bear mine."

I ran my fingers over my breasts, and his hard cock twitched as he watched. "A lovely sentiment, but the townsfolk would talk if we were not wed," I joked. "Magical beings are not as judgmental as humans when it comes to such things. And I've never cared much for other people's opinions."

He shrugged as he wrapped his hand around himself, gently stroking. I reached out to replace his hand with mine and a hiss escaped between his teeth, his head tipping back in pleasure. "If you want to wed, we can wed. They'd only talk because they are jealous. I don't blame them. Even I'm jealous of me right now."

His gaze met mine, and I raised an eyebrow at him. He leaned down to kiss me, but I dodged it, teasing him with a rougher stroke before pulling his face to mine. Our tongues met in a sensual dance, tasting and touching each other before I took a tiny nip of his bottom lip. "I'm afraid I'm going to need a better proposal than that, Constable Sheehan. Until then, I'll settle for no less than two orgasms tonight. And I'm sorry to say, your perfect hair is not going to last long."

His grin spread slowly, like a predator about to devour its prey. "I can handle two," he said. Both he and his very large manhood standing tall, he whistled. "Hell, I might have to aim for three."

Scooting back so my head rested atop my pile of pillows, I spread my legs invitingly. He climbed onto the bed and prowled towards me, sliding his fingertips up the insides of my legs as he approached.

"I think you've had enough to eat, Michael," I said, gliding my palm up and down his shaft, before squeezing it gently. "I've been dying to know how this would feel inside of me, Constable. I don't think I can wait another minute to find out."

His lips crashed into mine, our tongues swirling together in a frenzied dance. He held himself above me with one arm as his other hand dug into my hair. Mine roamed up his chest and over his shoulders before grazing down his biceps and squeezing them. Breaking the kiss, he looked down at me and smiled. "You're sure?"

Cupping his cheek in my palm, I answered. "I've never been more sure of anything, Michael."

Resting his forehead on mine for a moment, he kissed me again as he situated himself between my legs.

I had thought about what making love to him would be like. I had known it would be fierce and passionate, and I had been impatient for a glimpse of that lawful authority. The juxtaposition of that assertiveness and his need to ensure my comfort and pleasure made for the perfect lover.

I was safe. Protected. And possibly happy?

Chapter Eight

Anna and I had only shared conversation, so why did her relationship with Constable Sheehan bother me? He was a good man, true, I didn't fault her for that. But it felt...wrong. Not because it was him. Because it wasn't me. She was gorgeous, but that wasn't all. She was brilliant. Strong. And something drew me to her. Something familiar and right. Our conversation had breached a subject I never discussed, and it sounded like she hadn't either. Though Michael had also lost a parent, he had been much older. He didn't know what it felt like, and I doubted he discussed emotions with her. It wasn't him. It couldn't be, because of his job.

She was all I could think about on the bumpy coach ride back to the enclave and while teaching my astrology lesson the next morning. Even the smell of teenage sweat couldn't pull me from it, despite not being able to get its putrid taste out of my mouth. We needed some women in the enclave to influence these young men and their awful hygiene. My classrooms were scented with frankincense for that very reason.

"Alright, boys. You each have a stack of star charts for the year you were born. Find the one for your birth month and compare it to those around you. Using your textbooks, I want 500 words on how your star chart correlates to your traits."

One of my best students raised his hand. "Professor, these are potion recipes. You didn't give us star charts."

"He looks lost. Maybe a pretty witch put a love spell on him?" Another one said, causing the class to snicker.

They weren't far off. I got the boys settled with the real star charts. I was distracted. I didn't notice the adults entering my classroom as our session concluded. I didn't comprehend a word Elias or Aiden said until the latter elbowed me, bringing me back to the real world.

"Did you hear my request, Killian?" the elder asked.

"I'm sorry, sir. My mind is still trying to piece together all the clues about the dead bodies. I'm afraid I got lost in thought."

Elias released a frustrated sigh. "We need you to get closer to Anna. Find out if she's in communication with her Aunt Astrid. I suspect Astrid is seeking revenge on Dracht, and maybe Anna is aiding her. Or knows where she is. Either way, find out what she knows. Do whatever you have to do to get us this information. Do you understand?"

"I don't need to. She believes her aunt to be dead. She's never met her."

"Do you believe everything any pretty witch tells you?" Aiden asked.

"No. But I believe the honest and helpful ones. She's done nothing but aid the community since she got here, including the investigation. She has nobody left. I know exactly how that feels."

"You have had us since you were a child, dear boy. You're not alone." Elias placed a hand on my shoulder in a fatherly gesture.

"I know, but it's...different."

"Use that to your advantage. Bond with her. I'm sure you're right, in which case, you get to spend more time with her," Aiden added.

"You don't have to convince me. You know I always do as you

ask. Do you really think it could be her aunt? What makes you think so?"

"There are murmurings among the legacy families that she cursed them. She was a powerful witch, but a hex beyond the grave? That type of magic is too rare for me to believe."

"Alright, I'll pay her a visit tonight." Anna had extended an invitation for anytime I needed to talk about my past. It was the perfect opportunity.

"Thank you, Killian. I am more and more thankful we found you that terrible day when you were a child."

While I was glad they had found me, something about him constantly telling me about it irked me. It had been over twenty years, and I wasn't a child anymore. It was like he didn't want me to forget I owed him. Like everything I did since then hadn't made up for that.

Later that night, I changed into my most comfortable attire and borrowed a horse to ride to Anna's. There was no sense in taking an entire coach for myself. My familiar, Sion, normally stayed in the enclave, but he could be of some assistance—since most witches find foxes adorable—so he trotted along beside us. It was a brisk, early fall evening. The sun set earlier now, and the green leaves were fading as their chlorophyll depleted. This was my favorite time of year. When I arrived at Leighis Chateau, I was grateful to find that the constable's coach wasn't there. I tied my horse up to the post outside and hopped up the few stairs, knocking twice.

A quiet, middle-aged man in a dark waistcoat and paints opened the door almost immediately. An older woman with a stern face stood beside him. "Can I help you?" the woman asked.

"Good evening, madam. My name is Killian Tine-Radharc,

and I'm here to see Miss Anna Leighis. She extended me an invitation to chat whenever I should need it, but if she's not available, I can come back another time."

"Come in, Killian," a sultry voice said from behind the old woman. "Thank you, Mrs. Yates. Would you mind bringing some refreshments to the sitting room?"

"Of course not, dear. I'll be along shortly."

"And who do we have here?" she asked, looking down at my dark red fox, his white chest puffed out in pride.

"This is Sion. I hope you don't mind. He's been trapped inside the enclave for weeks, and he enjoys the fresh fall air as much as I do, ay boy?" Sion swished his tail in confirmation.

"Of course not." She squatted and held out her hand to him, and he sniffed it and then let her gently pat his head before he rubbed himself all over my ankles like a cat. She whistled, and a dark wolf bounded down the stairs, tail wagging. "This is Ranai. Ranai, would you like to come join us and entertain Sion while we chat?"

The enormous canine bowed her head in acceptance.

Anna smiled at me and gestured to follow her, and I complied. We entered a small sitting room with four cushy chairs surrounding a round table. She sat first, and I took the seat next to her instead of opposite. I needed to be close to her. My body often felt like it needed to be close to women, but this was the first time my heart and mind agreed.

"Is everything alright?" she asked, resting her elbow on the arm of the chair to prop up her head. The gesture had her leaning a little closer to me.

"I don't know. I feel...off lately. I'm sorry for intruding, but I know it's safe to talk to you. I don't always feel comfortable speaking about certain things within the enclave."

"Like feelings? I find men like Elias and Aiden tend to be scared of that kind of thing."

"Is Constable Sheehan the same way?"

She shifted in her seat, crossing her legs and adjusting her skirt. "Everyone has their strengths and weaknesses. Did you come here to talk about Michael?"

"I'm sorry, it wasn't right of me to comment on that. But no, I needed to be in good company. With somebody who understands me. Even though the enclave is crowded, sometimes it feels so lonely." I ran my fingers through my hair. It had recently grown out enough to touch the top of my ears, so I fussed with it more.

"You didn't strike me as somebody who would be lonely," she said, eyes flicking up and down my body. "I'm sorry to hear that," she added with a sympathetic nod as her eyes held mine.

Something about her pity at this sent a jolt of electricity through me. I was glad when her housekeeper entered, breaking the tension. She placed a tray of cheese and fruit down with a kettle and two teacups.

"Thank you, madam."

"You're welcome, sir. Anna, I'll be in the kitchen should you need anything else."

Sion and Ranai lay on the floor between us, each at their master's feet. They had only just met, so they were getting along but wary of each other and kept their distance.

"I have to ask. Are you jealous of me and Michael?"

"If I said yes?"

Ranai sat up and stared at me, a low growl rumbling in her throat. Anna eyed her suspiciously before gently stroking her head.

"I don't think she likes me very much," I said, frowning.

"That's so strange, she's been so friendly with Michael. I'm sure she'll come around."

"Have you considered that Michael might be the one committing these murders?"

"Don't be ridiculous, Killian. He's too good for that."

"His job is innately violent. And he's the first to know a body is found."

"I'm an excellent judge of character. I can assure you it's not Constable Sheehan."

We sat in silence for a moment, and it was clear by her crossed arms and sour face that I had taken the discussion too far.

"Was there something specific you wanted to talk about, or did you just need the company?" she finally asked.

"I'm so sorry, I didn't realize how late it was," I said, standing up. "I didn't mean to impose."

"Sit down, Killian. You obviously came here for something."

I paced around a few steps, running my fingers through my hair. My heart told me that I could open up to her, but Hecate forbid if Elias and Aiden find out. Taking a deep breath, I decided to trust my gut. "In all honesty, Elias asked me to get closer to you. I have no idea why, but something is off. I thought you should know he wanted me to watch you. And if I'm frank, I wanted to see you again. I enjoy being around you."

"Why are you telling me this?"

"I'm not sure. Elias found me. The Triumvirate raised me. I owe them so much. They've made me who I am. But my instincts tell me you're a good person and that there's no reason for me to watch you. They think the reign of terror on Dracht is your aunt's doing, and that you may know where she is. Or that she's around. That you're aiding her somehow, but I know that's not true. I know it. Maybe they're trying to get me out of the way? Or they've noticed how I stare at you and thought it would help."

"And how do you stare at me?"

"Come on, Anna. I know you've noticed."

She smiled, and my heart almost exploded. "It's still nice to hear once in a while." Her expression dropped and turned hard. "Do you trust me, Killian?"

"I do. I don't know why I do, but I do."

"I believe Elias and Aiden are trying to turn the town against me. I don't know why, but the constable and I overheard them talking about it. That's why they have you getting closer to me. They know my Aunt Astrid is dead. I'm fairly certain the Triumvirate chased her out of town. Who knows the lengths they would've gone to find her, but my mother stopped hearing from her long ago. That's why I'm back. I need to know why. I need to know who. She did nothing to deserve any of that. Maybe she died of natural causes, but at least I'll have closure. And if I make a few friends along the way and help everyone in Dracht stay safe and happy, that's all I need."

I nodded, my heart racing with panic thinking that Elias and Aiden would find out I had told her. But she wasn't surprised. And she didn't ask for anything from me in return. She was a good person. But perhaps Elias and Aiden weren't who I thought they were? But I had known them my entire life. They had raised me. My eyes darted around the room as thoughts raced through my head. I couldn't make all of this add up. None of it made sense. It was time the other Triumvirate members let me into their inner circle.

"You okay? You looked like you got lost in there," she said, pointing to my head.

"I'm fine, just processing. I'd better head back. If I hear anything else, I'll let you know. And thank you, Anna. For listening."

"You're always welcome here. Actually, I'm glad you came tonight. I'm planning to throw a Mabon festival at my house this Saturday. I'm inviting witches and warlocks, but I'm also inviting the humans. I'm not sure how well that would go over with Elias and Aiden, so I haven't informed them, but I would really like it if you could be there. I think showing solidarity is important during these uncertain times."

"That's an excellent idea. I wouldn't miss it for the world."

I considered giving her a hug or a kiss on the cheek, but I second-guessed myself because she might suspect me of using my powers on her.

"Have a good evening, Anna." I tipped my head towards her and silently summoned Sion to follow me out.

Mounting my horse, I looked down at my familiar, and he shook his head.

"Don't worry, I know what I'm doing. I hope."

Chapter Nine

Michael

Anna had invites made up quickly, packed with all the information the humans would need to celebrate Mabon. Time and place, what to wear, what to bring, and what to prepare for. It would bring both factions together and help make sure everyone supported Anna, should things turn ugly.

When I arrived after my shift, a few guests were filing in. The outside of the house had been decorated, both sides of the steps lined with apples, gourds, acorns, pine cones, and ears of multicolored corn. The smell of myrrh and sage wafted out of the house each time the door was opened by Anna's butler. On either side of the door, a homemade broom leaned up against the house. Everyone knew witches couldn't fly, but the myth frightened the hell out of human children.

Excited whispers filled the air. Humans. Dozens of them. Thrilled to be invited to a witch celebration for the first time in the history of Dracht. Most of them already loved Anna thanks to her healing services, but I couldn't wait to see what waves she made with ideas like this. I entered the house with a huge smile on my face until I turned the corner. Killian leaned back against the wall, arms crossed, and his irritating, unkempt hair flailed every time he turned his head a fraction of an inch. Anna stood beside him in a free-flowing, burnt-orange dress. She laughed along with whatever story he was telling the three women surrounding him.

The next thing I knew, I had been knocked to the ground by a giant, dark shadow—Ranai. One woman let out a small scream, and a few of the other humans gasped, concerned until I greeted her. "There's my sweet girl. I missed you so much," I said, sitting up and scratching her behind her ears. I turned to see Killian scowling at me. *Interesting.* A red fox was tucked behind his ankles, distancing itself from the wolf. I noticed Mrs. Yates moving quickly up the stairs with a gentleman I didn't recognize, and they were smiling grandly at each other.

Anna left Killian's side, holding a hand out to help me up. She was much stronger than I expected and lifted me with ease.

"What's his problem?" I asked, tilted my head in the warlock's direction.

"Ranai isn't fond of him yet."

"Good. She's an excellent judge of character." I smiled back down at the loyal beast and scratched her side as she leaned against me.

"I'm glad you're here, I think we have enough people to get started. I need to grab something, but can you round everyone up to meet in the kitchen? I'll give a quick speech, and then everyone can get to it. I'm just not sure where Mrs. Yates is."

"I saw her head upstairs with an older gentleman," I commented.

Anna giggled, then whispered something to her lady's maid, who nodded and began to pour drinks.

She peeled off toward the sitting room and I did as she said. She wasn't long, and when she returned, she drank down the orange, fizzy liquid from a small vial. I startled as she began speaking, her voice now amplified.

"Thank you so much for coming. I'm so excited to bring together witches, warlocks, and humans for our first holiday celebrating as one. It's an honor to help bring Dracht together, and I hope this tradition will continue. I'd like to start out by sharing about Mabon and why we celebrate it."

She paused, looking at everyone with a smile as she took my hand and gestured for me to help her up onto the worktable.

"In essence, Mabon is very similar to your Thanksgiving. It's the autumn equinox, when the sun and the moon, male and female energies, are in balance. The nights will grow longer, the days shorter, and the air colder. So we take the time to reflect, give thanks to Mother Earth for our bountiful harvest, and think about the balance by honoring death as nature prepares for a long, dark winter."

She lit a small flame in her hand, which was rewarded with a chorus of surprised but pleased gasps from the crowd. She held a bundle of common garden sage in her other hand, which she lit and waved around in front of herself, allowing the gentle aroma and smoke to permeate the room, mingling with the scent of roasting vegetables. Though it smelled nice, I didn't feel any different, and I didn't understand the point of it.

"In old Gaelic magic, common garden sage represents wisdom, but also cleansing. I invite you now to close your eyes, think about everything you want to let go of. Anything that hasn't served you in the past. We leave it here and prepare to move forward. Next, think of what you are most grateful for, whether it be the warm food that fills your bellies or the loved ones standing around you. Take a moment to be grateful for what the gods and nature have provided and give your thanks."

Closing her eyes and tilting her head back, she let the room be silent for a few moments—the only noise the crackling of the stove. I pondered how thankful I was that I had come to introduce myself the day she arrived. I was also very thankful my mother remained in good health.

"As some of you may have noticed, I've decorated with the lovely harvest Mother Nature has bestowed upon us. I'd like to take this time to give her thanks for what I've prepared for you all today. There are refreshments in each room on the lower floor.

Please eat and drink your fill, get to know each other, and take the time to be grateful for everything we will accomplish together—all citizens of Dracht, united as one. Thank you for joining me in my home, I can't tell you how much this means to me."

Now that she had finished her speech, I finally had the chance to take in my surroundings. She had cleaned the worktable since I had been here last. My brain replayed what I had done to her here, and I couldn't help but grin. She caught my eye, fully aware of where my thoughts had wandered to.

The whole thing was a massive display, beautifully decorated with burnt-orange, deep cranberry, and walnut-brown candles with a wolf statue as the centerpiece. The smell of various sweet cakes and treats lining the table made my stomach grumble as Ranai nudged her nose into my palm.

Two warlocks and a witch entered the kitchen as most of the humans filtered out. All three were wearing their finest clothes and directed warm smiles at Anna.

"Flur! Alder! Caltain! I can't believe all three of you came!" she said cheerily. She wiped her hands on a towel and gave each of them a joyous hug.

"As if we would miss your groundbreaking party that will no doubt piss off the Trimvirate," the shorter warlock with red hair and a beard said, eyeing Killian.

Killian nodded. "Elias and Aiden are very upset, Alder. I, however, think it's a brilliant idea."

Silence filled the room until the short, curvy witch broke it, pushing a box towards Anna. "I brought a selection of bite-sized treats. I know you said not to bring anything, but I couldn't resist. I threw a few of your favorites in there, too."

"Thank you, Flur. You know I can't say no to anything you make. I'm sure you already know Constable Sheehan. Michael, this is Flur, Alder, and Caltain. Three of my good friends. Flur here owns the bakery in Witch's Way, and Alder and Caltain own the magical supply shop there."

"I've seen you around, but it's nice to officially meet all of you." I shook each of their hands, but Flur pulled me in for a hug. I had never been treated this well by magical beings before, and I knew it was Anna's impact.

Anna was taking a tray of roasted vegetables out of the oven, but there was a tray already out and cooling. I picked up a lukewarm piece of roasted carrot and fed it to Ranai, who scampered off like she was absconding with a stolen good.

Chuckling, I turned back to Anna, who had her eyebrow raised at me. I shrugged. She handed me a glass filled with an amber liquid with bubbles rising to the top and a faint scent of apples.

"Don't worry, it's only spiced cider."

"So, Mabon is basically a celebration of the season changing?" Taking a sip of the sweet liquid, I smacked my lips at the delicious flavor.

"That's the simplified explanation. We like to celebrate each change by thanking Mother Nature for all she gives us. As far as our holidays go, I thought the tamest was the best first experience for all the humans in Dracht. Be glad it's not Beltane. That's a bunch of drunken dancing, fire, elderflower champagne, and sex." She elbowed me at the end of the sentence and looked up at me through lowered lashes. For a moment, I forgot we weren't alone until the slug ruined the moment.

"That one might be my favorite," Killian said from behind me.

"I wouldn't mind it so much if it were only you and I." I took her hand in mine and kissed the back of her knuckles.

"What's wrong, Constable. Your parents didn't teach you to share? I don't mind sharing."

The thought of the warlock naked anywhere near Anna—or myself—sent a shiver through my body. "Certain things aren't meant to be shared."

She cut him a glare, then turned back to the spread of food on the worktable before us. Carefully curating the items she selected, she placed a collection of roasted vegetables and cubes of each cake on a plate and handed it to me. I wasn't sure how they would taste together, but popping one of the orange blocks I assumed was sweet potato into my mouth, I found it sweet and a little spicy. They were perfectly paired with the light but fruity pieces of cake.

Killian waited a moment, watching, then decided to make his own plate. I eyed him in victory, earning a scowl. Both of my women—Anna and Ranai—had chosen me over him. I had to enjoy it a little.

A few human women joined us, thanking Anna for opening up her home and for sharing this sacred ritual with them. Our plan was going well. Then they turned to Killian, and I was floored by their brazenness. It was clear they were interested in him, but Anna rolling her eyes at them affected me more than I liked to admit. Jealousy didn't look good on me. I had been furious when I realized she had invited him, but he was our best hope at staying in the loop on the Triumvirates' doings. I had to deal with it.

She left Killian and I alone for a while as she mingled throughout the kitchen and sitting room, chatting with guests. Whether witch or human, she treated everyone the same, and it gave my heart an unfamiliar tingling sensation. Killian and I sat in silence, munching on the array of foods in front of us for what felt like hours until she finally returned.

When she did, I put an arm around her, relishing the tickling sensation as my palm slid across the soft fabric of her dress. I tucked her into my side as she enjoyed her delicious treats, occasionally interrupted by a grateful human, warlock, or witch who wanted to thank her for a lovely day. After an hour or so, the crowd dwindled down, leaving only the two of us and Killian. *Great.*

At least I'd have the chance to ask what had been weighing on my mind. "Killian, the first day you three came to the morgue, how did you know ahead of my messenger what was going on?"

Snatching another cube of cake, he popped it in his mouth

and winked at Anna. "These are delicious, though I can't say I'm surprised, given who made them." He then turned to me, his eyes darkening. "Aiden had a prophetic dream. He saw the body with no eyeballs and informed Elias and I. Said we should hurry to the morgue before anyone tampered with it."

"Did either you or Elias have a similar dream? See any of the victims."

"Elias hasn't mentioned anything, but I haven't."

"That's a little convenient, isn't it?" I questioned, crossing my arms.

Killian stood up straighter, looking down at me over Anna's head. "What are you implying, Constable?"

"He says he has a prophetic dream that nobody else on the Triumvirate has, and you just...believe him? Seems suspicious to me. If I recall, he was also the one to identify the bodies, despite their unfortunate states."

Anna turned to me then, her sparkling green eyes full of questions. "Are you saying Aiden is your top suspect?"

"Right now, we don't have a top suspect, but he's certainly on my list. As are you, Mr. Tine-Radharc." I had told Anna he wasn't when we were out to dinner, but I didn't want this sniveling rat getting comfortable.

Killian snorted. "Were you not the first person to find the bodies? That's rather convenient, wouldn't you say? It's certainly why you're the top suspect on the Triumvirate's list."

"That's absurd. I'm the head of the Dracht Watch," I said matter-of-factly.

"Perfect station to get away with murder, wouldn't you say?" He moved closer to me, his arm brushing Anna's as she stood between us.

"Gentlemen, I think that's enough. I know you both well enough that I am sure neither of you is the killer. Neither of you have the motivation or the character to carry out such a heinous act. I think we've had enough alcohol for the evening and too much social interaction. Perhaps we should call it a night?"

"I think that's a wonderful idea. Good evening, Killian. I can escort you out," I said, grabbing his arm and dragging him to the door.

"This is Anna's home. I'd prefer her to show me out if you wouldn't mind."

"Actually, I do mind."

"Michael, that's enough. Killian is my guest."

I dropped the weasel's arm and turned back to her with a heavy sigh. My foot tapped, waiting for her to kick him out.

"I had a lovely evening, Anna," he said, placing a kiss on her cheek. She let him. It took every ounce of self-control not to punch him square in the nose. "Inviting the humans was a brilliant idea. An excellent way to bring everyone together, given how scared they are."

"Thank you, Killian. Good evening," she said, nodding at the butler to open the door and gesturing for Killian to exit with a tight smile. After he left, she whirled back to me. "Was that really necessary?"

"Yes. You're mine."

She crossed her arms and lifted one brow at me, seeming taller than me for a moment. Her jaw clenched. "First of all, I belong to no one but myself. Secondly, Killian is a guest, and that is all. He is also aiding us—against his own people I might add—and your behavior was absolutely uncalled for. I expect better from you from now on. Is that clear?"

"Crystal. Are you ready for bed, or would you like me to help you clean up first?"

"Mrs. Yates will handle the cleaning, but I think you should go. It's been a long night for all of us."

"Anna, don't be like that." My head dropped as she held up a hand to stop me.

"I'm not mad. I think it's sweet how jealous you are of Killian..."

"I'm not jealous of that creepy warlock," I interrupted.

Her glare stopped me in my tracks. "Yes, you are. But you

shouldn't be. I just need a good night's sleep. Why don't you stop by for dinner tomorrow? Just you and me, okay?"

Pursing my lips, I nodded at her. She placed a single kiss on my lips and gave me a sad smile before the silent butler opened the door to show me out.

Chapter Ten

I had barely slept the night before. My heart raced and my mind spun, trying to sort out these feelings. I shook my head and sank deep into thought as my fingers mindlessly prepared potion ingredients. I regretted throwing Michael out. His jealousy had me wanting him to throw me against the wall and prove how much I belonged to him, right in front of Killian.

But Killian...I swore I had felt a shock through my whole body when he kissed my cheek. I feared he had read me, but my father's journals made it clear that their power only worked with a touch of their hands. He had kept his hands to himself the entire evening. I had only felt something like that once before, when I was too young to understand it, and it hadn't worked out.

What a mess my life had become. A pileup of murders, a powerful group of warlocks conspiring against me, and now I was stuck in this conundrum of the heart. If only this goddess-forsaken potion would sort itself out. Many humans believe that love potions *make* the person of your choosing fall in love with you, but there is no such magic. In old witch's tales passed down through generations, it is said that love potions are created to determine your one true love. Like a litmus test of love. I'm determined to figure it out. Not just for solving the puzzle that was irking me, but because it would be an honor to my human mother to be the witch who goes down in history for such a prestigious discovery. At least officially, anyway.

There have been whispers of which ingredients should be included—ranging from the spicy and delicious to the downright disgusting, immoral, and illegal—but no documented information about what works. Needless to say, I've only tested the items on the lower end of the spectrum. Love is meant to be beautiful and special, so it made sense to me. This morning, I hoped it would inspire me to sort out my feelings. But first, I needed more components. And caffeine.

I hadn't found my way to Bubbling Brews before, but as I entered, I knew I'd be visiting often. The nutty aroma filled my nose, and I closed my eyes to breathe it in deeper. I tightened my shawl around my shoulders to fight off the chill. I opened my eyes again and took in my surroundings. The shop was set up differently from any place I'd ever been. As soon as you entered, there were small tables with two chairs, but along the back was a long bar top and stools. Behind the countertop a cheerful-looking man with medium-length, ruffled hair whistled a tune as he flitted about, his melody the only sound.

The store was otherwise empty, so I approached to see what offerings I had to choose from. "Good morning, sir," I said.

"Good morning, you must be Miss Leighis. The name's Declan. So nice to meet you. What can I get for you?" he asked, wiping his hands.

"I'm not sure, what do you recommend?"

"I don't know about you, but I'm a mood drinker, so it changes. Do you prefer coffee or tea?"

"Both, but I normally make my own tea. I'm in a coffee mood."

"Any particular flavor addition suit your fancy?"

My eyes widened. "I've only had plain coffee. I didn't know there were options."

"Oh, my dear, I'm about to open your eyes to a world you'll

never want to leave. Have a seat, and I'll give you a few samples." He placed a few miniaturized mugs in front of me and poured coffee into each of them, placing a creamer jug beside them. He topped each cup with a different substance. One with ground cinnamon, one with a liquid that smelled like vanilla, and one with what looked like caramelized and browned sugar. "Try them and tell me which is your favorite."

Skeptical, I tilted my head at him curiously, but his genuine smile had me picking up the first mug and taking a sip. Cinnamon. Absolutely delicious. With cream swirled in and the powdered spices on top, the pale brown drink slid smoothly down my throat. The warmth filled my insides, the spices and flavor dancing along my taste buds.

"Wow."

His smile grew, and he nodded knowingly as another patron entered. "Let me help him, and then I'll be back to find out which you like best."

Though all were fantastic, the cinnamon remained my favorite. A little sweet, a little kick, and full of warmth and joy.

I arrived at Magickal Arts and Hearts just in time to watch Caltain flip the sign to "open". He smiled through the glass door when he noticed my arrival and held it for me to enter. "It's so lovely to see you again, dear. Looking for anything special today? Herbs? Ingredients? Advice?"

Tilting my head, I held his eyes. "What makes you think I need advice?"

He pursed his lips. "Partly your melancholy demeanor this morning, partly rumors from your lovely party."

"Where is Alder?"

"Home. He started feeling ill last night."

"Would you like me to look him over? I am a healer, you know."

He smiled sadly at me before looking down at a vial he was fiddling with. "I'm sure he'll be fine. I checked on him last night and then spent the night here so I wouldn't catch whatever he has. I didn't want to leave him, but he insisted. Now, have a seat and tell me what's wrong."

I sat on a stool along the main worktable as he produced hot cups of tea from seemingly nowhere.

"How did you know Alder was the right person for you? Your one true love?"

Alder pulled a box out from underneath his side of the table. "True love potion? I had a feeling you'd be working on it, so I took the liberty of preparing a box of potential ingredients. Alder and I never figured out the potion ourselves, but then again, we only had eyes for each other. One warlock for each of us, no human constable to compete with," he said with a wink. "Trust me, dear, I'm not judging. Had there been a constable who looked like Michael Sheehan, he would've given Alder a run for his money. But for us, we just knew."

"But how? A feeling in your stomach? Electricity when you touch? Feeling safe when you're near him?"

His friendly chuckle resonated through me, calming my anxiety. "It's different for everyone, but I think it's all of those things. I could be myself, and he accepted me, as I do him. We wanted the same things in life, had the same goals. My time spent with him was always a pleasure, and every second away filled with thinking about when I'd see him next. Like he completed me. I know you've been around Dracht with Constable Sheehan, have you spent the same amount of time with Killian, or were the rumors just that?"

"I've been seeing Michael often. Killian is more of a business relationship."

"Ah, yes, the murders."

I nodded. "He did come to my Mabon party at my request,

and we've been working together on the investigation. He came to my house to chat one other time," I said, tipping my head to the side, trying to keep my voice in a flat, factual tone.

"Oh my, how scandalous," he said, crossing his legs and leaning in to put a hand on my arm. "How did that go?"

"It wasn't scandalous. It was only to talk."

"Mhm."

I couldn't help but smile back at him. From his facial expressions, I knew he wasn't judging me. He genuinely wanted the gossip and was loving every second.

"When I came to Dracht, I had no intention of dating. No interest in men. I just wanted to fulfill my duty and hopefully feel a little closer to my Aunt Astrid. I don't have anybody left but my wolf, Ranai. Michael showed up on the first day and made me feel welcome. He's a gentleman, and very handsome, and even though I don't need protecting, he makes me feel safe. He's made it very clear he feels the same way."

"But?"

"But..." I shook my head, unsure of what to say, my eyes burning from trying to hold back tears.

"Killian makes your tummy feel like butterflies are in there?"

I could feel my cheeks flush, but I didn't bother to hide it as I shifted my legs to seat myself more comfortably. "I felt an actual spark when he kissed my cheek. And he's so...different from Michael. He's much more flirtatious. He's a romantic, and I can talk to him about how things make me feel. Michael is very practical."

"Does Michael give you butterflies in your tummy, too?"

I fiddled with the collar of my dress, a single tear falling from my eye. Caltain wiped it away.

"I take that as a yes. Well, dear, I think you're going to need everything in this box for your experiments." He pushed the box towards me. "Some of those items are...difficult to obtain and a little unsavory. You didn't get them here, yeah?"

My fingers loosened from their death grip on my teacup as I

took the box from him with a wide grin. I slid a few coins across the front counter and snatched up the box before he could push the coins back to me. "Go home and check on Alder. If he isn't feeling better, please do call me. I couldn't live with myself if anything happened to either of you."

"Of course, dear," he said as I reached the door. As my hands gripped the knob he added, "Anna, I recommend choosing ingredients that remind you of the bond you share with each of them. It should help you refine it correctly, if the old witch's tales are to be believed."

I met his eyes with a pinched brow. He winked at me and headed into the back room.

Arriving back home, I sorted through the ingredients Caltain had given me and put most of them away in my apothecary cabinet. Most of it was for healing. Coltsfoot and slippery elm for sore throats, feverfew and sorrel leaves for colds and strengthening immune systems, lavender oil to cure insomnia, and dried mesquite to burn for purification. But he hadn't been kidding that some of this was a bit unsavory, much of it rare and slightly illegal. Spider legs, rattlesnake venom, graveyard dirt, blood of a virgin, ground heart of widow, fingernails of a rake. I wasn't going near any of that stuff. I grabbed a few of the items and headed to the kitchen to begin.

1 teaspoon of paprika to invoke passion
A dash of iron filings for attraction
2 drops of blood from the witch's left thumb, pricked with a thorn
Half a lime, squeezed to release inhibitions
4 orchid petals to increase allure and give a competitive edge
A tablespoon of catnip to energize the potion and speed up results

A pinch of tamarind seeds to bring out their wild side

Holding my palms out and upward, the vial centered between them, I recited the spell I had been drafting.

"Torn between two, one fiery red and one dressed in blue. Show me my destiny, oh goddess of night, for I do not know which one is right."

I heard the shattering glass before I felt the explosion, the ingredients now covering my face and the top of my dress. Fortunately, none of them were caustic. My head dropped, and I let out a huff, my hair now surrounding me in a chaotic mess.

Mrs. Yates drifted into the kitchen, took in the mess, and let out a sigh. "Perhaps you should take a break. The constable sent a messenger to request your presence at the morgue. They found a new body this morning. You go get changed and sorted, and I'll clean up this mess."

Blowing the errant strands of hair out of my eyes, I nodded. "Serendipitous timing, indeed."

Chapter Eleven

Elias drifted into my morning lesson with a scowl, the children eying him in fear. "Mr. Tine-Radharc's classes are cancelled for the rest of the day. You are all dismissed."

Aiden entered shortly after the last child had passed through the doorway. "You summoned me, Elias?"

"There's been another victim. Alder O'Faolin was found dead this morning by his husband, eyeballs removed."

"We lost another one? How are we going to..." Aiden started, trailing off as his eyes flicked to me.

"Going to what?" I asked. "Look, I can tell you are hiding something from me. How am I supposed to help with the investigation if you're not telling me everything? There are three members of this triumvirate, you know. A triangle of trust. Have I not proved myself to both of you?"

Aiden opened his mouth to speak, but Elias held up a hand. "He's right. He deserves the truth. We've been trying to build up our strength and the magical strength of Dracht. To do so, we needed to link the strongest members of the magical community with a powerful spell. Many who had been doing research for us have fallen victim to this assassin."

My head jolted back as if I had been slapped. "Why didn't you tell me sooner? It has to be somebody who is in on this plan. That should make the suspect list shorter."

"I'm afraid that won't help. We haven't been forthcoming, and most of those helping us aren't fully aware of how our powers work. Somebody knows far more than they should," Aiden informed me.

"We need to get to the morgue quickly. I don't trust Anna and Constable Sheehan to be there without us, and the mortician is close with the latter," Elias said.

My eyes must've been full of mistrust as I glared at Elias.

"I promise, Killian. We will tell you everything. Right now, you know what's most important. We must go." His hand on my shoulder no longer did anything to assuage me.

"Fine, but confirm what you suggested. Alder was working with you?"

"Yes, every victim so far has been," Aiden confirmed, earning a scowl from Elias.

When we arrived at the morgue, Constable Sheehan was already in with the body, consoling the grieving husband. Michael rolled his eyes when he saw me before turning back to Caltain. Aiden, Eilas, and I hung back, waiting, presumably, for the arrival of Miss Leighis. The door swung open, and Anna walked in, hair in a neat bun atop her head and wearing a simple black dress.

"Constable, I got your messenger. Another body has been found, who..." she trailed off, realizing there were others in the room. "Caltain, what's wrong?"

The crying man dabbed his eyes with his handkerchief and moved, allowing her to see the face of the body covered in cloth.

Her eyes widened and she froze. "No. No, it can't be." She ran to the body and put her hands on either side of his face, as if she were trying to force her healing powers into him. "Alder, wake up. You have to wake up." The man's face was pale, a stark contrast to the bright red of his beard and hair. With no eyeballs in the sockets, his ghostly appearance was chilling.

Caltain sniffled and pulled her away as he shook his head in despair. "I found him like that this morning, if I had called you last night instead of leaving him..."

"This is *not* your fault," she said firmly, gripping the lanky man by the shoulders. Tears streamed down her face, and I wanted to destroy whoever had made her feel this way. These warlocks were her friends, and someone had taken one of them away from her.

He pulled her into his chest for a tight hug as they both sobbed, the rest of us watching in silence. He stroked her hair and pulled away, taking a deep breath as he held her gaze. He nodded and gave her a sad smile. "I have to make funeral preparations. Alder wanted to be cremated and have his ashes used to plant a new tree in our yard. I'll let you all get back to the investigation."

"We're going to figure out who did this, do you hear me?" Anna asked, still holding onto him.

He nodded as fresh tears poured out of his eyes. The taste of bile burned my throat. I had seen a number of dead and mutilated bodies at this point, but this was the first victim that had any relation to someone I knew.

"I mean it, Caltain. None of us will rest until the monster is found. In the meantime, if you need help with preparations or need to talk, stop by or send a messenger to fetch me. Any time, day or night. You're not alone."

He hugged her again and mumbled something about closing the shop for a few weeks as he stumbled out.

"Are you alright, Anna?" I asked, grabbing the clothed part of her arm. Despite the lack of skin-to-skin contact, I relished her warmth. I hadn't encountered Alder many times, but on the few occasions I had, he had been sincere and kind. It didn't surprise me that Anna had been close with him. Whatever Elias and Aiden had been doing must be for the greater good for Alder to have agreed to participate. So why were they hiding so much from me?

She turned to me and nodded, then tilted her head deep in thought. "Actually, no. I'm not okay. That's a friend of mine lying on that table. Not a stranger. Somebody I cared about. Somebody who was well-loved in this town."

Michael moved as if to stand between us, but she pulled away and strode over to Elias. Despite being a few inches shorter, she managed to look down her nose at the elder warlock. "I don't know what your involvement is, but you're not telling us everything. And now," she pointed to Alder's body, "somebody I love is on the autopsy table. Unless you'd like to be next, I suggest you share some wisdom with us. Now!"

Elias' mouth slowly tugged into a smile. "I assure you, Miss Leighis, we had nothing to do with that man's death."

"He has a name. And I'm sure you know it." She didn't back down, keeping her face inches away from his and never breaking their gaze. Flickers of flames danced at her fingers, but Elias was the leader of the Triumvirate—I had never seen him back down or show an ounce of fear to anyone.

Aiden rocked back and forth beside me, almost knocking over a pitcher of water. The tapping sound caught Anna's attention, and she spun to turn her gaze on him instead. She approached him slowly, keeping her eyes locked on his. When she stood almost toe to toe with him, she asked, "Something you want to get off your chest, Mr. Bates?"

He glanced at Elias, then back at her, and shook his head. She had turned from sad to furious in moments, and my chest tightened, worried what she might do to Aiden. I had never seen a witch brave enough to stand up to any of us, and here she was, doing it to all of us. I had never wanted anyone more.

Michael took one of her hands, focusing her ire on him instead. "Caltain didn't find any signs of forced entry, neither did my men, when I sent them to investigate."

"Which means Alder let them in. He knew them. Perhaps worked with them?" She questioned, turning her gaze to Elias once more.

"Caltain mentioned you came to see him yesterday. Why wasn't he with Alder?" Michael asked.

"Alder wasn't feeling well. He told Caltain to focus on the shop, so he planned to spend the night there instead."

Michael's eyebrows lifted. "It's almost like Alder knew something bad was going to happen."

Anna nodded furiously.

"Perhaps it's the Dapper Reaper?" I suggested.

She spun to me, eyes filled with heated anger. I wanted to tell her that Alder had been working with Elias and Aiden on whatever this crazy plan of theirs was. But I couldn't. At least not in front of them. I did, however, need to defuse the situation.

"You can't be serious," she said.

"Who is the Dapper Reaper?" the constable asked.

"It's a legend that witch and warlock parents tell their naughty children to keep them in line. A boogeyman who wears a tailored suit and top hat. He steals away his victims in the dead of night. He's not real," she said flatly.

I shrugged my shoulders and gave her a look that I hoped conveyed the message I was going for. *Shut the hell up and I'll tell you later.*

She let out a sigh, and her shoulders sank. "I guess that makes more sense than it being one of you incorrigible jackanapes."

Michael glanced at her with his eyebrows pinched before noticing me assessing him. Elias and Aiden weren't the only ones keeping secrets, and he definitely looked suspicious of my exchange with Anna.

Chapter Twelve

Michael

I somehow knew from the gloomy fog that the morning wasn't going to start off well. The cobblestone alleyways were lit by a soft, silver glow as the lamps fizzled out with the rising sun. The droplets stuck to my skin as I walked, smelling like eucalyptus as my feet slid across the wet stones.

I had been woken by one of my men and told to hurry to the market. Someone was causing a ruckus. Donning my uniform and rushing the few blocks there, I arrived in time to find a familiar man standing atop one of the vendor carts, shouting at the crowd. I arrested him weekly for public intoxication and monthly for being a public nuisance.

"The Triumvirate is killing their own. Do you think it will stop there? No! They'll come for us next! The magic folk cannot be trusted. We must band together and do something."

Approaching him, I crossed my arms and looked up as he met my eyes.

"Get down, Rory, you're making a fool of yourself," I said flatly.

"Ah, the witch-fucker. Why should I listen to you? You're part of the problem."

"Anna is an upstanding citizen who heals the ill and injured, including humans, whom she treats with respect and dignity. Whatever sick story you're trying to spin, leave her out of it." My fingers squeezed into fists as I tried to prevent myself from doing anything stupid.

Rory climbed down and approached me, stopping when his face was an inch from mine. "You're a traitor to your kind, Constable. Their magic is a danger to us all."

"You're wrong. Anna is here to help, as are many of the magic users of Dracht. You're safe. Everyone is safe," I said, raising my voice and spinning to the crowd to assure them.

"Keep telling yourself that, Constable. But mark my words, they're coming for us next." And with that, he swung at me. He caught me off guard and connected with my forehead, but his intoxicated state threw him off balance. Though his blow had landed, the pain was minimal, except for a cut from his thumbnail.

After getting him under control, I handed him off to one of my men. He could sober up in one of our cells, but in the meantime, I had to make sure he was the only one who believed this nonsense. I scanned the market, questioning each vendor and patron. Though some shared Rory's feelings about the Triumvirate, they had all had positive experiences dealing with Anna, so I breathed a sigh of relief.

I sprang up the three stairs to the front door of Leighis Chateau with more pep than my body felt. These last few weeks had been draining, and Anna's invigorating presence was the only thing keeping me going.

The butler let me in, and Mrs. Yates led me to the sitting room where tea and pastries had been set out. Anna sat sipping from her cup and absentmindedly swirling a glass jar with some kind of tincture in it, her sullen face proof she was thinking about Alder's death. Ranai sensed me first, bounding over from where she had lain by Anna's feet, and rolled over for a belly rub. I happily obliged, offering a few sweet words for my loving canine. "Good morning, Anna."

She looked up at me, tilting her head to the side. "Are you injured? You have a giant gash on your forehead. Was it from asking around about Alder's death?" Placing her teacup down, she approached me, removing my hat and running two fingers over the wound. It tingled, but not unpleasantly, and the pain ebbed away.

"It was only a scuffle with a patron hassling a market vendor. Nothing to worry yourself over. Nobody has had any information on Alder. No witnesses. I'm sorry."

"Don't worry. We'll find something. There, it's healed," she said, kissing where the injury had been and placing my hat back on my head.

"I'm sorry I didn't make it here last night with all the commotion."

"It's alright. I called it an early night after checking in on Caltain. I'm sorry yours didn't go smoothly."

"Did you speak to Killian after we left the morgue?"

"No, why?"

"I suspected he might come here after you played along with his diversion. What was that about anyway?"

Shaking her head, she said, "I have no idea. I had the sense he wanted me to drop it. Like he had something to tell us, but he never got around to it."

"I'll see if I can find him today," I said with a heavy sigh.

She took my cheeks in her hands and looked into my eyes. "Have you been sleeping, Michael? You look terrible."

"Not really. Too many things to investigate."

"Nonsense. You can't investigate without a clear head, and you need sleep for that. I think we need to find you a hobby, too."

"I have hobbies," I said, my tone more clipped than I would have liked.

"Do you? What are they?" she asked with a sassy grin, crossing her arms to glare at me. I was glad for the temporary shift from her sulking.

"I play chess."

She tipped her head in derision. "That's not a hobby, that's more work."

I shrugged. "It's fun. Have you ever played, Anna?"

"No. It always looked too boring."

Moving closer to her, I tucked a wavy strand of hair behind her ear. "You should give it a chance. It's a complicated game that requires a strategic brain. I think you'd be excellent at it. Two play-ers, black and white, clear rules. Each piece has its own method of moving, and the aim of the game is to protect the king at all costs."

"Not the queen?"

My smile grew wider, and I saw her take in my dimples. All the ladies loved my dimples. "The queen can move however she likes. The king can move only once space at a time."

"Well, at least it's realistic," she said, pinching my side.

I leaned in and kissed her on the lips.

"Go up to my room for a nap. But first," she walked to her apothecary cabinet in the corner and slipped open one of the small drawers, pulling a vial filled with yellow liquid from it. "Drink this. It'll help you feel more refreshed, even on little sleep. This is only for today. I expect you to get real sleep from now on. Understand?"

"Yes, Mother," I said, with a smirk.

Her amused attempt at a glare fell flat.

"Are you going to join me?"

"I'm afraid not. But I'm sure Ranai would be happy to. I have some tonics and powders to make up. I'll wake you in two hours, and we can get back to the investigation."

I nodded and followed Ranai up the stairs to Anna's bed.

Downing the potion, I kicked off my boots and placed my hat on the side table with the empty vial. I nestled under the top comforter, and Ranai curled up next to me as I drifted into a peaceful sleep.

Waking to a gentle nudge to my face, I opened my eyes to find Ranai staring deep into my soul. I swore she smiled at me, then jumped off the bed and bounded down the stairs. The smell of roasting meat wafted into the room, and my stomach growled loudly.

I found Anna scurrying about in the kitchen, flitting between the worktable and the stovetop, wearing an apron. I leaned against the doorframe and watched her in her element. She looked so feminine and delicate, and though the former was true, I knew better than to believe the latter.

"Well, don't just stand there, make yourself useful and come taste this."

"Last time you cooked for me, I ended up naked very quickly."

"I don't recall you complaining about that," she said, her lips pursed to hold in her wicked smile.

"Oh, I would never complain about nudity between us. But we should be working on our investigation."

"You've been doing too much of that. The horrors of Dracht can exist for one night without your intervention. You're teaching me to play chess tonight."

My eyebrows raised in shock. I tasted the spoonful of sauce she held out to me, feeling the squish of a mushroom as I chewed and swallowed. It was sweet yet salty, with a strong beef flavor. "Delicious."

"Good. Now sit. I'll make us each a plate, and then you teach me to play."

"Do you have a chess set?"

"Mrs. Yates picked one up for me. It's in the sitting room."

I sat down, and she placed my plate in front of me. On it sat a thick, round steak glistening with juices. A luscious brown sauce swimming with chunks of mushrooms dripped down the sides. Next to it was a heap of butter and parsley-glazed carrots. I practically drooled as I snatched up my fork and knife to dig in.

We ate in silence, sharing glances and smiles, and I couldn't help but feel lucky. This was the life I had always dreamed of. Coming home from work to a hot, delicious meal and the woman I loved. I had just never pictured it with a witch with immense powers and a more impressive heart. I wasn't sure if I believed in fate, but somebody was looking out for me.

Chapter Thirteen

Running low on many of my items, I decided to visit Caltain. It had been two weeks since Alder had been murdered. Mrs. Yates and I had checked in on him at home a few times, but Flur told me that he had begun returning to get the store back in order. I had to see it with my own eyes. The trek there had been pleasant, the streets empty due to the chill in the air. The previously green trees were now spotted with red, amber, and gold, with leaves falling like confetti as the breeze drifted through. Smoke curled from some homes' chimneys, and the scent of baked apples drifted out from others.

We were too far from the bay to smell the waves, which reminded me that I needed to visit the market with Michael again. Pulling up outside, I smiled at the open sign and a solemn Caltain sweeping dust out the front door. He still looked miserable, but at least he was back to work.

Climbing out of the carriage, I approached him with tight lips. He looked up with a nod. "Well, aren't you a sight for sore eyes? Let me finish sweeping, and I'll get you whatever you need. I just got a delivery last night, and I should be restocked. Still clearing out some of my expired goods though."

"That can wait. I'm here to see how my friend is doing," I said, handing him a polished piece of amethyst, often given to mourners to bring comfort in times of loss.

He huffed a miserable laugh. "Same as three days ago when you stopped by to check on me."

"Yes, but you were home. Now you're back here. I'm happy to see that."

"I do have rent to pay."

"And you know I'd pay it for you if you asked. You don't *need* to be here."

He let out a depressed sigh. "I *need* to keep my mind off things more than I need to pay the rent."

"I think you also need a cup of tea," I said, snatching the broom from his hands. "You make the tea, I'll finish cleaning."

He snorted but took in my serious glare and did as I asked.

With the distraction of my depressed friend gone, music in the distance delighted my ears. I left the shop in search of the sound and turned the corner to find Killian perched on a small staircase surrounded by witches. His fingers delicately plucked the notes on his guitar in a beautiful melody, captivating his adoring fans. He met my gaze with a wink, but I rolled my eyes and returned to Magickal Arts and Hearts, the cold metal knob unpleasant to the touch of my ungloved hand.

Caltain was still in the back getting the tea together, so I rummaged through his wares, picking out anything that had spoiled and tossing it into an empty bin in a corner. At the sound of a door swinging open, I turned, expecting a patron, but locked eyes with Killian instead. Still holding his stupid guitar.

"Get tired of them throwing themselves at you?" I asked over my shoulder as I kept picking through the items.

"If I didn't know any better, Anna, I'd say that sounds like jealousy," he said teasingly.

Glaring at him over my shoulder, I wanted to wipe the prideful leer right off his face with my fire. He crossed the store in a few long strides and leaned his back against the shop counter.

I hadn't answered, but he was apparently glad to fill the silence. "What are you doing?"

"Helping Caltain clean out the spoiled wares. He's in no state to be doing this himself."

"She's a meddling little witch, is the real answer," Caltain accused as he entered with a teapot and three cups. "I thought I heard a third voice, so I brought an extra cup. Have a seat, Killian. Any news on Alder's murder?"

"Nothing new since I saw you yesterday, my friend."

Friend? Since when? I spun to face them, my eyes flicking back and forth between them.

"Killian has kindly checked in on me almost as much as you have since..." His eyes dropped to his teacup. He picked up the teapot and poured some tea into each cup, fighting back tears.

"What happened to Alder was horrific. Nobody should have to endure losing the love of their life. If you don't want to talk about it, I'm happy to keep you company and help you get the store sorted. Having it open will help keep you distracted and hopefully ease the pain over time." Killian placed his hand over Caltain's in a soothing manner, my friend clearly not caring about Killian's ability to read people. "Or perhaps you would like to talk about him. Keeping the memory of someone alive is important. If it wouldn't be too upsetting, I'd love to hear the story of how you fell in love."

He had used his powers, but Caltain's pleasantly surprised look made it seem worthy. I took a seat on the open stool with my jaw hanging in surprise.

He smiled warmly at Killian and pondered before answering. "Before he and I had met, I had...explored my sexuality with both men and women."

"As we all do," Killian joked.

Caltain's shoulders noticeably relaxed. "But the day I met him, I got this tunnel vision. I saw nobody else. Well, I *saw* them, but not like I *saw* him. And he saw me. We could be ourselves, we could be honest, and I *knew* with every fiber of my being that I was safe. Maybe that's not what true love is, but it sure felt like it."

Killian's smile grew, and it tugged at something in my heart. I knew he was telling the truth, but it surprised me how much Killian cared for someone whom I had believed he barely knew. "Did you get butterflies in your stomach or feel tingles when he touched you?"

My gaze met Killian's, and I saw heat and a mischievous twinkle in his eyes. He knew what he did to me, and I hated that.

"In the beginning. Over time that dwindles, but that flame never flickered out. He was still the only one I had eyes for, even when things got hard. Lately he had been...secretive. Distant. Part of me was concerned that there was someone else in his life."

"I don't think that was the case. He loved you more than anything. I always saw that in his eyes. Maybe he knew his time was limited and wanted to spare you." I added, resting my head on his shoulder.

He placed a friendly kiss on the top of my head. "That's what I'm choosing to believe. What does love look like to you, Killian?"

I poked Caltain in the side with a sturdy finger, causing him to squirm.

Killian took a sip of his tea to hide his grin. "I think it's as you said, fully accepting one another for who you truly are. Though, there is something to be said about the magnetic pull of attraction when you meet someone. Like a fire burning in your heart. A need to be close to them. A need to protect them."

As I listened, I pictured Michael. He had asked me out instantly upon meeting me, both of us feeling that attraction. He was an excellent protector, that was certain. And he had never taken our difference in class, wealth, or status into account. Not to mention the fact that I was a witch and he was a human, he accepted me without a second thought. But apparently Killian did too.

When our tea was gone, we finished cleaning out the ruined

wares and organizing the new delivery. I packed up a few items I was low on and forced more coins than required on a reluctant Caltain before sipping on the fresh cup of tea he had poured for each of us.

My eyes flicked to Caltain's brass ogee clock, and my heart dropped. "Shit!" I yelled, jumping up. "I'm late to meet Michael."

"Tell Constable Sheehan I said hello," Killian murmured snarkily, mouth inside his teacup.

I wouldn't be doing that.

Running across the street, I skidded to a halt outside of Bubbling Brews. Inside, Michael was seated with his cap on the coffee bar next to a steaming mug. His eyes met mine, and he stood with relief as I entered the shop. "I was beginning to worry that the Dapper Reaper had made you his latest victim." His voice didn't carry any humor, but it rarely did.

"I've been fearing that myself lately. I'm so sorry," I said, standing on tiptoes to kiss him on the lips before taking a seat.

A warm cup of coffee swirled with milk and topped with a sprinkle of cinnamon was placed in front of him. "He told me who was joining him, but I wanted to make sure it was hot when you got here. Your usual, Miss Leighis!"

I had returned to Bubbling Brews almost daily to try a different flavor of coffee or tea. It was my newest fixation. A whole new world.

"Thank you, Declan. Just how I like it!" I smiled at him, and he left us to chat, interrupting only once more to drop a small plate of miniature pastries between us. "On the house, as a thanks for the ongoing investigation. Regardless of what the Triumvirate thinks of humans, you're always welcome here, Constable."

"Thank you, Declan," Michael said politely, watching him walk away.

"Do you hear sentiments like that often in Dracht?" I asked him.

"More and more since my father died. Since we overheard

Elias and Aiden that day, they haven't kept up the appearance of tolerating humans. More magic wielders have been informing me of their hatred for my kind. Others, however, have shown support. Their respect—and possibly fear of your power—have certainly helped my case," he said, grinning at me. His perfectly styled hair was on display, not a single piece out of place. "What had you running late?"

"I stopped in to visit Caltain. He's finally reopening the shop. We were cleaning and sorting out the spoiled goods. I lost track of time."

"How is he doing?"

"Not well. But he's putting on a good show."

"Perhaps you should've brought him along. I can't imagine being alone in that state to be very good for him."

"He's fine, Killian is with him."

Michael took a swig of his coffee and popped a pastry into his mouth, his eyes turning to look at me. "Killian was helping you two?"

Shifting, I rested my knee against his. "He's been checking on Caltain since Alder died. I think he was even flirting with him." I tossed Michael a look that I hoped conveyed how scandalous it sounded, Killian flirting with someone who had just lost the man they loved. His eyes conveyed the jealousy he was failing to hide. Perhaps I had put too much lime and paprika in the last potion.

"Killian would flirt with a dead rat."

Giggling, I wrapped my arm around his. His elbow resting on the bar top made it easy. "I suspect you might be right. But if it gives Caltain a boost, I'm not going to fault him for it."

He kissed me on the lips. A whistle came from Declan behind the front counter.

"Don't worry, he's only teasing. Public displays of affection are not as scandalous among our kind," I assured him.

"I know. Killian painted a very vivid picture of some of your holidays at your Mabon party."

We broke apart reluctantly and went back to our drinks and snacks.

Michael barely looked at me the rest of our date, and I feared I should've kept Killian's visit a secret. I didn't want lies looming between us. Secrets were hard to keep and destroyed relationships. I didn't need that in my life.

Chapter Fourteen

KILLIAN

I don't know why I enjoyed getting under Anna's skin so much. Maybe it was how her nose scrunched up when I annoyed her. Or the way her voice almost squeaked when she realized how I made her feel. She pretended to hate it, but I could read her well enough without my powers to know how badly she wanted me. Michael had simply gotten to her first. He was handsome, kind, and intelligent. But he was boring. I think she liked the excitement I gave her.

With a grin on my face and Sion happily trotting next to me, we took a long walk through the streets of Dracht. Waving at every witch and warlock I passed, I took in the cool breeze and the aromas of the shops along Witch's Way. Pumpkin, apple, cinnamon, nutmeg—the zesty spices filled the air and delighted my tastebuds. Sion took pleasure in rolling through every pile of leaves we found along the way.

It took us about an hour to make the trek back to the enclave, and all the acolytes had already been sent to bed. I loved when the halls were empty. I could make my way back to my room without being asked a million questions. The worst part about being a teacher was that everyone felt the need to learn from you. Sometimes it was sweet, but when all I wanted to do was go to bed, it was just plain irritating.

As I approached our council room, there were voices murmuring inside. Aiden and Elias. Without me. I eased closer to the door, pressing my ear to the smooth wood to listen. I could barely make out their muffled voices.

"We need to bring Killian in on our plan, Elias. He's proven himself time and again."

"I disagree. He's grown too fond of that little witch. I fear his loyalty is no longer to us."

"Then what do you suggest we do?"

"I think it might be time for the Dapper Reaper to find her."

"And if he finds out we killed her?"

"He won't. It will be easy to pin it on whoever is committing these murders. Just make sure whoever does it removes the eyeballs and makes her look as brutalized as the other bodies. We can't let this land on us. Understand?"

"Yes, sir. Then we can bring Killian in on our plan?" Aiden asked.

"Of course. He'll be fully on board if it's *her* killer we're trying to take down. We need his loyalty to be stronger, not split."

Their boots shuffled towards the door. Carefully shuffling away from the door so my boots didn't clack, I quietly turned the corner and made a run for it. I headed straight to my bedroom and locked myself and Sion in. I let out a huff of air and dropped my head. I had to warn Anna.

Hecate help me, that was close.

As their footfalls reached my door, I swung it open with a big smile. "Ah! Elias, Aiden. Good evening to you both. It looks gorgeous outside. Thought I might take a stroll into Dracht. Would either of you care to join me?"

"That's very kind of you, but at my age, I'm too tired at this hour," Elias said, patting my shoulder.

I turned to Aiden with a grin and hopeful eyes. "I'm afraid I must retire, too. Any destination in mind?" he questioned.

Taking a deep breath and tightening my cape, I said, "I think I'll see where the evening takes me. Perhaps I'll find myself in a beautiful lady's bed." I raised my eyebrows suggestively. They were used to my antics. "Good evening, fellows. Perhaps I'll see you in the morning."

Storming out of the mountain, I rushed to the first horse I could find and raced towards Leighis Chateau. The crisp chill of autumn was settling in, despite the thick cape I wore over my clothing. Smoke filled the air with an applewood aroma. The empty streets were lined with decorative pumpkins and gourds atop tied bundles of hay. The peaceful setting was an uncomfortable contrast to my racing heart.

Everyone was inside avoiding the chill, so my trek was unimpeded. For once, the door did not swing open prior to my knocking and Anna answered instead of Mrs. Yates. Unfortunately, Michael was also there.

Despite having ridden a horse all the way, I gasped for breath as she let me in. "I overheard Elias and Aiden talking. They're planning to kill you and blame the Dapper Reaper. You *need* to be careful. Don't go anywhere without myself or Michael."

"I'm perfectly capable of guarding her, you don't need..."

"I'm perfectly capable of guarding myself," she cut in with a raised voice. She crossed her arms and glared at him as if she would burn through him. "I was joking when I said I'd be the Dapper Reaper's next victim. I have no idea what I did to put myself in their path."

"I don't believe it's them committing these murders. They're going to use him as a scapegoat. I have no idea when, but I'll find out whatever I can."

"Why are you helping? Aren't they your family?" Anna asked.

"They raised me, but I'm not loyal to them when they plan to take an innocent life. You have done nothing to deserve this, and the Triumvirate is meant to stand for what is right and just. This is neither."

"And you're certain the rest of the victims were not at their hands? Any of them?" she asked, her green eyes imploring me to share everything I knew. And I would. I'd do anything for her, and I think she knew that.

"I have no idea what I believe anymore."

She put her hand on my forearm and locked eyes with me. "Get on their good side and earn their trust. Find out what they know and what they're capable of. I fear it's far worse than you think, Killian. For that, I'm sorry."

Michael stood behind her with his arms crossed, looking like he wanted to rip my head off for being here. Or because she had touched me. My powers would stop him in an instant, but if it came down to a purely physical fight, I didn't stand a chance. I nodded and looked at him. "I know she can defend herself, but don't you let her out of your sight? Understand? I'll find out who they're assigning to this mission and make sure it doesn't happen. You have my word."

Chapter Fifteen

Michael

I was grateful that Killian had come to warn us of the assassin, but if he hadn't had a reason, I would've ripped his head off for showing up here so late. The unease in the town was growing—that much I knew from the rumblings on the streets—but for the Triumvirate to plan to murder Dracht's beloved healer? I shook my head to break free from my thoughts as she closed the door behind the warlock.

"Thank you for not causing a scene."

"Why would I cause a scene?"

"I know how sensitive you are about Killian…"

"I am *not* sensitive. I just don't like the way he looks at you."

Her lips turned up as she stalked closer, hips swaying like the seductress I knew her to be. "I know you don't." She ran her fingers through my styled hair, shaking it loose of the pomade I used. "Your hair is getting much longer."

"I need to get to the barber, but I've been too busy between investigations and spending time with you." I raised my eyebrows at her as she fiddled with the ties on the back of her dress. I looked around for Mrs. Yates before remembering that she had gone to bed the moment we had returned.

"I could cut it for you. If you're not opposed to joining me in the tub, that is?" She dropped her dress to the floor and revealed that she had been wearing nothing underneath. She began to climb the stairs towards the washroom, peering over her shoulder at me while I watched her ass bounce as she ascended. I undid my brass buttons as I stalked up the stairs after her.

When she picked up speed, I raced after her, and she shrieked when I caught her. I ran my hands all over her body. I had only succeeded in removing my coat before I caught her, but she reached to undo the ties of my pants, dropping them to the floor. By the time we made it through the doorway, we were both naked. A light fog from the magically heated water filled the room. Droplets clung to my skin, mixing with my sweat.

She grabbed her scissors and a comb as I climbed into the hot tub. I could feel my sore muscles relax, and a soothing, herbaceous aroma filled my nostrils. A hint of mint cooled my tongue.

"I put in some lavender, jasmine, hibiscus, and some dried rose petals. The tingling is from the tea tree oil. Speaking from experience, not only is it soothing for your hard-working muscles, but I find the mix to be...invigorating." She ran the hand not holding the barber tools over her breasts and down her stomach, trailing her fingers down between her thighs as I watched.

"I highly suggest you cut my hair first, or neither of us is going to be...invigorated enough for it after."

She climbed in, shoving me forward so she could scoot behind me, and her breasts pushed up against my back. The stiff peaks of her nipples rubbed against me, my cock protesting the delay. She leaned close to my ear and whispered, "I'm glad one of us is thinking logically."

She began trimming my hair and humming a tune to herself.

"I didn't know you liked music," I said.

"I don't normally, but this tune has been stuck in my head since I heard someone play it on a guitar down in Witch's Way," she commented.

"Speaking of Witch's Way, have you received word about the ongoing situation?"

"They don't talk about it with me much, other than thanking me for helping with the investigation. Have you heard anything from the humans?"

"A lot. They're scared. We've always feared magic, but the imbalance of power has never felt this severe. Elias is unhinged if he believes taking your life is a step in the right direction. I fear what else they're capable of, and so do the rest of my kind."

Her fingers gently eased the pomade out of my hair as she swiped the comb through it, snipping the ends of each section and dropping them into a small dish she had set on the rim of the tub. She caught me peeking curiously and said, "Hair makes excellent nesting material for birds when it gets chilly. The chickadees and robins always take it. No sense in wasting it. Do you feel like *we* are of a different kind? Does it bother you that I'm a witch?"

"It doesn't bother me at all. It's a little thrilling to know what you're capable of. You could end my life in a single heartbeat, but I trust you. And strangely enough, it makes me feel stronger. I want to protect you from every horror that lies outside of these walls."

"It's so strange that you worded it like that. Since we met, when you are very close to me, I also feel stronger. Like I have more energy or power. I've never felt that before. It scares me a little," she whispered at the end.

"I'd say that's a good sign. Besides, Ranai is very fond of me," I winked at her over my shoulder.

She grinned and pushed my cheek so I was facing forward again. "Hold still. I'm almost done, and I don't need to heal you from a scissor wound before we get to the fun part of the evening."

"And what might that be, Miss Leighis?"

"Well, Constable, if you must know, it starts with you drying me off with a towel, your hands, and your tongue."

"I like the way you think, Mo Chridhe."

She finished trimming and combing, then tossed her barber tools at the bathroom sink, the scissors sliding into the basin and clanging around. "Close enough," she said, nudging me to turn around and face her. She whispered a spell and I watched the remnants of hair rise to the top so she could scoop them out. A nifty trick. "I'm not ready to be dried yet. I'd prefer to stay this wet for a while if that's okay with you." Her gaze filled me with heat and my cock stood at attention. She reached into the water to grip me, stroking up and down as she moved her lips to mine, tasting me ever so gently.

My hands went to her hips, and I pulled her chest flush against mine, her legs straddling me with ease. As the fervor of her kisses increased, so did the speed of my hands, caressing every square inch of her as she moaned into my mouth. Her floral smell pushed me towards a lustful frenzy. My lips curled through our kiss at the noises I was able to coax from her body. My cock nudged at her entrance, and I looked to her for permission. There was not a doubt in my mind this was where we were heading, but I would never cross that line without her permission.

She nodded, lifting herself to adjust over me. She gripped me once more and lined me up perfectly before she lowered herself with torturously slow speed. Swirling her hips to make sure I was seated fully within her, she began to slowly bounce herself up and down in my lap, and her grip on my shoulders and mine on her hips was a dance that had a magic of its own.

We moved in rhythm, at a slow pace. I wasn't one for romance, but this was more enjoyable than anything I had ever felt before. She wasn't just a witch, but a goddess: the way the water dripped off her hair and down her breasts, the way she rode me like she wanted nothing else in the world, the way her back arched as she took her pleasure from my body without a shred of inhibition.

I never wanted this to end, but my release grew closer by the second. Her eyes met mine between kisses, and ecstasy flared in her deep-green irises. Her release was imminent. I slid my hand between us, swirling my thumb over the sensitive bundle of nerves between her thighs as she continued to gyrate her hips around my hard cock.

"Fuck, Michael. I'm right there." Her eyes closed and her head tipped back, but I grabbed her chin and tilted it back to me.

"Look at me. I want to hear you, and I want to watch your eyes as you cum for me, Mo Chridhe. Don't hold back. Never hold back with me."

She didn't. All it took was two more swirls of my thumb, my words, and our held gaze for her to find her release. As her body pulsed around my manhood, I couldn't hold back. My grunts mixed with her moans in a beautiful melody.

I felt it then. The boost of energy she said she felt from me. I felt it from her as well, like a swell in my chest that made me feel like I could take on an alley full of warlocks. I could die right now and be a happy man. I realized at that moment that I would die for her. And something inside me locked into place.

Chapter Sixteen

KILLIAN

The smell of smoke startled me awake, and the taste and feel of ash was heavy on my tongue. I frantically scanned the room for any signs that it had breached my bedroom. It had not, but the eerie silence disturbed me. Why was nobody screaming? *The children!* I ran down the hall to the dormitories, but the smell faded the closer I got. It had to be coming from the other direction, but the only thing that way was the library.

I changed my trajectory and sprinted, skidding to a stop outside the double doors, emanating out puffs of black smoke. Flinging them open, the intense heat hit me like a wall. Flames engulfed the entire restricted section in flickers of orange and white. Sharp crackles filled the room as the books burned like a pile of dry autumn leaves. An occasional pop sent sparks flying across the room. Only the three members of the Triumvirate and select historians were allowed to access the books in that area. The chalky-tasting smoke clawed at my throat as I prepared to unleash my water powers to put it out.

Elias gripped my hand to stop me from fighting the flames as he stepped out from behind a bookcase to the right that had not yet caught fire. "Not yet. Let them burn. We removed everything we needed to keep. All our history. But these need to burn. The fire is controlled. It won't reach anything else."

I couldn't decide which question to ask first.

Aiden came out from the left with a heavy sigh. "This has to be. There are too many dangerous words in there. Miss Leighis has been asking too many questions. It wouldn't be long before she demanded access or had Constable Sheehan force his way in with the law on his side. We couldn't take that risk."

"What the hell was in there that makes you think that?"

"Plenty. Dark magic, mostly, among other things," Aiden added.

"And you think *she* would use it against us? She's trying to save Dracht from whoever is causing this murderous rampage, and this is your solution? What are we hiding?"

"We have nothing to hide, dear boy," Elias added, resting his palm on my shoulder.

"Bullshit!"

He pulled back in shock at my outburst. "We asked you to get close to her, but perhaps that wasn't wise."

Shaking my head, I met his eyes. "This has nothing to do with her, Elias. I'm a member of the Triumvirate, too. A spot I earned by being top of my class since I was a child, following every order, and passing every test you put me through. I have never wavered. And yet, I have not earned your trust. What have I done to wrong you?"

"You've done nothing wrong, my child."

"Then tell me the truth. It's the least I deserve." The fire popped and crackled like the blood in my veins, but it didn't spread from the two shelves that were burning. Somehow, they had truly contained it.

Aiden tilted his head questioningly at Elias.

Elias pinched the bridge of his nose and nodded back to him. "We're afraid Anna is going to try to end the Triumvirate. Break us apart. Take us down. We cannot let that happen. There are reasons that we've ruled the magical community for centuries. To keep the order. Without us, Dracht will fall into chaos. They need a leader to make the best decisions for everyone."

"And there were books in there that would tell her how to do that?"

"Honestly, we don't know. We aren't sure what she's capable of, but we know she's suspicious of us. She knows Alder was working with us, and she's not going to let his death go."

"I can't say I blame her. Her friend is dead because he was working with us. And the constable?" I asked.

"What about him?" Elias questioned in return.

"Are you concerned about him as well?"

"No. We chose him for a reason. He is pliant and cooperative." Elias' voice was quiet, and his nose wrinkled.

"Chose him?"

"More like, pushed him towards the position. He was younger and easier to control than the rest of his father's men. Their minds had already been poisoned by the senior Sheehan's hatred for us," Aiden added.

They didn't say it, but their tone made me wholeheartedly believe they had killed Michael's father. Were these really the men who had raised me? I couldn't imagine Anna doing what they suspected. There was more hidden here than they would admit, but at least I had earned their trust. I had to keep it if I was going to get anything useful for Miss Leighis.

"What do you need me to do?" I asked, trying to keep my drumming heart and sweaty palms in check.

"Keep an eye on Anna and the constable. Find out how much they know about our plans."

I nodded before they left the room, my heart heavier than lead.

Once they left, I used my water to put out the rest of the flames, watching ominous, white smoke billow as my breathing evened out. The oxygen levels crept higher as the fire ceased its selfish devouring. Crogan, the gray-haired head librarian stepped out of the shadows between bookshelves, startling me.

"What are you doing?" he asked.

"I can't leave the library burning," I said, shaking my head.

He leaned closer to me, lowering his voice to a whisper. "If I thought I could've stopped them, I would have."

"I know. I was too late."

"Go. I'll deal with this. Don't let them see your displeasure."

"Thank you, my friend. I'm so sorry. I know how much you cared for these books."

He snorted. "That's the least of my worries right now. I'm late for a date. The wrath of an angry witch is scarier than burning books."

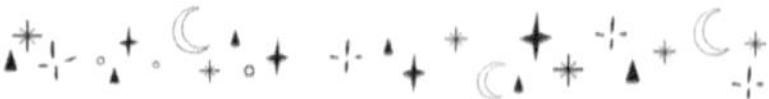

I had to keep my distance from Anna until I had enough information to share with her. Proving my loyalty meant staying within the enclave except for when they asked me to trail her. That was fine. I had an assassin to find before he found Anna, and I was certain he was also within these walls.

Killing him wouldn't help my cause with Elias and Aiden, so I needed a plan to incapacitate the poor cretin and make sure there was no link to my involvement. There was nobody I could ask for help either. *It's just me and you, Sion.* He nodded, scurrying off to collect intel. He was loyal and fucking brilliant. Perhaps the two of us would be enough. I wasn't sure I could handle losing her.

"Fuck, my class starts soon," I said, eying my box of supplies. I wasn't the best with potions or poisons, which was why I taught astrology and the gift of sight, but I had the basic knowledge provided by the enclave. I needed a lesson to keep my class busy while I brainstormed more of my plan. I mentally cataloged my ingredients and hurried towards my classroom.

I entered before the magical chimes signaled that class was to begin. This session was full of young men between the ages of twelve and fourteen, and they were right pains in the ass.

"Good morning, gentlemen. Today, we are practicing smoke scrying. One person at each table please grab a large candleholder and your choice candle for your group. I'll come around and light them. Using your quill and parchment, I want each of you to write what you see in the smoke and what you think it means. Please do so every three minutes as the smoke changes. A few minutes before class is over, I'll call you back to share your readings. Is everyone clear?"

Groans went around the room as one warlock from each table scuffled to collect a candle and await their lighting. One impatient student tried to light the candle himself, somehow catching the hair of the boy next to him on fire instead. I quickly put out the flames by conjuring a large scoop of water in my cupped palm. I rubbed the salve I always kept in my pocket on the burn on his forehead, right at the hairline.

"Liam, I take it you weren't listening when I said I would light the fire?"

"You were taking too long, Professor Killian."

I shook my head at my most frustrating student. "Patience is one of the most important lessons you'll ever learn, young man. All good things take time, and if you're not willing to wait, then don't bother. But don't be surprised when the good things don't come to you, ay?"

The boy looked down in shame, and I felt a tinge of guilt, but it was better than what I wanted to say. I nearly told him he'd never make it to the Triumvirate, so he may as well quit now, but a living being was nothing without hope.

Eventually, I got all the boys settled with smoke swirling in the center of their tables. I pulled out a tome on poisons, cross-referencing the items I had catalogued in my head. I spent thirty minutes sifting through pages before Sion entered, his tail swishing. He had discovered my target. I let a big smile take over my face and snapped the book shut. "Alright boys. We can skip the sharing. Leave your parchments for me to check and blow out your candles. Class is dismissed early. Enjoy the rest of your day."

I had a warlock to frame.

Chapter Seventeen

Unknown Narrator

Magic comes at a cost. Especially dark magic.

The cost of the Triumvirate's unraveling plan? Dracht was dying. Though the death and decay of winter was approaching, the decline of the flora was rapid this year. Even the fauna had begun to struggle as food became scarcer. But not a single soul in Dracht had noticed. They were too self-involved.

The only way to defeat dark magic is with more dark magic. The price of saving our planet was taking down those who would destroy her. One by one.

This had started as revenge. Revenge so sweet and fulfilling that I knew deep in my bones I had become pure evil. But all of that changed when I realized there were more important things at play. Survival of the entire species. The balance of power. My plans were no longer tuned to those who had wronged me, but instead, to all those aiding the Triumvirate.

I had only one choice left. I had to end them. Now.

They knew this was coming. They just couldn't figure out who to target. So they had destroyed the entire knowledge base that could help me. Perhaps, for the first time in my life, I couldn't do this alone. Maybe I needed help. But from who? Who would ally with the assumed Dapper Reaper?

As if anyone would go around taking lives dressed in a fancy suit. Didn't they know how hard it was to get blood out of clothing?

Chapter Eighteen

Anna

Before heading out for the day, I checked my wares.

"You still haven't formulated a stable one, have you?" Mrs. Yates asked from behind me.

"You know what I'm working on?"

"Of course, and I understand why. Tune your ingredients specifically for Michael or Killian. Your formula is too vague and unstable."

I rifled through my apothecary cabinet, reviewing my inventory, wondering what in Hecate's name would be right for either of the men. "I'm heading to Witch's Way to stock up. I'll be back soon."

"Of course, dear."

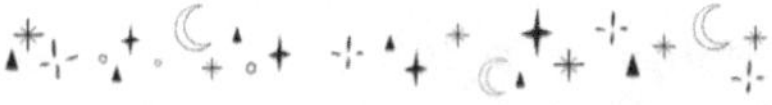

Parading into Magickal Arts and Hearts, I found a far less depressed Caltain organizing the display on his countertop. "Well, look at you, sprucing up the place. It looks almost as good as the façade you're putting on."

"Customers prefer cheerful proprietors, haven't you heard? Speaking of which, shouldn't we be celebrating?"

It was my birthday, and Caltain was the only one I had told. I pinched my lips and let out a sad huff before picking up a pair of scissors. I snipped off the ends of the herbs he had been laying out and placed them into the jars full of water. "Given the state of Dracht, it doesn't feel right to be celebrating. Have you heard from Killian lately?"

Placing a finger over his lips in thought, he said, "Come to think of it, not in a week or two. You have a lovers' spat?"

"Very funny. I'm concerned Elias and Aiden have done something. I worry about him alone in that dark mountain fortress."

"Do you, now?"

I glared at him over the herbs I was holding. "I care about everyone, you know."

"Some more than others," he said with a chuckle. "There was a fire inside the enclave, but nobody has learned what burned. No rumors of any deaths though, so that's hopeful."

The Triumvirate were close-lipped about the powers of their members, but fire magic was rare. Had the fire been intentional or accidental? And why hadn't more news of it made its way to the community? I had so many questions, and if anybody had answers, it would be Michael.

There was a scratching at the door, and I opened it to find Sion. I held out my palm, and he smiled at me and licked it, letting out a happy bark before scurrying down the street and throwing himself in a pile of dead leaves.

Caltain approached behind me, and I turned to face him. "What was that about?" he asked.

"I think that's Killian's way of telling me he's okay. I hope."

"I guess he cares about everyone too?"

I elbowed him in the ribs as I passed him to return to my seat.

We worked a while longer before the door swung open and I heard the clacking of boots behind me. Caltain tilted his head in confusion. Behind him, a flash of light bounced across the wall, like the sun shining off metal. I whirled, and a man holding a knife lunged for me.

I lit flames and hurled them at him, ducking out of the way of his blade. I grabbed his arms, spinning to throw him against the counter. His back slammed into the edge, and he winced, and a small grunt passed through his snarled lips as the flames flickered out from his clothing. Fireproof.

"You're going to pay for that, bitch," he growled.

"Oh, I don't think so," I said sweetly.

Caltain smashed a large potion bottle over the back of his head and the man turned. Thankful for the distraction, I grabbed the back of his head and slammed him face-first onto the counter-top. His unconscious body slumped to the floor. Tearing his durable clothing open to expose his skin, I lit him on fire. I crossed my arms and watched him burn, the metallic taste of his blood stinging my tongue.

"Aren't you going to put him out? We should call Michael."

"Nope."

I turned to Caltain, his eyes narrowed on me.

"This man just tried to kill me. I'm not waiting for Michael. We let him burn."

"Where did that come from?"

"Well, I don't think he's the Dapper Reaper. I'm guessing this is the handiwork of the Triumvirate."

"I didn't mean him. I meant you."

With a sigh and a heavy shrug, I said, "I think well under pressure. And he deserved it."

"Remind me never to get on your bad side."

I raised one eyebrow at him. "I guess you forgot the first time we met. I did light that man's carriage on fire."

As the man's body turned to cedar-scented ashes from the scorching witchfire, I grabbed a broom and a bucket from behind the counter.

"Leave the bucket here. Warlock ashes sell well." He scooped some into a small vial and stoppered it, handing it to me. "Here's your share, I'm sure you can find something fun to use it for. I'll keep the rest as payment for having to clean up this mess."

With a smile, I handed him the broom.

"I still think you should tell Michael, and Killian."

"I will." As soon as I figured out how to prove who this asshole was working for.

Chapter Nineteen

Michael

News of the enclave fire came in trickles, barely useful enough to formulate a theory. All I had learned so far was that it was contained to one room and there had been no deaths or injuries. The folks I had spoken to believed it had been a simple mishap that had been quickly dealt with. The humans, however, felt something more sinister was afoot.

I made it my mission to get ahold of Killian, or to figure out exactly *what* had been burned. The Triumvirate had much to hide, but I was concerned this had to do with their plan to assassinate Anna. My best path forward was to coax Killian out without alerting the more dangerous members. I formulated a plan as I approached the giant doors at the enclave gate, grateful for the warmth of my thick uniform.

"What can I help you with, Constable Sheehan?" The guard asked from the top of the tower.

"I'd like to speak with Mr. Tine-Radharc."

"And what matter would you like to discuss with him? He's a very busy man."

"It's about his friend, Caltain. I'm worried about him. I'm sure Killian will want to hear more."

I stood outside for what felt like a century before the door swung open. I was relieved to see the warlock's hairy face, something I never thought could happen. He rushed towards me, panting. "What's wrong with Caltain?" he questioned loudly.

"Caltain is fine, I needed a reason to speak with you without alerting the others. Can you walk with me so they can't overhear us?"

"Of course, but look concerned to keep up the ruse. Is Anna alright?"

"She's fine."

"Why isn't she with you? One of us should always be with her. I stopped the first assassin, but I haven't figured out who they assigned next."

"She's fine, Killian. She can take care of herself, and there are plenty of people to aid her. I needed to ask you about the fire. Was that you?"

"I'm afraid not. Elias and Aiden set the restricted section of the library ablaze. There was nothing I could do to stop it."

"Why would they do that?"

"I haven't been able to figure that out. It's why I haven't left. They're concerned that my *loyalty* is to Anna instead of them. I need to keep my distance from her and stay focused. It's the only way I know to help. The books had information about stopping their plan or making someone else more powerful. They claim they were aiming to destroy black magic. I'm still looking into it."

I nodded at him. He was honest and decent, but it irked me that his loyalty was with her. She was mine, and I didn't like it. But if it kept her safe, I'd tamp it down. "I'll let her know. Now, about this assassin?"

"He didn't stand a chance, just some charlatan who convinced Elias he could do the job. I sent my familiar to gather information, and Elias and Aiden were discussing it while I was teaching a class. But I wasn't going to let him anywhere near her. I may have set him up for theft from the private archives. Made it look like he had been trying to save the tomes they were trying to burn."

"Can't they use their powers on him to see that you set him up?"

"If it had looked like that from his eyes, yes. His last memories after I drugged him were a bit foggy but showed him in possession of a stolen book they had hoped perished in the blaze." Killian said flatly.

Light laughter broke out of me before I could control it. Thankfully, we were nowhere near the gates to the enclave. "I didn't think you had that in you."

He turned, his eyes meeting mine. "I'll do whatever it takes to protect Anna. Do you have a problem with that?" It was rare for him to look so emotionless, and it was unsettling.

"I share your sentiment, warlock. My savagery knows no bounds when it comes to her. I'm just impressed by your cleverness. Have you ever played chess?"

"Of course. Never lost a game. Learned when I was a child. There's not much to do in the enclave, especially when it's often only men. Once I discovered the joys of a woman, I stopped playing."

"I can't see why you can't do both. Women and chess aren't exclusive, you know."

"There are only twenty-four hours in a day, Constable. I'd pick women over chess, all twenty-four of them, if I could."

"I'm sure you would. I, however, only have eyes for one woman, and we are both busy people. Our balance works for us."

"Balance. How romantic. I haven't heard you mention fiery passion, or lust...I bet you're as boring as chess in the bedroom."

I wasn't proud, but I edged closer to Killian and puffed my chest as I met his gaze, a hint of a threat lacing my words. "Believe me, our sex life is fiery, not that it's any of your business."

"Right," he snarked, and I wanted to punch the cocky expression right off his face.

"Figure out who the next assassin might be. Thank you for the information, Killian. I appreciate you keeping her safe."

"You're welcome. I know you don't like me. Truth be told, I'm not fond of you either. But I want what's best for Anna, and if it's you, so be it. If you ever hurt her, I will end you."

"Likewise, warlock. Now go make sure my girl is safe."

Chapter Twenty

I had promised Michael I would only take the coach to Witch's Way and back home and stop nowhere else without him. As condescending as that was, after the assassin, I abided by his silly request because he had been right. Back home, I paced the foyer awaiting his return. Why hadn't Killian been seen, and why had he sent Sion to see me? I assumed it was to let me know he was alive, but perhaps he was checking on me instead?

I peered out the window and breathed a sigh of relief as Michael hopped out of the coach and bounded through the growing mounds of dead leaves on the stairs. Before he got fully through the door, I barraged him with questions. "Did you hear about the fire? Caltain didn't know much. Is Killian alright? His fox came to see me, so I know he's alive. Or was. What do we do?"

Without a word, he grabbed me in a huge hug and kissed the side of my head. "I did. Killian told me about the fire. He's fine. I went up to the enclave and requested to speak with him on a trivial matter so Elias wouldn't intervene. They burned part of the library—no deaths and no injuries. Killian is working on finding out what they were burning, but he confirmed Elias and Aiden set the fire."

The stress melted off my arms. Michael pulled back, and his

eyes met mine. "Should I be concerned at how relieved you are that he's alive?"

"Were you concerned when I was worried about Caltain?"

"Yes, but for different reasons. Caltain is your friend; I know it hurts you to see him upset. What happened to Alder was horrible."

"I care for everyone in this town. Deeply. Except Elias and Aiden, if I'm being honest. Did he say anything else?" Between my trips to the human market, Witch's Way, my party, and caring for humans, witches, and warlocks alike as a healer, I had come to know so many of them.

"He had the first assassin locked up, but he hasn't figured out who is coming for you next. I'm afraid we're stuck on high alert."

"Well, we don't have to wait to figure that out. Caltain and I took care of it."

Michael's eyes lit with anger, and his cheeks reddened immediately. "What?"

"A warlock attached me at Caltain's shop. He's dead. I'm fine. Tell me what else Killian said."

"I'm not just going to let you change the subject."

"Then check me over, Michael. I said I'm fine. Caltain will confirm it if you like. The man didn't stand a chance against the two of us. Now tell me the rest of what Killian said before you find out just how strong my fire is."

He snorted and did his best to hold in his amusement. "They're concerned about his loyalty, so he's keeping his distance to find out what he can."

My heart sank at that confession. The warlock annoyed the hell out of me, but for some reason, I knew I'd miss him. I hoped Michael couldn't read it on my face. I smiled placatingly and kissed him, his arms wrapping around my waist to pull my body flush with his.

"Can I ask you something...strange?" he said, an uncharacteristically boyish expression on his face.

"Of course."

"Have you ever used your fire powers...in the bedroom?"

I tilted my head, my eyebrows pinching as I tried to determine how serious he was being. "Is that really something you want an answer to?"

"It is. I was thinking, if you're open to it, that we should spice things up a little. Let things get more...well...fiery."

Pulling back in surprise, I said, "You're human, my fire could really hurt you."

"What a shame I don't know a witch with healing powers," he said, his voice getting deeper in tone. He lifted his eyebrows in encouragement.

Running my finger down the row of buttons on his uniform, I looked up at him through my lashes. "I could heat up some wax and give you a nice massage."

"Mmm. That sounds nice."

"You're sure about this? It doesn't seem like you, Michael."

"But you've done it before? Wouldn't it be something you enjoy? Something we can do for you?"

"The wax massage, no."

"Then how *have* you used your fire?"

I sighed, knowing this was not going to end well. "In the heat of passion, I've accidentally let my flames take over my hands and burned...someone."

He brushed my hair behind my ear and kissed me. "I'm not mad you've been with others before. So have I. I just want to make sure you're enjoying our relationship. But apparently, I don't get you...heated enough to turn on the fireworks."

Michael tried to pull away, but I grabbed both of his cheeks and pulled his face a breath away from mine. "You absolutely get me heated. You have *no idea* how difficult it is to rein in my fire when you get me worked up. But I would never hurt you, and letting my control slip is too big a risk. I fight it. Every single time."

Through a smile, he asked, "Really?"

Grinning back and pushing my body up against his, I

confirmed. "Yes, really. But if you want to try it, just say the word. I'll bring some salve up to the bedroom in case we get out of hand. Don't say I didn't warn you."

The bed shifting woke me the next morning, and I opened my eyes to find Michael watching me sleep, wearing a grin and nothing else. Though I had gone easy on him the night before, the salve and my healing powers had eased his pain, but hadn't wiped away all the scorch marks my palms had left. I traced my fingertips along them, forcing another wave of healing into his marks.

"Leave them. I like having a reminder of how hot I get you."

I was about to answer when someone knocked on the door.

"I'd better get going," Michael said. "I have to visit my mother before I check in at the constabulary."

He kissed me goodbye as I got up, wrapping my robe around my naked body while he dressed. He greeted Mrs. Yates quickly before easing past her to leave.

"Sorry to wake you so early. There's a telegram from the coroner."

"Thank you, Matilda." I took the note and sat on the bed, flipping it open to read aloud. "He's got one with eyeballs intact."

Chapter Twenty-One

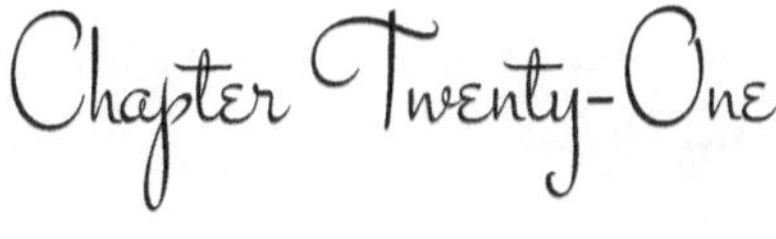

For once, I was the first to arrive at the morgue. No Elias or Aiden. No Anna. Not even Constable Sheehan. Only the coroner was there, unlocking the door at the crack of dawn, all bundled up in a warm jacket. The half-bare trees swayed in the strong winds, and they ruffled my hair into an unruly mess.

"You're going to want to see this one, Killian. It appears the killer was interrupted and never took the eyeballs out. I have to get some paperwork, but you can head in and get started.

I bounded through the door to see it with my own eyes. Thanks to the cold, the body of the tall, bulky male didn't carry the putrid odor the others had. I rushed to the corpse and grabbed its wrist. Closing my eyes, I dug into their memories.

He ran through the woods, chased by two sets of footsteps. One human, one not. He screamed and panted, but to no avail. Sparks of lightning flicked from his fingers in crackles, but he was struggling to gather his magic, despite it being just one day past the full moon.

Sparing a quick glance behind him, the only thing in the background was a seemingly abandoned house with a single lamp lit inside. It was built into the hill and no longer had glass windows or a door, just bare openings that gave it a distinct, haunted look. It sat on a stone slab, but a menacing tunnel of crumbling rock loomed beneath it. The black roof was battered, and even the withering vines growing up the stone face screamed death and despair. Had he escaped that terrifying place?

His turn cost him—an unseen rock tripping him to his doom. He fell to the ground, face down in moss. If only he would flip over so I could see who...

A furry, black paw moved into view and an angry, female voice reprimanded the victim. "Why do men always run? Do you enjoy the coward's way out? I wasn't finished with my questioning."

I knew that voice, but it couldn't be. But that paw belonged to...

The victim flipped over, staring straight up at the treetops. The nearly-full moon was bright and fully visible now that most of the leaves had fallen from the trees. He took a deep breath and tensed as footsteps edged up to him. A sputter raked his insides as he coughed up a gob of blood. He turned his head to stare directly at yellow, glowing eyes and a maw dripping with blood. An angry growl came from the wolf's throat. Moments later, Anna's face broke into his plane of sight, her eyes a glowing peridot.

I let go of the body, unable to watch what came next. It couldn't be. She wouldn't. I spun to run to tell the others, and found myself staring into the same eyes, inches away. How she had gotten into this room without me hearing or smelling her, I had no idea.

"I had hoped I'd be the first one here. It seems we have a problem, don't we Killian?" Her face devoid of emotion, she lit flames in her hands and pulled them back, ready to fire at me.

"It can't be..."

"Nobody suspected dear, sweet Anna. Anna who helps heal the whole community. Anna who throws parties to bring humans and witches together. It couldn't possibly be the delicate little witch who just moved to Dracht and is helping with the investigation. It's fucking pathetic how blinded men are by a pretty face and a tiny bit of bare skin. Not one of you even considered it could be me." She crept towards me, walking around the body. I held up my hands placatingly, circling around it away from her.

"Wait! There's still time before the others get here!" I whisper-yelled, launching myself towards the coroner's tools and picking up a scalpel.

She tilted her head to the side as she watched me scoop out both eyeballs and hold them out to her. "The coroner let me in, but he hasn't seen the body since last night. Destroy them quickly, and we can say this happened before we got here. We arrived together and found it like this. Quick, Anna. You have to do it now."

"Why?"

"Because they'll know if you don't."

"No, you idiot. Why are you helping me?"

"I'll explain later, there's not time right now. They'll be here any minute. The promise of answers is too good."

She took the oozing eyeballs from me and engulfed them in flames, tossing the remnants in the nearby sink and running the water to clean off her hands. She gestured to the sink, and I did the same, wary she might end me. The outside door slammed, and she grabbed my hands, using her fire to dry us both off. Elias and Michael walked in, side by side, Aiden following behind.

Elias froze, taking in the state of the body. "What the hell happened? I thought the coroner said the eyeballs were left."

"That was what I was told too. I arrived at the same time as the coroner. The killer must've broken in to finish the job and impede our investigation," I answered.

Michael eyed me with pinched brows before turning to Anna. "What are your thoughts, Miss Leighis?"

"I walked in right behind him. We found the body this way, and we're as shocked as you are. I don't see any signs of forced entry, either. Who else has the keys to get in here?"

"Other than the coroner, only myself. I'm afraid we don't have magical wards or locking mechanisms, so any witch or warlock could've found their way in or out without our knowledge," Michael said, running his finger between the back of his neck and collar.

"Where was the body found? The coroner mentioned the killer had been interrupted. By whom?" I asked. Unfortunately, I hadn't watched the man's memories long enough to glean that for myself.

"A mushroom forager came upon the body late last night. His wife was with him, and he sent her to inform the coroner where the body was," the constable said.

"Knowing how important a body with the eyeballs still intact would be for this investigation, you waited until this morning to inform us and posted no guard?" Elias said, standing toe to toe with the constable, an angry finger pointed in his face. Despite being inches shorter, he still managed to look down at him.

"I wasn't informed of the body until this morning when I arrived at the constabulary. I wasn't on duty overnight; I was at Leighis Chateau."

"What a convenient excuse, Michael," Elias spat.

"If you think he's lying, why don't you read him, Elias?" Anna questioned, a sassy smile on her face. She clearly knew we couldn't read him. None of us had ever been able to figure out why.

"Well, we're back to square one. Aiden, go fetch the coroner. I want to ensure that neither he nor Michael knew about the body last night. I also want to get more information on the timeline," I said, hoping to restore the peace and reduce any suspicion they may have of me.

I wondered if Michael knew it was Anna. I suspected not, as he was always an upright citizen who followed and defended every law. Perhaps their relationship was a sham. Keeping him on her side was a wise move to keep her protected and abreast of the investigation. She was cleverer than any of us had given her credit for, which was terrifying.

While the constable and coroner kept Aiden and Elias busy in discussion, Anna crept towards me and whispered. "Stop by my house this evening, after sunset. We need to talk."

I nodded as she continued past me, maintaining my position as far from Elias and Aiden as possible. I leaned my back casually against the table, hoping neither of them could hear my racing heart. I needed to get out of here before I gave myself away.

"Have you four learned anything productive, or has it just been more accusations?" she asked, glaring at Elias as she reached Michael.

Conor spoke directly to us for the first time during this investigation. "The wounds are too fresh for it to have been last night. His eyeballs had to have been removed within the last three hours. The killer must've barely beat us here."

Elias whirled on him, making the man cower. "Your only job was to keep that body intact."

Michael put himself between the two men, gently pushing the coroner away from the angry warlock. "He is the coroner. And a human. He is not the law, and he wouldn't have stood a chance against whoever did this. It was my duty, and I failed. I'm going to go speak with my men and find out who else knew. Then I'll go speak with the forager to see if he told anyone else."

Anna sighed and brushed her hands down the lapels of the constable's uniform. "It sounds like it's going to be a long day. You should get some rest, maybe spend some more time with your mother after. Spend the night at your place so I don't keep you up?"

He nodded and kissed her lips, then placed another on her forehead. "I'm sorry, Mo Chridhe."

"Don't be sorry. Duty first, Constable," she said with a wink. She pulled him away from Elias and Aiden, just close enough for me to hear. "I'll stay home so you don't have to worry about me. Send me a messenger if you need anything, alright? I'm going to stop by Flur's to stock up first, then I'll head straight home. I promise. And, Michael. Be safe, okay?"

"Always."

Anna and Mrs. Yates hadn't heard me sneak into Leighis Chateau, and neither had Ranai. I cautiously approached the sitting room, where loud voices were emanating from inside.

"You're going to wear a hole in the floor if you keep pacing like that," Mrs. Yates snapped.

Anna's footsteps halted. From where I stood, I could see her peering out the window. Half the room was illuminated by the sun that was beginning its descent behind the cliff, and the rest of the room was lit by the warm glow of the recently lit fireplaces. Sage and smoke perfumed the entire house.

Clearing my throat and crossing the threshold, I startled both ladies. The housekeeper excused herself to make us tea. "Good evening, Anna."

"We have too much to discuss for small talk. Why did you help me?" I had barely made it a few inches into the room.

"That's a long story. Were you responsible for all of those deaths, or only the last one?"

"That's a long story," she said, using my own words against me. "I have all night, Killian, but I suggest you start talking. I get rather irate without my beauty rest."

"If we're going to be talking a while, may I sit?"

She gestured for me to take a seat across from where she sat in a very cozy-looking chair. The cushion was plush and inviting, and the deep maroon suited her skin tone. Instead, I sat in the one next to her. Scooting to the very edge, I rested my elbows on my knees, only inches away from her.

"Right. To the point then. Elias killed my parents. He then took me in as if he were my savior. Aiden knew and never spoke a word to me. I only learned this around the time of the library fire. The two men who had raised me as their own were the men responsible for my being an orphan. They also implied they killed the last constable. Michael's father."

Shaking her head, she asked, "How in Hecate's name have you not confronted them about this? Made them pay?"

I looked down and picked at my fingernails, doing my best not to shed any tears. "I simply couldn't reconcile the two. How could the same men who raised me and helped me build this life be the ones who put me in this spot in the first place? How could they be both good and evil at the same time? Were my parents truly evil, and were they doing something good?"

Our gaze met as she assessed me. She slid forward and patted my forearm. "I think we are more alike than you know. How do you feel about them now?"

My eyes flicked down to where her hand made contact with my skin, then back up to her face as I smiled. "I've made it very clear to them that I'm unhappy about their lies and omissions. I've also made it clear to them that their mission against you was a waste, although it turns out I was wrong. Have I shared enough for some in return?"

"After you finish answering this one. How do you feel about them now?"

"I want them dead. And not in a nice way. They intended to murder you for reasons I can't understand. I want them to feel the same pain they inflicted on my parents."

"Do you think it was painful?"

"I know it was."

"How?"

Mrs. Yates entered the room and placed a tray with two teacups and an assortment of baked goods on the table in front of us.

I shook my head, picked up a teacup, and slid back into the chair, changing the subject. "It's your turn, Anna."

"Astrid," she said as I took a sip.

Choking as I nearly spit it out, I looked at her with wide eyes. My glance flicked to Mrs. Yates, who was wearing a huge grin.

"Don't worry, she knows. There is no Anna. Tell me warlock, do your powers work on animals?"

"They do."

"Ranai can give you a better viewpoint. She's witnessed all of it," she said, gesturing with a nod towards her wolf. The large creature approached me, holding out a paw as if to shake my hand. I gripped it and slipped into a vision.

I was inside Leighis Chateau, watching through the window. A baby, only a few days old by the looks of it, was being yanked from Mrs. Yates's hands. Ranai was trapped inside the mansion. Her breath fogged up the window, fighting against the frigid cold outside. She barked furiously at the two men in green robes. One took the little girl from the housekeeper, the other kept Anna face down on the cobblestone street with his magic. They had twenty other men with them, some warlocks, some human. Both faces were familiar from paintings hung in the hall of the enclave, the Triumvirate members that Aiden and I had replaced.

Anna broke free of her magical hold, launching a fiery attack on the men who had surrounded her and Mrs. Yates. She burned two of them alive while the other fought back. She screamed, she cried, and Ranai scratched at the glass trying to get out.

Black smoke swirled, transporting me to another setting. Again, Ranai was peering through a glass window, whining loudly and scratching frantically. The baby lay on an altar in a home that had once been the former Triumvirate leader's, three men chanting around her within a circle of fire and wind. A young Elias looked directly into my eyes. Ranai's eyes. He smiled and drove the dagger through the child.

The smoke swirled again, this time the black mixed with red, and I was back at Leighis Chateau. Anna was furiously packing a bag as Mrs. Yates peered out of the upstairs window.

"They're here," the housekeeper said. "I had the driver wait a few houses down. I'll keep them distracted. Go out through the stairs in the wine cellar and out the back. Hurry!"

Anna did as she was told, Ranai racing beside her in case

anyone attacked. She climbed into the coach as Ranai took one last look at their home.

The black and red smoke now swirled with blue, and I was transported to another place. Ranai scanned a town, often glancing up at Anna, who was wearing a hooded cloak. It was only a brief glimpse before the smoke shifted me to yet another scene.

Ranai was in the woods, bounding towards the deserted house from the vision in the morgue. Just inside, Anna hovered over Alder, who was tied to the dilapidated stone table.

"I don't get it. You and Caltain seemed like such nice people. My friends. Normally, I'm an excellent judge of character. How could you be hiding something like this from him?"

"Caltain and I are very different. He is a far better man than me. He deserved better, but I couldn't stay away. He knew nothing about what we were doing. He wouldn't approve," the restrained man scoffed.

"Of course not, he despises dark magic. But you, you're just full of it. That's why you reacted so badly to your potion."

"And you figured it out quickly, didn't you, little witch? I was worried you'd tell him, but like calls to like. You're full of dark magic too. I can hear it coursing through your veins. Such is my gift. It's why I had to help Elias. The humans are a scourge on Dracht. Why are you killing us instead of them?"

"Humans? Is that what Elias and Aiden's plan is all about?"

Alder cackled but said nothing.

She tilted her head, face twisted in a grimace. "Don't worry, I'll get it out of you," she said, picking up a knife to flay the skin from his forearm like she was peeling a potato.

Letting go of Ranai's paw, I came back to reality. Anna watched me intently.

Chapter Twenty-Two

"I fled Dracht forty years ago when the Triumvirate kidnapped my baby. They slaughtered her because of a prophecy. They believed she would be the most powerful witch of all time, which would end their magical reign of terror. They intended to kill me too. So I ran, mostly hiding in New England. Though I had never met him, Elias was the youngest member at that time. I know he was involved, thanks to Ranai."

Killian looked frozen, eyes wide with terror and jaw hanging open like a fish at the market.

"Are you alright?" I asked.

He nodded and began pacing around the room. "How can you be Astrid? Astrid left forty years ago and was already older than you look. And why is your housekeeper not surprised?" Once he finished his barrage of questions, he stopped pacing.

I ran my tongue over my top teeth as I considered how much to tell him. "Dark magic is very powerful. The Triumvirate acquired a lot of power from the death of my daughter. But something as traumatizing as losing a child snaps something inside of you. I'm afraid I lost my humanity that day. I didn't care what I had to do to make them pay. Or who I had to become. I hunted down every book I could and learned every ounce of dark magic possible. The only way to extend your life is with severe trauma and the blood of someone you love. In my case, my newborn child."

He held my gaze, but his lips pinched.

"Ending more lives and taking in their souls can rejuvenate your youth. So much so that you can reverse the aging process. Ground linden flowers help too. But every magic has a cost. I had to anchor my life to another. Bound for the rest of our lives. If one of us dies, so does the other."

My housekeeper tipped her head at him, then left the room to let us talk.

"That's why Mrs. Yates knows. Does it slow her aging as well? Surely people would have noticed that."

"She ages more slowly than a normal witch, but she will live longer. My age changes would've been noticeable, so I've spent the past forty years moving between different towns populated with witches to research. Taking a life here or there from the legacy families of Dracht that fled after the purge. And once in a while, other criminals and just plain awful people."

"And the creepy house the victim was running from? Where you tortured Alder?"

"Belonged to a dark magic witch who had lived as a hermit when I was a child. She died many years ago, and the house fell into disrepair. It's deep in the woods of western Dracht, closest to Leighis Chateau. Nobody would be able to get to it without me knowing. I used it for reconnaissance before I moved back as Anna. Now I use it to question people before I take their lives. There's still evil within those walls, so it feels right. Their body parts come in handy for the potions I've needed as well."

He nodded, letting it sink in, but didn't speak. Mrs. Yates returned, setting down a jug of water and some cups. I motioned to her as I continued.

"Mrs. Yates and her familiar, Cliste, the owl outside, have guarded and kept this house up while I was away. I bided my time and planned my revenge. But I knew how powerful the Triumvirate was becoming, and I had to be smart. I started hunting down members of the legacy families whose ancestors had been involved in my daughter's murder and my persecution. But when I discovered so many folks aiding their master plan, my choice of victim became so easy."

He silently held my gaze, his face unreadable.

So, I continued. "The torture was a means to get information to learn what Elias and Aiden were up to, but none of them knew a thing. I will admit, killing Alder really hurt me. But he wasn't who Caltain thought he was. I saw the nefarious things Elias had him do. When I was done with them, I felt a tinge of guilt for their families, so I dumped them where they'd eventually be found."

"Was anything you told me about your family true?"

"My father did die when I was very young, but he was a powerful warlock. I was only three years old, so I don't remember him. The only stories I know are from his journals my mother used to read me. That much was true. My mother, however, died when I was thirteen. I had an older brother, but he had no magic. He wanted no part of this legacy and fled. I stayed with him from time to time after I was forced out of here, but he died eighteen years ago. Other than Mrs. Yates, I've been alone since then."

He was close enough that I could reach him if I scooted forward, so I gripped his hand in mine. His eyes lit up a bright yellow, startling me. I dropped his hand and jumped back into the chair so hard that it almost flipped backwards. Mrs. Yates backed up a few feet until her back hit the wall.

He jumped up and started pacing. "NO! Nope. Absolutely not. Hecate help me, that's why you looked so familiar." He flailed his arms around as he spoke, as if the more he moved, the less real this would be.

"Sit down before you wear a hole in my floor! I already yelled at Astrid for that today, I don't need you doing it, too!" Mrs. Yates snapped.

"I shared my story, now it's your turn. Why did you freak out, and why did your eyes light up?"

"I need to show you something. You'll never believe me without witnessing it. Do you trust me?"

"For some odd reason, I do."

He smiled and took my hand, his eyes lighting up again, but not as brightly, like he was controlling it. He swirled his other hand, and golden sparkles formed a whirlwind in front of us, circling into an oval portal.

It was my turn for a jaw to drop. "You're a timewalker?"

He nodded, and the smile he gave me tugged at my heart.

"The moment I met you, you felt familiar, but I couldn't put my finger on it. I'd seen you in the past, but you were older. You were Astrid. I can see it clear as day now. But there's a different scene I need you to see. It's easier if you close your eyes and walk through. Are you ready?"

I nodded and stepped through the time portal.

When we came out on the other side, a younger Killian, perhaps nineteen, sat with an older woman at a small table. There were five candles lit and spread out between them in a circle, and various herbs placed between them. Worried that they might see us, I dodged behind the wall instead of remaining in the doorway. Older Killian rolled his eyes and grabbed my arm to pull me closer.

"Relax. They can't see us. My timewalking is only visual; we can't change anything."

"Ever?"

He tipped his head side to side. "It's possible to change time, but it requires dark magic and far more energy than I expend for this. That's something I haven't been willing to do. Not even to save my parents," he whispered.

"But that's how you know it was Elias."

"It is. I can go back in time and watch any memory where I was present, or a memory I've seen from someone else. I can also go back to a specific time and place if it's described to me well enough, but it's complicated. She's about to start. Come listen."

The woman rubbed her hands together, all the metal bracelets adorning her wrists jangling as she did so. She closed her eyes and began to rock lightly, front to back. A few moments later, her eyes opened and landed directly on mine. Like she could see me, regardless of Killian's belief. Her piercing gaze bored through me before her eyes rolled back in her head.

"Find the woman who brings the glow to your eyes.

First, you must wade through all her lies.

From her, your spawn of power will rise.

Once the mother has passed her test,

The daughter's power will exceed the rest.

But fear the Triumvirate who believe they know best."

The memory froze, with a young Killian looking terrified. Older Killian shook his head and smiled. "Elias and Aiden were raising me, and I hadn't yet learned they killed my parents. I didn't know I'd be inducted into the Triumvirate at that time, but I was so scared of their power. My daughter would be their target. As time went on, I thought about the prophecy less, but it bubbled to the surface again when Elias nominated me to take the newly opened spot. But I hadn't met that woman. Never thought I would."

"You said you had seen me in the past, and I looked older. How did that happen?"

"Elias and Aiden took me to another town. They were searching for someone. They had received information about a woman who had left Dracht years before and was hiding out there. They never told me anymore about it, but piecing it together now..."

"When did you see me?"

Crossing his arms, he snorted a laugh and stared off into the distance, recalling the fond memory. "I was young and foolish, and I had snuck out of the inn at night for a romp with one of the cute little witches there. One of the prettiest girls I'd ever seen. I hadn't noticed anything at the time, but when I went back to the memory, I saw a woman in a hooded cloak creeping past the inn. I followed to find her paying a man with a horse and carriage to help her get out of town quickly."

"So instead of replaying one of the fondest nights of your life, you followed the old woman in a hooded cloak?"

His deep laugh rumbled right through me. "I had to follow. I felt drawn to you, like you were pulling me with you. I felt that again the moment you walked into the morgue. Don't you see, we're meant to be together. We're going to have a child."

The memory realm was shrinking in on me, all the air within it evaporating and suffocating me. "I'd like to go back, please. How do we go back?"

His shoulders sank as he took in my worried look. He reached to take my hand again, but I paused.

"Did you read me when we walked through here?"

"No. It's not right to do so without your permission."

"I didn't know you could control it."

"Not exactly something Elias wants to be public knowledge. Keep that between us, eh?"

"Please don't ever read me without my permission."

"Wouldn't dream of it, Lasair," he said, holding his hand out to me.

Men and their pet names. Could be worse than flame.

Did I feel pulled to Killian? Yes. But Michael...Michael made me feel protected, cared for, and safe. Something everyone wishes for in a relationship. And he was such a loyal and honest man. Killian had so many secrets. It was too complicated. And how dare Fate dictate who I belong with. How dare she make his hand shoot electricity through me as we passed back through the portal into our own time.

I immediately snatched my hand back, and his lips pinched. His sad eyes searched mine, but I had no answers for him. "I think you should leave."

"We have more to discuss than our future child."

My throat bobbed as I swallowed every detail I didn't want to think about. "We'll talk tomorrow. I need some time to process.

"Of course, Lasair. Sleep well."

As Killian opened the door to exit, Ranai waltzed in. Her glance flicked between me and Killian as he left. She shook her head at me with a tiny growl and bounded up the stairs.

"If it makes you feel any better, I don't want to feel this way either!" I shouted up after her. "Curse you, Hecate and your Fates."

It was so hard for me to leave Anna's...Astrid's house. We had so much to talk about, and I hated leaving things the way we had. We were connected. I *knew* it was deeper than lust. But did her heart already belong to Michael? It couldn't. With what I had learned about her, the constable couldn't offer enough to keep her happy.

I couldn't go back to the enclave. Elias and Aiden's powers of sight didn't work on me—one of the reasons I believed they had inducted me into the triangle—so I wasn't concerned they'd learn the truth. I just didn't want to be away from *her.*

Though I understood why she needed time to process—it was a lot to handle—I wish she had let me stay to process with her. Waiting to learn her thoughts was going to kill me. Rather than toss and turn all night, I decided to walk all the way back to tire myself out. It worked, and eventually, I drifted off to a restless sleep.

The next morning, I took one of the smaller coaches to the coffee shop and Flur's Fancies. I picked out a few pastries, got two cups of liquid energy, and finished my journey to Astrid's house. She said we would talk today, and I wasn't going to wait any longer. I held my breath, hoping Michael hadn't beaten me to her.

Mrs. Yates opened the door as I approached, with her arms crossed and a scowl planted on her face. "She could've used a few more hours."

"I couldn't. I brought these to make it up," I said, holding up the two cups and bag of goodies I was struggling to grip with both hands.

She tipped her head, and I followed her to the kitchen where Astrid was frantically mixing powders and liquids into a vial. She rolled her eyes as I entered, but they lit up once she got a whiff of what I had brought. "Wise choice, warlock. I may just let you keep your life today."

Holding back my smile, I ran my fingers through my hair. "I'm sure you don't want to start with the obvious, so I thought I'd tell you the most important. Elias suspected you were helping Astrid. Even if you weren't, he fears you. They burned the entire restricted section in the library. He claims they were books on dark magic that, in the wrong hands, would be disastrous for the Triumvirate. He believes you want to take them down."

"And if I do?"

I crossed my arms and leaned back against the worktable, eyes scanning her entire body. "Then I believe we belong together, Lasair."

Her glare cracked my heart.

Holding up my hands, I said, "I'm sorry. I know you and Michael are...whatever you are. I'll wait as long as you need, but I know how this ends. With us together. But for now, we have the same goal. Take down the assholes that took our loved ones away."

She nodded, sipping her coffee between bites of pastry, and making tiny, pleased moans she didn't know she was making. I did. Heat burst through the lower half of my body while chills ran up my arms. The nutty, chocolate fragrances mixed with her delicate floral ones filled me with desire. Goddess, how I ached to know what her lips tasted like. What the rest of her tasted like.

"I don't know the full plan, but it's my understanding that the warlocks and witches you killed were working with Elias and

Aiden to bond together. I'm not sure how, but I assume through dark magic. It's supposed to make them stronger."

"Like they're anchoring their lives to all of them."

"That's what I believe, too."

She sucked in a loud breath and exhaled, the tiny tendrils of hair hanging from her bun blowing off her face in the rush of air. "So, timewalker, any other secret powers I should know? And do the others know?"

"Elias and Aiden can't read me. They don't know of my time-walker powers. My mother was a powerful water witch, and my father a powerful fire warlock. I have both abilities, but they're not as strong as my other talents. Everyone at the enclave knows of my elemental powers as well as my seer abilities."

"You said you didn't learn they had killed your parents until you were older. Why did you hide your timewalking?"

"After *Astrid* left Dracht, there were more prophecies and more witches driven out during the purge. They were hunting for timewalkers. To eliminate them. My parents taught me to hide this secret."

"Did you know Elias and Aiden can't read Michael, either?"

I nodded. "I did. But I can. They don't know that either."

Her eyes narrowed, and she flipped open her recipe book and scribbled something down. "Are you keeping a record of what I say to use against me, Lasair?"

"No. You just gave me an idea for a potion is all."

I raised one brow at her. Her pleased expression proved she enjoyed getting under my skin as well. I loved every second of it. I crept towards her, giving her every chance to stop it. To push me away. I needed to kiss her. I needed her to feel what I felt. I knew she did, but she wouldn't admit it. But I needed her consent. When I was a few inches away, she met my gaze. Brushing loose tendrils behind her ear, I stared deep into her eyes.

She stared back with glassy eyes for a moment, but then stepped back and shook her head.

"I don't get why you keep fighting it. Tell me you haven't felt the same pull? Tell me you think that prophecy is utter bullshit. How can you stand there and keep denying what we have?" Anger flared inside of me, urging my fire magic to set the room ablaze.

"It's complicated, Killian. I feel something toward you, but I love Michael. You wouldn't understand."

"You're right, I don't. How can you say you love him when he barely knows you? You barely know him. You don't even trust him enough to tell him who you really are, Astrid."

"Astrid?" a deep voice asked from the doorway to my right. I hadn't heard the door swing open. For such a large man, and a human at that, Constable Sheehan sure had a way of sneaking up on you. His face contorted in confusion as he pieced it together.

Astrid struggled to find the right words, and as his face turned from confused to knowing, she finally found them. "Michael, I can explain..."

Throwing both hands in the air, he slowly backed out of the room. "I don't need to hear any more."

Astrid's face fell as her eyes filled with tears. I struggled to understand how this heartbroken woman standing before me could be the one who had just murdered a whole slew of witches out of revenge for something that had happened to her decades ago. And for a human no less. As far as humans go, Michael was a decent one, but what could he possibly offer her that I couldn't? Not a god's damn thing.

"I have to go after him," she whispered, like she was intentionally buying him time to run.

"You have to kill him. He's a liability. Mister Do Good will put the pieces together about you being the murderer now, and Bates and Hornsby will get wind of it immediately. You have no choice."

Shaking her head as the tears fell harder, she simply said, "I know."

Chapter Twenty-Four

Michael

Anna was Astrid? Anna *is* Astrid. But Astrid had disappeared forty years ago. Anna didn't look a day over twenty-five. I knew very little about magic, but there was only one logical explanation for how she could be not only alive, but also so young. Dark magic.

A million thoughts barreled through my head, the puzzle pieces clicking together as I stomped through the empty streets. If she had lied to me about who she was, what else had she lied to me about? My thoughts were so loud that I didn't hear a thing around me. Not the buzz of the magical streetlamps flickering off as the sun rose, not the clamor of wheels on merchant carts in the distance, and not the murderous witch silently stalking up behind me as I turned down a vacant alley. A ball of fire missed my head by mere inches and singed the top of my hat. The smell of burning wool irritated my nostrils.

I whirled on her, only one word at a time making its way through my clenched teeth. "How. Fucking. Dare. You."

"I can't let you tell anyone, Michael. This secret is too big."

"Clearly. I was good enough to have dinner with. To sleep with. But not to get the truth from you. But your little warlock minion? Really? He earned that from you? But not the man who loved you? Who *you said* you loved? Why had I not earned that right?"

She bounced another small ball of fire back and forth between her palms, the air reeking of sulfur. Her eyes looked glassy, but I had a hard time believing the tears were real. That any of this was real. "We both know you wouldn't have accepted that I had killed those people. It doesn't matter why I did it. In your eyes, there's only right and wrong. Killian understands me. Would you have even listened to my motive?"

"You never gave me that choice."

"It was to keep you safe. Now, I have no other choice."

Didn't she? She was right. What she had done was inherently evil and wrong. Could I have lived with knowing who she really was and what she had done? Would any reason make me forgive her? I only knew I couldn't live with the fact that she trusted Killian to know her truly, and that betrayal hurt more than this fiery death would.

"I really did love you, you know. I meant every word I said, Anna. Astrid. Whoever the fuck you are."

"I know you won't believe me, but I love you too."

"Bullshit. I'm sure you used me for the latest knowledge of the investigation. Who better to get close to than the man running it? The single human that could keep you off the suspect list."

"At first, that was true. But you're the best human I know, and you've earned the love and respect of everyone in Dracht. You made me have hope for your kind. I had no intention of falling for you, Michael, but I couldn't help it."

Anna rarely showed emotions. But the Anna I knew wasn't a murderous witch. My brain couldn't believe her, but my heart was trying to force me to. There were no words to express how I felt, but nothing I said would matter anyway. I was a liability.

"You have no idea what the Triumvirate did to me. With every fiber of my soul, I don't want to do this, but I have no choice." She drew back the hand holding the ball of flame and prepared to launch it at me, tears flowing down her face. Before she could launch it, she was slammed to the ground by a blur of black that had come out of nowhere.

Before Anna could stand back up, Ranai stood between us, growling with a deep, angry hatred towards her master. I didn't know how long Ranai would be able to keep the witch at bay, so I ran for my life.

✦ ☽ ✦ ✦ ✧ ✦ ☽ ✦

I arrived at the constabulary, Ranai by my side. My men startled at the sight of her. I had grown so accustomed to her steady presence that I had forgotten how most people reacted to the large carnivore. "It's alright, she's protecting me."

"From what?" my second-in-command asked.

My mouth opened to tell them. To tell them I knew who had killed our victims. To tell them to be on the lookout for the witch who had attacked me. To order her to be put under arrest. But my traitorous mouth did none of those things.

"Nothing you should worry about," I replied instead. I patted Ranai on the head and headed to my office to think.

It was why I had come here, wasn't it? I had come straight here instead of going home. She was a danger, wasn't she? My heart felt split between the woman I had come to know, and the one I had just realized she was. Had she been using me this whole time, or was that only how it had started? Why did I feel so conflicted? Each victim had been working for the Triumvirate, whom my father had never trusted. Elias, Aiden, and Killian had worked so smoothly with me. Had I missed something?

I couldn't help but listen to something deep inside me that told me if she really wanted me dead, I would be. I'd seen the bodies of her victims. She was controlled, meticulous, and brutal.

She wouldn't have missed.

Chapter Twenty-Five

When I returned home, I found that Mrs. Yates had kicked Killian out. I was so grateful that I dug my face into the crook of her neck and broke down. She wrapped both arms around me tightly and let me sob for a few minutes before bringing me back to reality.

"Did you kill Constable Sheehan?"

I shook my head, which was still tucked into her.

"Good. He'll come around once he realizes who the true villain of this town is."

Pulling back, my wet eyes met hers. "I'm the villain, Matilda. It doesn't matter why I did what I did; he knows how many lives I've taken. He's never going to forgive that. Killian... understands."

She rolled her eyes and tapped me on the shoulder. "Go upstairs. Take a nice hot bath to relax. When you're done, we'll go check on Caltain and get more supplies for you to tinker with."

"Where's Ranai?"

"I thought she was with you."

"She attacked me before I could harm Michael."

With a twinkle in her eye, she said, "Of course she did. Now go. Don't dwell on it. All will be fine in time."

When I got upstairs, my tub was already full of water. Heating it with my flames, I stripped down and climbed in, the water scalding my skin. With the gas lamps off, the room was as dark as my soul, except for the flickering flames beneath the tub. If my life weren't linked to Mrs. Yates, I might've drowned myself. Instead, I sank down under the water, holding my breath as long as possible to feel the pain. When it started to burn my lungs, I launched back up and took a panicked inhale, my tears starting again.

How had my traitorous heart gotten so attached to someone that I knew it wouldn't work out with? Michael was a good man—kind and pure and always doing the right thing. I was a monster. Out of necessity, yes, but no matter the reason, a monster is still a monster. I took more deep breaths until they evened out and the pain ebbed from my tight chest. I hastily washed my hair and body and got dressed.

When I got downstairs, Mrs. Yates was waiting by the door.

"Is Ranai back?"

"I'm afraid not."

My chest tightened, but this wasn't the first time she had been mad at me. I attempted to see through her eyes, but I came up empty. She was either too far away or was blocking our connection. I had a feeling she'd be gone all night. Likely even longer. She'd come back. She always did.

Roth helped us both into the coach, and we rode to Witch's Way, the half-bare trees eerily still. The skies were dark and dreary, and storm clouds loomed closer by the hour. The sign on Magickal Arts and Hearts said closed, but the lights were on, so I peeked in. Caltain was seated at the front counter with his head in his hands. I tried the door and gently swung it open. He looked up and started with "We're closed..." before he realized it was me. He hurried across the shop to throw his arms around me, his red, swollen eyes overflowing with tears.

This was the one-month anniversary of Alder's death. Anniversaries of that nature were never easy. We stood clutching each other and sobbing until Mrs. Yates cleared her throat. "I'm so sorry for your loss, sir. We thought we'd see if you needed anything. I'd be happy to offer my services should you need help managing the store until you get back on your feet."

"I appreciate that, dear, but I wouldn't want to take you away from Anna."

"I don't mind, Caltain. We're at your disposal. How are you holding up?" I asked him.

"About as good as can be expected. Keeping busy in the shop helps, until I find something that reminds me of him. And then I just shut down. Yesterday and today have been the worst in a while."

"I understand. Can I suggest that you close for a week and see how you feel?"

He nodded, then searched my face. "What's wrong?"

"Nothing."

"You look heartbroken—something happened with you and Michael?"

I nodded. "We're done. It's not a big deal."

"Oh, sweetheart, I'm so sorry. Come have some tea with me. We can sulk together. You're welcome too, Matilda."

He went into the back room and came out with a steaming kettle and three delicate cups, the scent of mint tickling my nostrils. We pulled up stools to sit with him.

"Alright, now that we're settled, tell me what happened."

"He finally realized how different we are. I knew it could never work."

Caltain raised an eyebrow as he sipped at his brew. "Opposites attract, dear. You are good for each other. I'm sure he'll get over whatever happened and come back. You're clearly in love with him..."

"I am not!" I interrupted. Catching my tone, I started again. "I do *love* him. I don't think it was quite that serious." My nonchalant tone wasn't even convincing me.

"Mhm," both he and Mrs. Yates murmured.

"How have your love potions been going? Discovered anything about him or Killian?"

I shook my head and took a sip from my own cup. "Nothing has worked. None of my ingredients feels personal enough to either of them."

"Have you tried a lock of their hair? Or a possession of theirs? It doesn't have to be a normal potion ingredient. I think that's the trick nobody has been able to figure out."

"I'll have to think about it some more," I said, as glass shattered behind us. The large storefront window had blasted inward, shards and dead leaves flying past us and clanging off all the surfaces. Without thinking, I ran outside to see what had caused it.

Elias and Aiden stood in the middle of the cobblestone street, the former with a torrent of wind and snow circling around him. Bas, Elias' falcon familiar, flew in circles above, his eyes in the sky. Aiden's salamander clung to his lapel.

"Why in Hecate's name did you do that? Hasn't Caltain been through enough?"

"We're not here for Caltain, we're here for you," Aiden said.

"Unfortunately for him, it's collateral damage for being friends with you, Miss Leighis," Elias added.

"And what could you possibly want with me? Come to recruit me to your circle of victims that keep winding up dead?"

The streets were empty due to the impending thunderstorm, but I could see shop owners approaching their windows to determine the cause of the crash. I stared at the two warlocks, waiting for their answer. They hadn't noticed we weren't alone.

"We don't trust you, Miss Leighis. You've been asking too many questions. Digging into too many things. It is part of your family's legacy to step on toes, but you're stepping on the wrong ones."

"Is that so? Sooner or later this town is going to realize how evil you are. They may have forgotten what you did to my Aunt Astrid, but I haven't. You convinced the humans of Dracht to kidnap her child, whom you murdered, and then you sent them after her. Do you know what the Salem Witch Trials and the Dracht Purge have in common, Elias? You didn't burn witches. You burned women. Just like Astrid. All because she threatened your power. I know you've been recruiting magic folk to link to you."

"You know nothing of our plans," Aiden spat.

"Neither do any of the witches and warlocks in this town. Something that you need to hide from that many people sounds too nefarious for the magical leadership of our city."

"Our plan is for the greater good of Dracht, Miss Leighis. Something you wouldn't understand." The winds around Elias picked up, the sound raging into a deafening roar as it echoed off the buildings in Witch's Way.

"Ha! The greater good. Was it in the greater good to murder Killian's parents, too? And the last constable?"

If Elias was surprised at my knowledge, he and Aiden didn't let it show. "It was their choice to stand in our way. They knew that would be their fate," Elias said, eyes full of rage.

The shop owners stood in their doorways, taking in the shouting and the horrible truths. The roar of Elias' winds did nothing to drown it out.

"Do all of them know that is their fate for going against you as well? That you're responsible for the death of their loved ones? Respected members of this community?"

"It is not us killing them, and you know it, Anna," Aiden retorted, his fingers lighting with tiny sparks.

Now the library fire made more sense. As a fire wielder myself, it was clear his power was not as strong as mine. There was no way in Hecate's Hell I'd let them intimidate me, so I lit a large fireball in each hand and stared him down. "There is no proof it's not you. Every single one of them is linked to the Triumvirate. It's convenient that everyone who was involved with your plan is dead, is it not?"

Aiden's flames flickered as his hands trembled, but Elias held firm. He had been at the top of the magical food chain for too long, and he had no idea who he was messing with.

Mrs. Yates walked out of Caltain's shop towards me, and Elias took her in with an evil smile. The cyclone of winds around him began again as a lightning bolt struck the cobblestones a few blocks away. I launched myself between his attack and Mrs. Yates, throwing up a wall of fire to block his barrage, which never landed. Instead, the whirlwind bounced off a wall of fire and water thrown up by Killian, who had appeared out of thin air.

"That's enough!" Killian yelled. "Are you mad? The entire town is watching, and you attack a respected witch in the middle of the street?"

"We're here for Anna. Step aside and let us end this," Elias asserted, a second flash of purple light crashing into the stones. Closer this time. The shop windows rattled with the boom of thunder that echoed between them. The sky faded to a deep charcoal, filled with smoky whisps.

Killian's cloak swayed from the force of Elias' winds. "I stood by after I learned you murdered my parents. I'm not going to stand by and let you murder the woman I love."

My jaw dropped, and I wasn't alone. There had been rumors of Killian being seen at my house, but I didn't think anyone else knew Michael and I were no longer together. They didn't know how Killian *really* felt about me, because I thought he was just lusting after someone playing hard to get.

"You'd turn on your family for a woman who doesn't want you? It's clear who her heart belongs to."

Confirmed. They didn't know that Michael and I were over.

"It doesn't matter. Mine belongs to her. And you're not my family. My family died at your hands when I was a child. Then you raised me to believe your lies. If you want to take down Anna, you're going to have to go through me." As Killian formed a tiny wave of water in one hand and a dancing flame in the other, Caltain stormed out of his shop to stand next to him.

Two more flashes of white and purple struck the ground only

feet from us, startling most of the crowd. They were followed by an intense downpour, the droplets crashing into stone and ricocheting throughout the intersection. The rain hammered off the rooftops in a deafening roar. It was already chilly, but the damp, biting cold soaking through our clothing was almost unbearable. The metallic scent of ozone grew stronger. And yet the crowd remained, instead of taking cover.

"And me. We're done letting you abuse your power. And we're not letting you hurt Anna," Caltain said, his hair and clothing already soaked through.

Flur, who had been standing in her bakery doorway with her hands on her hips watching the exchange, scurried to join them. Her face was bright red with anger, the drops hitting her face sizzling a little as they struck. "You'll have to go through me too."

The street was a chorus of agreement as more and more shopkeepers and their patrons joined the mob to defend me, and my heart swelled with joy. Perhaps there was still some good left in this world.

"I think we should leave, Elias," Aiden said, taking the old man by the arm.

A flash of black and blue caught my attention. Michael stood in the alley with his arms crossed, leaning against the building. He looked concerned, and Ranai was glued to his leg. Our eyes met briefly before he turned and disappeared down the alley. Ranai shook her head at me and followed.

Chapter Twenty-Six

Michael

That whole day was a blur. It had been the worst few hours I'd ever had in my life. After Ranai had helped me escape certain death, she found me as I meandered through the streets on my way to the constabulary, trying to figure out where my life had gone wrong. She had remained by my side, and I was grateful for it. Despite my anger towards her mistress, digging my fingers into her fur brought me peace and comfort.

The Triumvirate hadn't denied the horrible things they had done to Astrid. They just hadn't known that Anna *was* Astrid. But they had done it. They had murdered her child and gone after her next. Who could do such a horrid thing? And they had murdered Killian's parents and raised him as their own.

When Elias had launched his attack on her, I froze. What could a human have done against that kind of power? But Killian? He jumped in and saved her. They belonged together. He was right. And I saw that now. It didn't make this hurt any less.

The past few months, I had been *sure* that the only villain in Dracht was the one responsible for all of the murders. I had that answer now—the woman who had stood by me in the morgue, feigning sadness at their loss. Promising retribution. How had I never seen it? But knowing the Triumvirate had some secret scheme made me think she was doing this town a favor. Was fighting evil with evil so wrong? Perhaps it was the only way. These thoughts made me question everything I knew about myself. The knots in my stomach were so large, I was constantly on the verge of being sick. I hadn't been sleeping, and my heart and mind were at war. The black-and-white chessboard of this murder investigation was growing gray and fuzzy.

Ranai followed me up the stairs to my rooms above the tavern. Fortunately, only one patron let out a squeal before I got her out of sight. Without a care for my sopping wet uniform, my rear slammed down on my bed, and I put my head in my hands. Taking a deep breath, I sighed and looked down at Ranai, who sat patiently by my feet. "I don't know up from down anymore. Is it true that the Triumvirate killed my father?"

Ranai nodded her head in confirmation. Like she understood me and knew the answer to my question.

"Did Anna know the whole time?"

Her head tilted to the side as if to say she wasn't sure.

"She suspects?"

Two head shakes.

"She just found out?"

Two nods.

"Killian told her?"

More nods.

I'm talking to a wolf. Get a grip on yourself, Michael.

I dried Ranai with a towel, then retook my spot on the bed. She gently rested her head in my lap and let me stroke between her ears, a few tears finding their way down my cheeks.

"Now what do I do, girl?"

Ranai curled up at the end of my bed.

"I guess rest should be first. We'll figure out a plan tomorrow." I changed into dry sleep clothes and tucked myself under the blanket, looking at Ranai. "The Triumvirate will get an ungodly amount of power if they succeed."

Two nods.

"I can't let that happen."

The large wolf shook her head a few times.

Snuggling up against her, I whispered, "I don't know what it is that makes me trust you so much. There's something so familiar about you. This whole time, I thought it was the command of Anna, but you went against her today for me. I can never thank you enough for that."

She grinned—all of her teeth showing—before nudging her nose into my chest for warmth and falling asleep.

The next morning, I felt surprisingly well-rested, but still had no idea what to do.

Ranai, lying on my bed, crossed her paws and watched me intently as I paced back and forth across my small room.

"Anna killed all of those people, but they were helping the Triumvirate. The same group who killed my father and are planning something sinister, right?"

I turned to the ebony wolf, who nodded her agreement.

"And they did terrible things to Anna and her child," I added.

The wolf's eyes glistened with tears, and she nodded, softer and slower this time.

"She's still a murderer, though," I said. My heart felt like it was ripping in two. "But I understand why she did it. Right now, she's not the issue. My father had been concerned about the Triumvirate gaining too much power. And he was right to be. It cost him his life. I know that now, and I won't let his legacy die with him. The Triumvirate has to be stopped."

Ranai let out a little howl of agreement.

Returning to my pacing, I reached the chessboard and picked up the black queen. "The queen can do whatever she wants," I whispered. Whirling back to Ranai, I spoke again, but louder.

"Nobody else in the town knows it's Anna. And they all love her. I know what she did, but none of that matters. She and Killian are likely planning to take the Triumvirate down, and that needs to stay top priority. We have to rally Dracht behind her. It's the only way. All the humans, warlocks, and witches adore her."

Ranai lurched up to stand on all fours, howling up at my ceiling.

"I take it you like my plan then?" I asked with a reluctant smile.

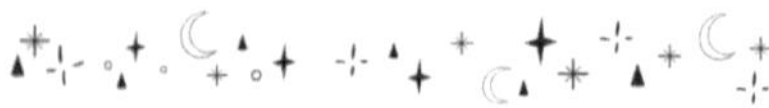

I spent the next three days visiting every shop in Witch's Way and every human I knew between the tavern and the market. I couldn't face Killian or Anna, but my plan would get to them through the likes of Caltain and Flur. And Ranai, eventually. I sent my men out to spread the story of how Elias and Aiden had attacked Anna and Killian. With the entire city of Dracht behind her, they wouldn't stand a chance. Not a single person had turned us down.

The Triumvirate had barricaded themselves within the enclave, and we weren't sure when they would show their faces again, but when they did, we would be ready. They had killed my father. I'd make sure they paid for that.

Chapter Twenty-Seven

KILLIAN

Adrenaline pumped through my veins throughout the entire trip to Leighis Chateau with Astrid and Mrs. Yates. The constant flashes of light and booming thunder weren't helping. Nor was the barrage of heavy raindrops ricocheting off the roof.

Immediately after Elias and Aiden left, Michael had left the scene with Astrid's wolf, and I wasn't sure how to feel. He shouldn't have been alive, but I was glad he was after hearing the revelations. He had needed to witness that, and now we *knew* we had nothing to fear from him. We had found Caltain a ride home, and I promised to fix his window. The two ladies remained silent the whole trip, but the scene kept replaying in my head.

I wished she would say something. Anything. But instead, she remained silent. Emotions warred within me. Not just anger from the silent treatment, but anxiety about what my life would become now. But the strongest were how scared I had been and how grateful I felt that we had all made it out alive. How close they had been to killing her. How horrified I had felt at the possibility of losing her. How quickly I had thrown away my entire life for the beautiful woman across from me. As we pulled up in front of the house, Astrid turned to Mrs. Yates and said, "Take the rest of the night off and get some rest. Take the next few days if you need them."

Mrs. Yates nodded as we exited the carriage. As we silently entered the house, Mrs. Yates headed off to her room, leaving Anna and I alone in the foyer. I awaited what I expected to hear, my fingertips fidgeting with my amulet that no longer meant anything.

"Thank you for escorting us home, Killian. And thank you for coming to our aid. My driver will take you anywhere you like."

"I threw away my entire life for you, and all I get is a 'thank you, good night' and I'm out to fend for myself?"

"It's complicated. Michael..."

"Doesn't want anything to do with you, *Astrid.* He made that abundantly clear when he ran out of here, and if it wasn't, you trying to kill him likely sealed that. He *hates* you. Why are you still holding onto that? I'm right here," I said, grabbing her arm and holding her hand to my heart.

Her throat bobbed, and her eyes dropped to the floor as she took her hand back. She bit her lip, drawing my attention to it. The urge to kiss her was almost overwhelming. "You can stay in one of the guest rooms. It wouldn't be right to leave you out on your own after all you did for me. Thank you."

"Look at me."

She looked up, fighting back tears.

"I know you're hurting, but this was for the best. You don't feel like talking about it, but fate wants us together. I want us together. I know you feel it—you can't deny that. I can see it in your eyes."

"No, I don't."

"Let me read you and tell me that again. Tell me you don't have feelings for me. Tell me I threw away everything for absolutely nothing. Tell me you don't want me to kiss you right now."

"I can't," she whispered.

"I know."

"It's your fault that Michael knows."

"It wasn't my fault. I had no idea he was going to barge in, but blame me all you like."

"I still hate you for it."

I smiled and leaned closer. "You don't hate me. Not even a little bit. It's alright to be angry with me, I'm sure it won't be the last time. But I think you also love me. And I think it scares you."

Her cheeks reddened as I brushed them with my fingers.

"Good things are usually scary. Otherwise, life would be easy."

Her eyes finally met mine, and I saw something crack inside them. Before I could ask her about it, her hands lit with flames. Two balls of scalding hot fire flew at me.

My fire and water burst into a shield around me. The wavering flames and wall of water bounced her attack off, my laugh a deep rumble aimed to get under her skin. "There you go. Let it all out. I can take it. More." The rage on her face made the hairs on my forearms rise, and warmth rushed to areas that shouldn't be involved in a fight. She had so much power. And no fear. It was incredibly erotic the way she wielded fire.

Screaming, she hurtled flame after flame at me.

"Fuck, you're sexy when you're mad. Keep it coming."

The flying blaze continued until the scream fizzled, and her hands hung limp at her sides. She panted as she stared at me, eyes alight with fury and hair mussed like she had had a rough and wild night. My cock strained to break free from my pants at the filthy thoughts that passed through my mind.

"That's all you've got, Lasair? I expected more from you," I said, taunting her.

She launched herself at me, our lips meeting in a fiery frenzy. Her arms wrapped around my neck and her fingers dug into my hair. Before I could think better of it, I scooped her up by her ass and slammed her against the wall. She ripped the front of my shirt open as I dug at the clasps down the back of her dress.

"Stairs," she commanded.

I raised my eyebrows but placed her on her feet. She hastily undid my pants and dropped them to the ground, then nodded. I didn't need any more confirmation. I bent her forward, her forearms resting on the stairs, and hiked her skirts up, relishing the view of her perfectly round ass in my face. She glared at me while I considered whether this was really how I wanted it to go.

"Is there a problem, warlock?"

"No problem, just enjoying the beautiful sight before me."

As much as I wanted to shove myself right in, I had been waiting for this moment for eons. I wanted to drag out the pleasure. Holding her ass flush to my front, I yanked down the front of her dress. I caressed one large breast, and my other hand moved around her body, two fingers sliding over her sensitive bundle of nerves.

Rocking with just enough friction to keep my hard cock satisfied, I closed my eyes and thought of my guitar to keep up my endurance. Gently swirling her nipple and strumming between her legs, her crescendo built against me. I leaned over her, moving my hands to either side of her head on the stairs. She arched her back and leaned into me, pushing her neck against my lips. I breathed in deeply, consumed by her scent. Placing kisses along her neck, I gently tugged her earlobe between my teeth and earned a hearty moan.

"Enough, Killian. Fuck me before I use my fire somewhere more painful."

I did as she asked, fully sheathing myself in an instant, as pure bliss coursed through me. The glow from my eyes lit up the whole staircase before I contained it, picking up the speed of my thrusts. She gripped the stair under her face as I bounced her, gripping her hips so tight it was going to leave marks.

"Hecate help me, harder, warlock!"

"I don't think you're in any position to be giving orders, are you?"

She tried to glare at me, but I thrust harder, pushing her into the stairs and slapping her bare ass cheek.

With a growl, she pushed us both back. I withdrew, and she spun to face me. Before she made another move, I sat her on the steps, leaning her back until my arms caged her head, pinning her wrists above her with one hand. With my other hand, I positioned myself to enter her again. "Did you want me to stop?"

"No."

With another grin, I thrust into her, her legs wrapping around my waist.

"I hate you," she whispered.

"No, you don't." I slowed my thrusts, moving my thumb to circle the nerves between her thighs.

Her lip curled into a smile before she could hide it. "You're not terrible at this, I'll give you that, warlock."

Leaning in, I kissed her and said, "I'll take it." A few more thrusts and we both tipped over the edge of bliss before I collapsed on top of her.

Chapter Twenty-Eight

TWO MONTHS LATER

Waking up next to Killian was so different, even after two months. The man was an expert on the guitar, and his skilled fingers had learned exactly how to strum the melody of my pleasure as well. Snuggling in the warlock's arms felt like being settled against a cozy fireplace. He was sensual and rough, which I enjoyed, but Michael had made me feel more protected. Safer. The constable's muscular arms had felt like a defense against the dangers in the world, where Killian's were a caress and a proclamation of feelings that I didn't have the right to express with my heart torn like this.

Killian was right. Michael didn't want me anymore. He hadn't tried to see me again, but considering the last time I had seen him, I had launched a fireball at his head, I didn't blame him. He hadn't asked anyone in Dracht about me either, other than asking them to side with me when the Triumvirate returned. That had been a brilliant political move. Though I was grateful, it was clear he was horrified. I was a monster. One that Killian knew and loved anyway. This was for the best. And exactly what fate—that evil bitch—had wanted all along.

Killian couldn't go back to the enclave. Elias and Aiden would hang him for defending me. They hadn't been seen or heard from in two months. None of the acolytes had either. No one had come or gone from any of the entrances of the enclave, but we knew it was still occupied due to the guards constantly on the gate towers. So Killian had moved in with me. Sion and Ranai were still standoffish, but they made do. They hadn't had much of a choice with the snow forcing us to stay in for days at a time. Ranai and I weren't back to normal, and she often blocked her sight from me, but I knew she was with Michael when she wasn't here. I couldn't fault her. But I was grateful when the snows forced her to stay with us.

Both of us had been frequenting Witch's Way more than usual to see what information we could glean, but the magical pipeline was silent. Occasionally, we discussed what we might do when they returned. Mrs. Yates and Caltain often joined our discussions, but the truth was, we had no plan. Killian had been enjoying the peace, content to ignore the problem that would bring our lives to a slamming halt. Peace never lasted for long, and that thought made me anxious.

So I prepared the only way I knew how—concocting potions for battle. Caltain had supplied me with whatever I needed and studied under me to learn my tricks when the snowfalls allowed. Once I'd finished each batch, he and Killian delivered them to various witches and warlocks in Dracht that we trusted to be on our side when the silence cracked. With everyone that cared about me forcing me to remain under house arrest—except my visits to Witch's Way—it was the only thing stopping me from going mad.

Though I didn't itch to kill again, I missed the rejuvenating rush of energy the dark magic gave me. Ranai was content to remain inside, but I expected that to change when the snows melted. She hated the cold.

After using the washroom and getting cleaned up with Libby constantly fussing over me, I returned to the bedroom to find Killian gone. My guess about where he had gone was confirmed when I got downstairs and found him hard at work over the stove. Weeks ago, when he had first commandeered my kitchen, I had struggled to come to terms with sharing my sacred space. I had let it slide after tasting the culinary creations he had come up with. I never had to worry about sharing this space—other than for sex—with Michael, because he preferred traditional gender roles. This had turned out to be a refreshing surprise.

"Good morning, Lasair. Hope you have a hearty appetite," he said, wearing only a low-hung pair of trousers as he cooked.

"Thanks to last night, I certainly do." I took a seat at the worktable, and he winked at me. Whatever was in the pan sizzled and popped, tiny bits of fat exploding across the stovetop. Killian gracefully avoided the scorching shrapnel. I would not have been so lucky. The smoky aroma filled the room, laced with a hint of sweetness. Cool winter air leaked in through the windows, breezing across the kitchen. I shivered and internally scolded myself for not bringing a blanket down. Instead, I launched a fireball into the kitchen fireplace, which had been down to smoking embers.

Mrs. Yates walked in and shrieked. "For Hecate's sake, I've asked you repeatedly to put clothes on before you come down here!"

He gave her his sunshine-bright smile. "Take a seat, Matilda, I've made enough for you too."

"I'll stay if you put a shirt on. As if there isn't enough scandal in the house of Leighis already," she whispered, putting her hand over her eyes to shield them.

"I enjoy a show while I eat. Do you take issue with the perfect planes of muscle down his torso?" *Although I do prefer a little more chest hair.*

Matilda swatted me as Killian handed me his cooking utensil. I kept an eye on the food while he ran upstairs to finish dressing. Their banter and his cooking had become an almost-daily routine, as was his playing guitar in the sitting room while I fiddled with my potions in the evening. It filled the days with cheer and peace, but something was missing.

I stirred the hash of potatoes, bacon, and eggs in the pan

before I was hit with a sudden wave of nausea. I emptied the contents of my stomach in the apron sink, and Mrs. Yates was immediately behind me, holding back my hair.

"My cooking isn't *that* bad," Killian joked, reentering the kitchen fully clothed.

"I don't think it's your cooking, I believe it's the new life growing in her stomach," Matilda asserted.

Once the queasiness subsided, I slowly turned to glare at her. She had been a midwife when I first met her, so I didn't doubt her knowledge, but this was not the news I wanted to hear. "What?"

Killian crossed his arms, a cocky grin on his face. "Her breasts *have* gotten larger."

My glare swung to him, but there was no fear on his face. Just mischief.

"Should I call the High Priest?" he asked.

"I'm not going to force you to marry me because I'm pregnant, you fool."

His face turned serious, and he held up his hands. "Nobody said you're forcing me into anything. I thought it was clear how I feel about you. I'm happy to marry you. I remember my childhood with my parents, despite how young I was when they died, and I remember every detail of growing into adulthood at the enclave. But living with you is the first time I have felt like I was home."

Without my consent, tears slid down my face at his admission. But was I ready for a child? Though I had the citizens of Dracht on my side, the Triumvirate could come out of hiding at any time, and nobody knew how much power they had amassed or what their plan truly was. As soon as the winter weather dissipated, we'd need to be on high alert. Bringing a child into these tumultuous times was a terrible idea. And to have such a monster for a mother. Thank Hecate their father was...

My stomach caught up to my brain, and I expelled the contents of my stomach once again. Hopefully, this wasn't a sign of things to come.

Chapter Twenty-Nine

ONE MONTH LATER

Michael

News of Anna's pregnancy spread like wildfire. I still refused to call her Astrid. Rumors went back and forth about whether it was Killian's child or mine, but nobody seemed to know the truth. I didn't want to know, and I was sure she'd never tell me. I was still counting my blessings that she had left me alive. But the pit of my stomach suggested that part of me wanted to be the father.

What would our baby look like? I imagined a beautiful little girl with wavy brown hair and bright green eyes like her mother's. Would she be human like me, or have incredible magical powers like her mother? But those thoughts weren't helpful. They only made me feel the hole that was consuming my life even more. Despite not having seen her in three months, my heart was cracked in half, and the time apart hadn't helped one bit.

Only half of the stores were open in Witch's Way. The awnings were adorned with icicles, and the roadways were filled with human and animal footprints through the snow left from last week's blizzard. My steps crunched loudly as I walked. I loved breathing in the sharp, clean air, but I could do without the burning sensation in my lungs.

I entered Magickal Arts and Hearts, dusted the snowflakes off my cap and sleeves, removed my gloves, and found Caltain restocking his shelves. His shop had been closed for some time, thanks to the storm, but the sign was finally flipped to open.

"Ah, Constable Sheehan. What can I do for you?"

"I was hoping to ask you a few questions. You've been through a lot, so I understand if you're not up for talking."

He gave me a sad smile and put down the box of wares he was holding on the dusty floor. "I'm starting to get back to normal. Finding out that the person you lived with for decades was aiding terrible people in a nightmarish scheme is not an easy adjustment. While I'm glad Killian told me, I'm still coming to terms with losing him, and it added to the confusion of feelings. Come, have a seat. Would you like some tea?"

Ahh, so Killian had come to talk to him. I doubted he knew who Anna really was though. "No, thank you. I won't stay long. Just a few questions."

"About Anna?"

With an eyeroll and an angry huff, I took a seat on a stool edged up to the front counter. "No, that's a lost cause."

"Are you sure? You look heartbroken. You should go see her."

"She's carrying Killian's child and wants nothing to do with me. It's a long story, but I'd like to talk about the Triumvirate instead."

"You're wrong, but we can change the subject."

What makes him think I'm wrong? "Does Anna talk about me?"

"I thought you wanted to talk about something else," he said, lips tipped up in that way I hated. "What would you like to know about the Triumvirate?"

"Since the fight in the alley, the two remaining members of the Triumvirate have secluded themselves in the enclave. Nobody has seen a single soul go in or out of the rock fortress. Have you heard otherwise?"

"There are rumors they've inducted a third member to replace Killian. A scared, young acolyte, no doubt. But that's the only news. There haven't been any deaths, so it seems it was the Triumvirate taking lives all along." Caltain looked down, swiping his finger through the dust adorning the top of the counter. "Including Alder," he whispered.

Though I knew the truth, I also knew the real problem was the Triumvirate. It wouldn't hurt to lie about this one thing, would it? I needed the town on my side. And more importantly, against them. "That's what I believe as well," I said, my fingers crossed behind my back. After their admissions in front of Witch's Way, they were easy scapegoats.

"I had no idea Alder was involved with them. He had been becoming more secretive. Coming home later and later. Telling me he was spending some nights at the shop to give me space, but when I'd open in the morning, there was no sign he had been here."

"From what I gather, the Triumvirate recruited like-minded warlocks and witches to bind their lives together. To give the Triumvirate more power. I believe that's what they did with Alder. I'm not sure if he did so willingly, because we've heard mixed accounts from other victims' family members."

His lips turned down in a confused frown. "Linking lives is dark magic I'm not familiar with, but I assumed having that kind of connection meant that if one died, the others did as well. They must've found a way around that. What else have they found a loophole for?"

There was a scratching at the door behind us, and I turned to see Ranai whining outside.

"Is that Anna's wolf?"

"It is. She's been turning up everywhere I go since..."

Caltain tipped his head knowingly. "I guess you and Anna aren't the only two that aren't over it."

I let her in, and she followed me back to the counter, lying on my feet as we picked our conversation back up.

"Be honest. You miss her."

"Of course I do. But she's a powerful witch with a complicated past. Killian...he's right for her."

"Her familiar doesn't think so. And if I'm being honest, she appears to be torn up about losing you. It's clear she has had feelings for both of you, but she wasn't ready to let you go."

"It's more complicated than that."

"Love always is. Is the child yours?"

I shrugged, then ran my palms over my face. "I have absolutely no idea."

"I'll find out for you."

"I appreciate it, but that's not necessary."

"Fine. At least take this box of items I set aside for you. I've labelled them with how to use them."

"What are they?" I asked.

"Petitgrain for your bathwater and valerian powder to help you sleep."

I eyed him, but he pushed the box toward me insistently.

"Back to why I came here. I've been trying to find out if there is anyone in the magical community on the Triumvirate's side. I feel a storm brewing, and when it hits, I need to know who will help me fight against them."

"You and your men have done a fabulous job of rallying the town. We had no idea of their abuse of power. Murdering your father. Killian's parents. Their own kind. Their behavior is unacceptable. Anna has been nothing but kind and helpful to each and every one of us. I'm not sure you could've gotten the town to rally behind you, but it was a smart move getting them to rally behind her. They meet here or at Flur's or the coffee shop to make sure we're ready when they finally emerge. We're all in this together now. I'll do anything I can to help. What do you need from me?"

"The snows will be melting soon. I don't think we have long. Let them all know the time of the Triumvirate is over. Prepare for war."

Chapter Thirty

ANOTHER TWO MONTHS LATER

KILLIAN

As I strolled back to Leighis Chateau from Witch's Way with my arms full of artisan beverages from Bubbling Brews and a box of goodies from Flur, I soaked up the warm rays and floral aromas of spring. The route was lined with pastel blooms and luscious green trees. Witches and warlocks waved as I passed, and I nodded in return. Even the humans had grown accustomed to my living with Anna—the witches and warlocks hadn't batted an eye—and the buzz about her and Michael had fizzled out.

I ran into him occasionally while making my rounds for information, as he was seemingly doing the same. He never said anything to me, but he never caused a scene either. Caltain had informed me that Michael had been mustering the town behind Anna and against the Triumvirate, despite the knowledge he possessed. He truly was a bright man, but a strong-willed one too. Had it been the other way around, I might've burned the town down to get Astrid back, but I didn't have his grace. He hadn't told a single soul about her identity or what she had done. He let them believe it had been Elias and Aiden.

Despite the snow's disappearance, not a soul had detected any activity within the enclave. Astrid's anxiety on the matter was only exacerbated by her hormonal shift. This anxiety was immediately apparent when I found her pacing in the entryway.

"Any news? Has anyone seen or heard anything?" she asked, snatching the box of Flur's baked goods out of my hands.

"Still nothing, I'm afraid."

"What in Hecate's name are they waiting for? Do they think we're all going to forget and go back to normal life?"

"I wish that were the most concerning option. My thoughts are much darker, I fear."

"That they're growing their dark powers?" Mrs. Yates said as she came to take the iced herbal tea jars from under my arms. We made our way to the sitting room and took our normal spots.

Astrid's belly was growing, and I felt our baby kicking regularly now, but watching her rest her hand and her drink on her belly always made me beam with joy. She had been rubbing mimosa oil over it for months to ensure a safe gestation, and so far, it seemed to be working. Mrs. Yates was convinced it was a little girl, which is what the seer had foretold. I had loved her fiery spirit from the instant I met her, but our bond had become so strong that I found everything she did endearing, even with her rising anxiety.

After she finished her drink and piece of cake, she threw off the blanket she had wrapped herself in to fight off the last of the winter cold. She struggled to rise from her sunken spot on her plush chair. I hopped up and offered her my hand, which she gently slapped away. "I'm not a whale, I'm just too far back."

Holding back my smile, I said, "There are plenty of other chairs you won't sink into as much."

"None of them are as comfortable."

Once she was up, she began pacing circles around the room. Her lady's maid fidgeted in the corner, like she wanted to help but feared Astrid's wrath. Smart woman.

"I can't take this anymore. In a few months, the baby will be here. Is that what they're waiting for? We need to do something. I can't live in fear of the same thing happening again, Killian, I just can't. They can't take my baby."

"I know. And nobody is going to let that happen. Dracht is on our side. Michael has been doing a wonderful job organizing it."

"But sitting here and waiting? It's torture. I've felt like a prisoner trapped here for the past few months. Between you, Matilda, and Ranai, I can't even visit Caltain or get a tea on my own." She scrubbed at her eyes with her fingers. "It's been five months, and we don't have a plan. We should have been researching. Plotting. Holding meetings. Getting organized."

"Michael's been doing that."

"But not involving us. *We* need to do something. I need to build up more dark magic..."

"Not while you're pregnant. We have no idea what it will do to the baby."

Ranai hopped up from her spot in the corner of the room and approached Astrid, scanning her as if communicating. Ranai's presence here for the last few months had been a rare gift, though Astrid wasn't sure where she went. I assumed it had something to do with Michael, but whenever I brought up Constable Sheehan's relationship with the wolf, Astrid changed the subject.

"I suspected my aging would speed up since I laid off the dark magic, but it hasn't. I've been aging normally. I'm not sure how long that's going to last. None of the books I read had any explanations for how this worked—it was all theoretical. The only reason I've put up with the three of you keeping me prisoner within my own walls is because I can't bear to lose another child, and I don't even want to think about what Elias would do if he got his hands on our offspring. But I'm restless."

"We'll deal with that when we get there. For now, I concede you may be right about preparing for their return. What do you propose as a solution?"

"Perhaps we can hold meetings here so I don't have to leave."

"Too risky. What if there's a single witch or warlock we can't trust, and we let them waltz right in here? We warded the house for a reason."

"I know you're against using dark magic, Killian, but the only solution I can see is to go back in time and save those books. We need to find out what they've done and how to undo it. Or find what they didn't want us to know about stopping them."

"Absolutely not."

"Can you at least go back and see what they discussed before they lit them ablaze? Maybe you can gather enough information that way."

"That sounds more reasonable." I lifted my hand and began my swirling motion and incantation. Nothing.

"Very funny, Killian."

"I'm not being funny. It's not working."

"What do you mean, it's not working? You told me they didn't know about your timewalking abilities."

"They don't."

"Then why isn't it working?"

"I have no idea, Astrid. They must've found a way to stop timewalking for this very reason. We're going to have to find another way."

There was a knock at the door, and I answered it with my flames in one hand and water in the other, prepared to strike. I opened the door to find the head librarian from the enclave standing outside.

Astrid lit her fire next to me and looked ready to pounce. He held up his hands placatingly.

"I'm not here to harm you. I have information," he said, before I could make introductions.

"And why should I trust you?" she asked.

"Because you have to. Elias is going mad. You and Anna need to stop him."

"And because he's a friend. The enclave librarian." I added.

"And because I trust him," Mrs. Yates said, coming from the kitchen to see what the commotion was about. "Good evening, Crogan."

"Fine. The three of us can handle an old librarian, if need be," Astrid said sweetly from behind me. "How exactly do you know him, Matilda?"

She picked at her apron as her cheeks flushed, but she remained quiet.

"We're lovers," the librarian said with a smile.

We both stared at Matilda, whose blush deepened in confirmation.

"Please, come in. We can sit and chat. I'm not fond of standing for long," Astrid added.

He peeked at her pregnant belly and then looked back at me with concern. "It's as Aiden suspected."

"News of my pregnancy hadn't made it into the enclave yet?"

"Nobody has been allowed in or out, Miss. I had to sneak out through the old tunnels."

"Tunnels? What tunnels? Do Elias and Aiden know of them?" Killian asked.

"Not as far as I know. I discovered them by accident one evening after studying the old blueprints of the enclave. I will not be welcomed back once they learn of my treachery."

We took our seats in the sitting room, and words flowed out of him in a torrent. "Elias is paranoid that you're coming for him. He's put the entire enclave on lockdown and inducted a teenager to take your spot. The poor boy is afraid for his life, but I couldn't get him out."

"What have they done that would stop my timewalking abilities?"

Astrid's eyes pinned me with a fierce glare for sharing that information.

"Don't worry. He's a friend," Killian added.

"You're a timewalker?"

"I am."

"How did they not know?"

"I'm thinking they do."

"They never mentioned it in my presence. They were afraid someone might go back and stop them, but your name never came up in that conversation. In the books they burned, they had learned some spell for blocking it that lasts as long as they live."

"Shit," Astrid said. She let out a heavy sigh.

"When I caught them destroying the restricted section, they told me there were books in there to stop their plan. Do you have any information about what was in them?"

"I've studied much of that section. The portion they burned related to using dark magic to link the life forces of many witches and warlocks together for ultimate power."

"I'm familiar with this, but linking lives together means if one dies, they all do. Elias and Aiden are still alive, even with their co-conspirators dead." Astrid absentmindedly rubbed her belly for comfort.

"In most cases, yes. But great sacrifice and the right spell weaving can link their soul to you, but not their life force. Strengthening you only. I don't know how, but it is possible." The librarian smiled up at Matilda when she sat on the arm of the chair he occupied.

"Why do they need all this power? What are they going to use it for?" I asked.

"Killian, have you ever heard them speak kindly of humans?"

"No."

"Elias despises them. He hates that we share power with them in Dracht. Since his induction, he's dreamt of a world without them. I believe he needed the power to eradicate the town of humans, unopposed."

"That's despicable," Astrid scoffed. "What can we do to stop them? Did your books provide that solution?"

"The only passage I can remember would require the sacrifice of a powerful life force. I'm afraid that's the only way I know of."

The look in Astrid's eyes struck fear in my heart. She had been through horrible and torturous events at the hands of power-hungry warlocks. I wasn't sure where she would draw the line in stopping them, other than not putting our child in danger.

"I don't like what you're thinking, Lasair. There has to be another way. We'll find it."

Chapter Thirty-One

We weren't going to find another way. The Triumvirate had to be stopped, and it had to be me to make the sacrifice. Whether this child was Killian's or Michael's, the baby was better off without me. They'd both make excellent fathers, and I couldn't let all the souls I'd passed to the underworld be my only legacy.

I *needed* my child to be proud of me. I *needed* one accomplishment that meant something. And now, if my estimation was correct, I had four months to plan how to do that. And I'd be damned by Hecate if I failed.

Not only would I have to sacrifice my life and Matilda's, but I'd have to become something worse to put a stop to their reign of terror. This would require some serious dark magic. It would be worth it.

Every night I woke in a sweaty fit. Dreams of my first newborn daughter being ripped from my arms. The knife piercing through her. Dreams of the child in my belly being cut from me by Elias. The only thing that had kept me from fighting back these past few months was the knowledge that I wouldn't live through losing another. And I never wanted Killian or Michael to know that pain.

Unable to sleep through the nightmarish thoughts, I stormed down the hall to find the old librarian asleep in one of the guest rooms. The room didn't look thoroughly slept in, so I suspected he had arrived recently from Matilda's room. The least I could do was let him stay after he had thrown away his life to warn us. Frantically, I shook him awake, hoping to get as much as possible out of him before Killian interrupted us.

"What's wrong, Miss?"

"I need answers, and I need you to not speak a word of this to Killian. Where else can I find books on the magic I'll need to derail Elias?"

"There are no other books that I know of. It wasn't only our library they burned. They sent me and others out to collect what we could from other cities as well. All of them have been destroyed."

"Do you recall anything else, Crogan?"

"Self-sacrifice is the only method I am aware of, and it requires extreme dark magic, exactly as you say. Killian is working on finding another method."

"We both know Killian's way isn't going to work. It's our only choice."

Rubbing my belly with a sad smile, I added, "As soon as this little one is born, it *must* be me. But Killian must not know. I need your help. It's the only way."

He eyed my stomach before his eyes flicked back up to meet mine, the gravity in them hopefully swaying his judgment. "Fine. Unless Killian finds a better solution before you give birth."

"I accept your terms. I'll make us something to eat while you tell me everything you know." Saying it out loud made me realize how ridiculous it sounded. How did one come to terms with giving up their own life? I had lost my first child, and it had broken me. The father had been a random dalliance during a drunken Beltane night, so I had been alone and had nobody to help me fight. Now I was intentionally going to throw my life away, leaving my child motherless. Possibly broken. But they wouldn't be alone. I couldn't think about that now. I really didn't have any other choice.

We entered the kitchen, and I heard a crash behind me. I whirled to find the librarian collapsed into a heap on the ground, convulsing. I hurried to his side and grabbed his cheeks, forcing my healing powers into his skin. It was too late.

Killian came barreling in. "Are you alright, Lasair?" He frantically checked me over with his hands before realizing what I was doing.

"I'm fine, you idiot. It's him."

"Poison?"

"Not that I can find. It feels like dark magic. There was nothing I could do," I said.

I held his hand to mourn his life. It felt warmer than it should have. Rotating his hand to expose his wrist, we found the Triumvirate eye etched into his skin. Black, spidery veins consumed the skin around it.

"A dark magic-proximity curse. He knew it would kill him, and he still came to warn us," I said, looking up at Killian. His face reddened by the second, flames flickering at his fingertips.

"Elias," Killian said with a growl.

Chapter Thirty-Two

Anna

"You really should brighten up, dear. Sulking is bad for unborn children," Matilda said. Her eyes were red-rimmed from Crogan's death, but she was taking it better than we had expected her to. Mostly because she had been channeling her sadness into nagging me more. She claimed that due to his age, she hadn't expected it to last much longer anyway. I knew better, but I wouldn't press her.

"The baby will be fine. There has to be a solution, or they wouldn't have burned the entire library to ashes."

Mrs. Yates disappeared into the kitchen and clunked down the stairs to the cellar. She returned quickly, panting as she clutched a tome. The corner of her lips turned up the teensiest bit. "They didn't burn the *entire* library to ashes."

My hand stopped absentmindedly rubbing circles on my swollen belly. "Out with it, Matilda."

"Cliste urged me to go into the cellar, and I found a stack of books and a note from Crogan on top. He had suspected they might be hiding something all those months ago. He had our familiars sneaking into their restricted section and stealing a book or two each night for months, storing them in your cellar."

My attempt at jumping up failed miserably, my rear end only

lifting an inch off the cushioned seat. "That damn owl. How is this the first I'm hearing about this?

"We haven't been down there since you got pregnant. I had no idea they were there."

"Killian!" I yelled, hoping he'd hear me from upstairs.

"You called, A stór?"

The humor he found in calling me his treasure instead of flame now that I was with child wasn't lost on me, but I was in no mood for jokes.

"It seems Cliste has been withholding information from us," I said, lifting a brow in the direction of the owl, despite a wall separating us. I knew she heard me.

"I'm not sure if I'd call it withholding, merely waiting until the right moment. In case you have forgotten, you are pregnant. Risking your own life, or even mine, is one thing, but I'll raise Hecate herself from hell before I let you risk theirs."

"I promise I won't do anything stupid until she's born. But we need a plan. We need to see if the books contain anything helpful."

She nodded and made me promise to stay seated while she and Killian combed through the tomes for anything that might be of help. They returned with six, handing me two of the smaller ones to peruse.

"You should rest a bit before we begin our research. I'll wake you when dinner is ready."

"I'm fine, Killian. This is important."

"If you weren't carrying a child, I would agree. A rested mother means a healthy baby."

"Don't start. If I were tired, I'd rest. We need to find a way to..."

"The Triumvirate has been around for centuries. They're not going to disappear. We have time to find a way to stop them. Our child, however, only has a few months of living inside your womb. The baby needs to be your number one priority."

"The baby *is* my priority. I don't need to be coddled. When you finish cooking, I will eat my fill and get some rest. I'm starving, and that is far worse for the baby than me being tired." My stomach grumbled in agreement. I was so hungry I felt I might wither away.

Flames flickered in his palm and in his eyes as he opened his mouth to speak again. "I really think..."

"I haven't eaten in six hours, and I fear death is imminent. Don't you *dare* spit that fire at me, Killian. I have no problem taking you with me straight to hell. Choose your words wisely, warlock."

With an angry huff, he spun on his heels and marched toward the kitchen. He was not going to win that argument. I flipped through a thin tome titled *Weaving and Breaking Dark Magic*. Many of the pages had been ripped out or singed into oblivion, but I took in whatever I could.

Half an hour later, he returned with a plate of food and an apology. "Hopefully this makes you feel better. I didn't realize how hungry you were, I know it's..."

"Bad for the baby. Yes. I know. Everything I do is apparently bad for the baby. Who in Hecate's name decided to let me have a child?"

"Destiny."

"She sounds like a fool!" I popped an olive in my mouth with a raised eyebrow, and he chuckled.

Killian sat in the chair across from me and we shared silent glances as we ate. I wasn't in the mood for talking. When we finished, he stood and took my plate. "I'll let you do some more research while I clean up."

Picking up the book closest to me, I scanned the title. *Sacred Architecture* was etched into the thick covered tome. How the hell was architecture going to help us? I began flipping through the pages, stopping on a hand-drawn sketch of a triangle. The strongest shape in architecture as well as magic, the book read. Probably what made the triumvirate so powerful. What kind of magic was needed to form such a bond? And what could be done to destroy that magic?

Ranai climbed into the chair with me, resting her head on my belly and looking up at me with adoration. She must've been frolicking outside and enjoying the start of spring, because her fur was thick with the fragrance of wildflowers and spicy bergamot. "It's not his, is it, girl?" I asked, tilting my head towards the kitchen.

She nudged at my belly with her nose and let out a whimper.

"I know. I miss him too. But it's too late. Even if the baby is his, he doesn't want anything to do with me." Despite growing close to Killian, I did miss Michael. I felt conflicted every damn day. It wasn't fair to either of them.

With her nose, she nudged another book that sat at the edge of the table. *Legacy Families of Dracht* according to the spine.

"You want me to read this one?"

She nodded. I cracked it open and began flipping. The early-evening spring sun illuminated the sitting room through the two large windows framed by deep burgundy curtains tied back with a golden cord. Out of curiosity, I flipped to the chapter titled *Leighis* first. None of the information there was surprising, but it was a nice trip down memory lane.

The Leighis family was one of the first legacy families to settle in Dracht, having faced the tumultuous trek by boat from Ireland. Aislinn Leighis was the first healer of Dracht, and her husband Tog was a mason. Leighis Chateau was the first to be erected, carefully constructed by Tog himself.

Before I could continue reading, the adjacent page titled *Litriu* caught my attention.

"Listen to this, Ranai. Iona Litriu was the first victim in the Dracht purge, twenty years before my own horrors. To think that had been going on for twenty years, and I had no idea. Iona was the eldest of four children and known for her outstanding hex and curse powers. There's no indication here of whether she used it for good or evil."

Her eyes were glued to mine, like she was trying to read my reaction. I attempted to flip the page, but she stopped me with her muzzle and tapped the page with her nose.

"Okay, I'll keep reading. The Litriu family and the Leighis family were close for many decades, until Iona fell pregnant. How do I not know who they are? It says here the Litriu family blamed my mother's influence for her *unfortunate situation* since the father of the child was suspected to be a human, rather than a reputable warlock. Though it was never confirmed, the Litriu family alleged that the father was Carraig Sheehan." My hand flew to my mouth, stifling my deep gasp. Chills rose up my arms, making every tiny hair stand on end.

I met the great wolf's eyes again, tears streaming down her face.

My throat bobbed as I failed to hold back my own sobs. "Is that why you're so attached to him? Are you Iona? You're Michael's grandmother? And you were friends with my mother?"

She stood up and licked my cheek, then hopped off the chair and ran towards the door. William opened the door and let her run out into the warm night.

Chapter Thirty-Three

Michael

"What's wrong, Michael?"

"Nothing, Mom. I'm just tired from work," I said as I handed her a fresh bouquet of violets for her table. The sweet smell was cloying, but they were her favorite. The deep purple was a stark contrast to her mostly off-white kitchen. I ran my fingers over the heart-shaped leaves, the velvety texture reminding me of one of Anna's dresses.

"Don't lie to me. You haven't been yourself the last few months. I can tell you miss Anna. Go see her," she said, placing her hand over mine across her small table.

"It's not that easy. Things are...complicated."

"Whatever happened between you two, I'm sure it's not as serious as you think it is. Go see her."

"I can't. She's pregnant."

"Is it yours?"

"I don't think so. She's with Killian now. They're right for each other."

She turned her motherly glare of truth on me but said nothing.

"I love you Mom, but I'm not in the mood to talk about it. Okay?"

"Okay, dear. Why don't you go home and get some rest," she said quietly. She gave me a sad smile and patted my hand.

I got up and put my hat and coat back on. I had come to visit her straight from my shift and still had my uniform on. Walking the few blocks back home, I stopped by the market for a stroll since the early spring vegetables were coming into season. Every smell, every smiling vendor, reminded me of how much I missed Anna. How much she had enjoyed shopping here. How much brightness she had brought to my life. How could I still have such strong feelings after all this time? I had had plenty of time to come to terms with what she had done. I knew her reasons. But she had kept them hidden from me.

The last few months, I had seen the shift in the town. The abuse of power from the Triumvirate. The rumblings from the witches and warlocks who remembered why Astrid had been driven out. They had told me the story of Astrid's departure. The kidnapping and brutal murder of her child. She had said she couldn't tell me the truth because she didn't think it would matter. I only saw black and white. But murdering someone's child? I might've gone on a murderous rampage too. But I wouldn't have been able to wait forty years to do it. And I wouldn't hide it from my partner.

From a few stalls ahead, screaming broke out. My instincts kicking in, I ran towards the ruckus to help. Among the vendors' stands stood a large, black wolf. When her glare met mine, she ran straight for me. The yells and shouting grew louder, filled with concern for my safety.

"It's okay. She's friendly. She's here for me."

She whined and rubbed up against me but then began yipping frantically.

"What's wrong? Did something happen to Anna?"

She turned her head towards Leighis Chateau, and my heart leapt into my throat. Something was wrong. Anna needed my help.

"Let's go, Ranai."

I found a coach driver willing to take me—and Ranai, reluctantly—to Leighis Chateau. With every squeak of the wheels and bounce of the cart, I felt more and more like my last meal was going to come back up. Was she hurt? Was there a problem with the baby? Had the triumvirate taken her? I should have fought for her once I knew the truth. I should've told her how I felt. Did I even know how I felt? She wasn't the worst villain in this story. The triumvirate was, and she needed to know that. What she had done was horrible, but in a weird, twisted way, I understood. After all this time, though, I struggled to come to terms with her being capable of such horrors. But what if it was too late? I wasn't sure I could live with myself if that were the case.

We pulled up outside of the manor, Ranai leaping from the cart and racing for the front door with me right on her tail. The door swung open, revealing Mrs. Yates inside. "About time. I'll keep Killian busy. She's in the sitting room."

"Is...she...okay?" I asked between pants.

"Physically, she's fine. But I'm disappointed it took you this long to find your way back here." She tipped her head at Ranai.

I glared at the midnight-colored wolf, filled with ire. "You tricked me?" I asked her. "You made me think something was wrong."

I swore she rolled her eyes at me as she huffed, then bounded up the stairs.

Keeping my footfalls quiet, I made my way to the sitting room. Stopping in the doorway, I leaned against the frame. She looked stunning. Her skin was glowing, and her hair framed her face like a halo. Her rounded belly only added to her beauty as she rested her book on it. Anna tossed the book onto the table in front of her while spewing a slew of expletives about its uselessness, and I snorted.

Her head snapped to me, her eyes full of confusion mixed with joy and possibly anger. "What are you doing here? Coming to arrest me for my crimes, Constable Sheehan?"

"Ranai found me. I thought you were hurt. Or the baby was hurt."

She stared at me for a moment, tears filling her eyes. "Well, as you can see, I'm perfectly fine."

"Then why did Mrs. Yates ask me why it took me so long to come back? Is Killian treating you poorly? I can have him arrested..."

She snorted a laugh and then burst into tears. I rushed to her, kneeling in front of her and taking her hands in mine. "What's wrong?"

Sniffling, she squeezed the words out in between sobs. "I'm... sorry..."

"Don't be sorry. I heard what happened to Astrid. To you. Did you really think I'd hate you if you told me the truth?"

"I didn't know what to think. I was afraid to lose you, but then I did anyway. And I almost..."

"But you didn't. I know you didn't want to kill me. That was all Killian's idea. I know how powerful and headstrong you are. If you had wanted me dead, I would be."

She burst into tears again and wrapped her arms around my neck, crying into my shoulder. I held her until her breathing evened out, rubbing her hair and placing gentle kisses on the top of her head. When she finally calmed enough to pull back, I asked the question that had been weighing on my mind for months. "Is the baby mine?"

She huffed a breath through her nose and smiled sadly at me. "Ranai seems to think so, but I'm not sure."

"Everyone else thinks it's Killian's."

She nodded. "A seer told him the same prophecy I was told about my child. Together, our child would take down the corrupt magic of the Triumvirate. Seers are never wrong."

"It can't be both of ours. Maybe you two are meant to have another one after? I don't want to think about that," I whispered.

She smiled at me and took my hand between hers. "I'm so sorry, Michael."

"What the fuck are you doing here?" An angry voice floated into the room. I guess Mrs. Yates couldn't hold him any longer.

I turned to face him. "Ranai came to get me. I thought Anna was in danger, so I came to make sure she was alright."

"She's fine. And it's Astrid."

Rolling my eyes, I turned back to her. "Now that I know you're safe, I'll go back home. If you need anything, you know where to find me."

She looked like she wanted to say something, but one look at Killian stopped her.

I placed one more kiss on her forehead and strode towards him. "Make sure my baby stays safe, ay warlock?"

Chapter Thirty-Four

KILLIAN

Stalking back into the kitchen, I paced around the room. My hands opened and closed, alternately igniting and extinguishing my fire and water. I tried to calm the burning embers inside of me, but all I could think about was launching my flames at the constable. *It couldn't be his baby, could it?* I could *feel* the extra magic inside of Astrid. It had to be mine. Doing the math in my head, I supposed it could be possible, but wouldn't she have realized she was pregnant earlier if it were his?

Before I had realized that Astrid had entered the kitchen, I picked up a potion vial and threw it across the room. It smashed into the brick wall, and tiny shards of glass exploded everywhere, stopped only by the wall of fire she threw, melting them into oblivion on the floor. She let out an angry huff, and I was shocked flames didn't shoot out of her mouth like a dragon.

"What is your problem?"

"My problem...is that asshole coming in here after he abandoned you months ago. He has no right to be here."

"Last time I checked, this was still *my* home, not yours. That decision is not up to you. And *you* and your big mouth are the reason he abandoned me. Ranai panicked him, and he needed to make sure I was alright. He had no malicious intentions."

"So, you've forgiven him just like that? Are you kicking me out on my ass now?"

"Killian. Please. Calm down. You're always so tranquil, except when Michael is involved."

"He irks me."

"He came to check on me. He knows we're together, and it's clear how we feel about each other."

Do you love me?" I asked, my heart stopping as I awaited the answer.

"Killian..."

"Do you love him?"

"This isn't fair."

"We're about to have a child, and *I've* made *my* feelings very clear. We aren't children, Astrid. And it's not like we've just met. You should know how you feel about me—and him, for that matter—by now." The volume of my voice increased with my heart rate.

"It's complicated."

"It's really not," I yelled.

She jumped back a step, startled by my outburst. Though she didn't speak, her eyes welled with tears as she firmly held my gaze. Even in the face of danger, she stood her ground. But she knew she need never fear me.

I hadn't realized flames were flickering at my fingertips again. I sighed and picked up another vial, examining the various herbs, powders, and other tidbits covering the worktable. My heart and mind were warring as my eyes skimmed across each item, but everything was starting to make sense. "That's what you've been tinkering with. You're trying to make a true love potion. You genuinely have no idea which one of us you love, do you?"

The tears broke free of her firm hold and she shook her head. My heart broke. Not because she may not love me, or she may love him, but because the uncertainty was hurting her. How long had she been dealing with this on top of carrying a child and living in fear of the triumvirate taking another person she loved away from her?

I crossed the room in three swift strides, engulfing her in my arms. She pressed her cheek into my chest as I stroked her hair, letting her cry as long as she needed. "Shh. It's okay. I'm so sorry for letting my anger get the best of me. It's just..."

Her head nodded slightly, and I smiled into her hair.

"It wasn't fair of me after everything."

At that moment, I realized something. If she told me she loved us both and wanted to be with the two of us, I wouldn't care. For her, I'd share. I needed her to not feel like this. I'd burn the whole world down to protect her and destroy anyone who hurt her. Even if that someone was me.

Later that afternoon, Caltain and Flur came over to work on battle potions. Flur also brought a number of sweet treats to appease Astrid's hormones. When she was distracted by baked goods, I pulled Caltain aside.

"Anna is getting restless. After Crogan's revelations, I fear she's going to do something stupid. He said the only way to take down Elias and Aiden is with great sacrifice, but there has to be another way."

"What are you thinking?"

"I want to break into the enclave," I whispered, peering over his shoulder to ensure Astrid was still preoccupied.

"Are you mad?" he asked, a little too loudly.

"Crogan told me how to get to the tunnels. I don't think anyone will expect me and Sion. I want to scout and see how many are still left. Maybe glean some intel and hopefully get the children out." And figure out why my timewalking no longer worked.

"I'm coming with you."

"I can't ask that of you, it's too dangerous."

"You're not asking. After what Alder did...I need to do something right. You don't know what you're up against. Two warlocks are better than one."

I nodded and turned to the ladies. Scooping up the box she had filled with potions already, I said, "We're going to head to Witch's Way and drop these off."

"We're also going to stop by the store and pick up more supplies."

Standing behind Astrid, I mouthed to Flur, "Keep her here," and hoped she pieced it together.

Hopping in the coach, we rushed towards Witch's Way. Though the day had been warm, the temperature was dropping rapidly as sunset approached. Keeping our promise, we delivered most of the potions and gathered more ingredients, but on the way out of Caltain's store, I almost walked into Michael. He looked like a shell of himself.

"Evening, Constable," I said, adjusting the pack filled with potions and explosives we had prepared for the attack.

"Evening, warlock. Up to no good?" he asked, forcing fake joviality into his voice. The ire in his eyes said otherwise.

"Actually, we're breaking into the enclave for reconnaissance," Caltain said.

"I want to get the children out too," I added.

"Noble. I'm coming with you."

"Absolutely not. You don't have magic, it's too dangerous," Caltain responded.

"Which is why I'll be on the opposite side of the enclave to distract them. While they're looking at me, you do your magic show. Just get those kids out."

"Where can we bring them?" I asked.

"To my shop for the night. In the morning, we'll place them in homes with the witches and warlocks on our side." Michael and I nodded at Caltain's suggestion and climbed into Astrid's coach.

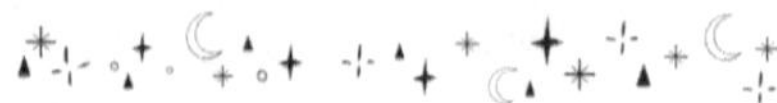

When we were close, Michael split off towards the front gate as Caltain and I headed to the tunnels. The sun had fully set, and the crescent moon through the clouds did little to light our path. Though the enclave had been almost entirely built into the mountain, the sewage system leaked out into a gutter that ran along the base. I followed it until it curved through a row of hedges. Scrunching my nose at the smell, I shrugged my shoulders at Caltain and pushed my way through the bushes, wading through the brown, mucky water.

I emerged on the other side, flush against a double wooden door held closed by a wooden beam across the outside. I tossed the beam on the ground and opened the doors enough to squeeze through as I whispered for Caltain to follow.

It was the first time I had met Caltain's familiar, at least to my knowledge, but the tiny mouse would come in very handy tonight. The wards hadn't been replaced since Crogan had escaped, so we snuck right in. He had believed he was the only one who knew of these tunnels, and so far, it seemed like he was right. The tunnel reeked of mold, and the floor was jagged, but neither of us wanted to risk using light in fear of revealing our approach.

We walked behind our familiars for ages, the pitter-patter of their tiny feet a contrast to the smacking of our boots. Eventually, the damp tunnel inclined sharply, leading us to a door. Muted light slipped through the cracks. We waited, pressing our ears to it. We could hear shouting in the distance, but no footfalls nearby. Michael's distraction at the entrance seemed to be working.

The small wooden door had a smaller version of the beam latch. Carefully prying open the door, we met a small amount of resistance, but I opened it enough to slip through. We emerged into Crogan's tiny, abandoned office, the door hidden behind a large tapestry. His office was between the library and the children's dormitory—the perfect spot for evacuating them.

The fox and mouse took off towards the dormitories to inform the children's familiars as we crept behind them. I slipped through the door to the first room and shook a child awake. "Liam, wake up. We need to get out of here," I whispered.

He wiped the sleep from his eyes and blinked up at me a few times. "Professor Killian? What are you doing here? Professor Aiden said you abandoned us for a witch."

"Does that sound like me, Liam?"

"No, Professor. Even when I lit your classroom on fire, you were kind to me. Since you left, it's been...scary."

"That's why we're here to get you out. But we have to hurry. I need your help getting the younger children. Take them to Librarian Crogan's office. There's a door hidden behind the tapestry with an owl sitting on a tree branch and the full moon. Get everyone out through those tunnels and run for the shops in Witch's Way. Do you understand?"

"Yes, Professor."

Explosions sounded from the front gate. We were running out of time. Caltain was just opening the last dormitory door. "I'm going to keep watch. Make sure to get every single one of them out."

He nodded and picked up the pace. Racing past the library, I reached my old room and rushed inside. Digging for the box under my bed, I pulled it out and smiled. This would do. I took one last look at the room I had spent the last few years in, and closed the door on what could have been.

Rushing towards the commotion, I reached a fork in the hall. A herd of warlocks flooded the building from both directions, and more shouting rang out as they noticed me. Taking aim, I chucked a potion down each hall and took pleasure in the loud bang and puff of smoke as they shattered. The men coughed and sputtered as I ran back towards the tunnel. I hadn't gotten the answer to what was stopping my timewalking, but hopefully, I had bought the children and Caltain enough time.

Running back, I was almost to Crogan's office when Aiden stepped out of one of the rooms. "Going somewhere, my boy?"

"Don't make me do this Aiden."

"We're not *making* you do anything. You made a choice. Albeit the wrong one."

I scoffed. "Bold words coming from one of the men who lied to me my whole life and pretended to care about me. I know you and Elias killed my parents."

"They were traitors to our cause. I see the apple doesn't fall far from the tree."

"Something I'm quite proud of," I said, calling upon my powers.

Instead of lighting his own, he charged at me, a battle cry resounding through the hall. I dodged his first swing, and his tightly balled fist slammed into the rock wall. As pissed as I was, I wasn't sure I could kill one of the men who had raised me. I wasn't a killer like they were. My only option was to get out of there, and without him knowing how. The kids needed more time.

"Old-fashioned hand-to-hand combat it is, ay, old friend?"

Aiden growled and dove for me again. I swung, my fist connecting with his face. He stumbled back but wasn't deterred. He landed a strike to my ribs before I could dodge it, and I doubled over in pain. I struck him again and shoved him, making him skid a few feet backward.

"Tell me, Killian. Is she worth it? Worth turning your back on the power? The family that raised you? The boys you teach?"

"I didn't turn my back on anyone," I gritted out painfully. "What you and Elias are doing is wrong. Can't you see that? You were going to kill an innocent witch. So many others are dead because of you. This isn't who you raised me to be. But yes. She is worth it."

He looked as if he would strike again when a bang rang out. Aiden slumped to the floor, unconscious. Caltain stood outside of Crogan's office. "I know you told me not to come back for you, but I've never been fond of following orders. Now let's go."

Caltain disappeared into the office, and I took one last look at Aiden's crumpled body. His chest rose and fell ever so slightly. He was still alive, but at least he wouldn't know how we had gotten in.

Chapter Thirty-Five

FOUR MONTHS LATER

"Wake up, Killian. My water broke," I said, shaking him awake. Of course, my baby had chosen the day of a full moon to be born. Her powers would be the strongest to break out of the womb. And of course, it was the hottest week of the year so far. I hated summer. My clothes were glued to my skin by my sticky, hormonal sweat.

His snore was stunted and loud as he jumped awake. Since he, Caltain, and Michael had rescued the children from the enclave, he had spent a lot of time tutoring them in the homes they had been placed in. His sleep was well-earned.

"Go get Mrs. Yates," I said calmly.

"Shouldn't we get you a doctor?"

"Matilda used to be a midwife—she's all we need. Now go!" I shoved him off the bed, and he landed on his ass, still groggy.

"Thank Hecate, these hormones will start declining."

"I heard that!" I yelled as he mumbled his way out of the room. "And they only get worse!" I added.

Mrs. Yates raced into the room a few moments later with a bucket of water and an armful of linens, Libby right behind her. She placed them on the side table and eyed me. "Which of your potions do you want me to get?"

"I prepped a special birthing one. It's in the bottom right drawer of the apothecary cabinet." It was my own mixture of chamomile and lavender for relaxation, blackberries for protection, and pomegranate for fertility and abundance. I had been taking it daily for the past two weeks. Judging by the constant motion in my belly, it had been effective. This version, however, had been made specifically for the birth. Ground cyclamen petals to ease the pain of childbirth, and ground red tulip petals to ensure a healthy delivery.

She returned with a vial in hand, and Killian came behind her sipping a cup of coffee. "Want some?" he asked.

Mrs. Yates eyed him. She had told him constantly she didn't think the liquid energy was safe for the fetus, so I had refrained since I learned of my pregnancy. They had allowed me herbal teas from Bubbling Brews only. He rolled his eyes and leaned his back against the doorway to watch. Mrs. Yates lit the yellow and red candles around the room that we had infused with fenugreek seeds.

I downed the surprisingly delicious potion, and Matilda lifted my nightdress to place both hands on my belly. Closing her eyes and checking with her magic, she said, "They're ready. Shouldn't be long now."

"They?" Killian asked, pushing off the wall to approach us.

"Yes, they. I keep telling you they. There are at least two."

"You did keep saying they, but you never told us you thought it was more than one," I said with a raised voice.

"I thought that was implied," she said with a sarcastic smile.

Off to the side, I heard them whispering, failing to hide their conversation from me.

"Are you going to call Michael? Should he be here for the birth?" Mrs. Yates asked.

"He hasn't come back since Ranai scared him. Unless she asks for him specifically, let's wait for the babies to come out and then decide."

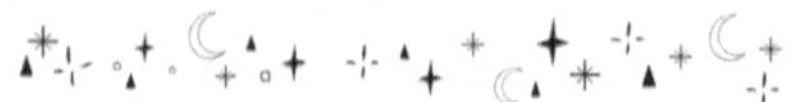

Though labor often took hours, and sometimes days, I was fortunate that mine was barely over four hours. Killian sweetly held my hand, even as I crushed it, throughout every contraction and every pained scream. When the first little one emerged, Mrs. Yates cleaned her off and had her wailing in no time. She handed her to me briefly as she checked me over.

My beautiful baby girl reeked of powerful magic. She had my ebony hair and Killian's deep brown eyes. Though it wasn't long, I was impressed by the sheer volume of hair this gorgeous newborn had. I didn't bother to hold back the tears as I held my little one in my arms. I had done this once before, but she had been ripped away from me so fast. I'd damn myself to hell before I let anyone hurt this precious soul too. Killian stood beside my bed, running two fingers through her little waves and brushing them across her cheek with a wide grin on his face.

"She's so beautiful. She looks fierce like her mama. What should we name her?"

"Tyra."

I stared deep into her eyes for an eternity until I felt the contractions begin again. "Take her, Killian. The next one is coming."

He scooped her out of my arms and held her snugly. He would protect her with every ounce of magic and love that he possessed. And he had an immense amount of both.

The next one was more reluctant, and I could feel how much larger she was. After Matilda cleaned her, she handed the quiet baby to me. She had a stoic, round face with Michael's sparkling blue eyes. She also had his straight brown hair. The tears broke free again, but this time because her father hadn't been here to see her come into the world. My throat bobbed, and Killian didn't miss it.

"She's not mine, is she? I don't sense any magic from her."

I shook my head to confirm his fears. "Meet Nyla. She is Michael's."

"Is that possible?" he asked Mrs. Yates in a shockingly calm tone.

"It is indeed. These two beautiful girls appear to have been conceived days apart. It's not common, but I have seen it before."

My heart felt like it was squeezing tight and expanding towards an explosion when Killian placed Tyra back in my arms. Holding both of them, seeing them so near to each other, made my heart full.

Killian stood beside me, sweetly caressing and kissing the three of us over and over. He didn't say a word about Nyla being Michael's. I don't think he cared. He was just happy to have so much joy in his life. That joy was interrupted by a very serious Matilda.

"We need supplies for the girls," she said, shoving a list at him. "And be quick about it. You know what to do."

"Yes, ma'am," he said, still wearing a proud smile as he rushed out of the room.

"I'll give you some time alone with the girls. Yell for me if you need anything," she said, an uncharacteristic smile adorning her face. "They're gorgeous, Astrid. I'm so happy for you." She nudged Libby with an elbow, both of them giving me privacy with my newborns.

The moment they left the room, every emotion I had been restraining poured out of me. Absorbing the warmth of the two beautiful creatures that I had made with two different men, I recalled the passage I had read all those months ago. That triangles were the strongest shape. I didn't think it was a coincidence that the Triumvirate was also a trio. I prayed that having twins—even if they were from different fathers—wasn't a coincidence, but I had to be sure.

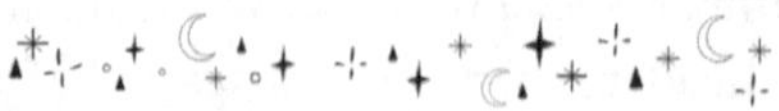

With both girls settled upstairs with our new nanny, Brenna, Mrs. Yates, Libby, and Ranai, I rushed downstairs to test my theory. Grabbing a few things from my apothecary cabinet, I rushed to the kitchen. I set two vials in my stand and opened the drawstring pouch of hair I had stolen from Michael when he had come to visit. I had hugged him so tightly that he hadn't noticed the few strands I had yanked off the back of his head. Carefully, I dropped them into the left vial.

Killian's hair was not in short supply, given our frantic love-making sessions. I placed a few pieces in the right vial. Into both, I finished the recipe I had been fine-tuning:

> 1 tsp. of ash from my witchfire
> A pinch of dried tangerine peel to invoke a lover who is a true friend
> 2 tbsp. of fennel seeds steeped in red wine to match Killian's sexuality
> ¼ cup of ground oathroot to represent Michael's loyalty and honor
> 2 crushed blackberries to deepen bonding
> 1 clockvine tendril to connect us across timelines
> Mix with a dove feather to bring long-lasting love

Slicing my palm, I dribbled blood into each. Placing my hands around each vial, I closed my eyes and whispered my incantation, begging Hecate to show me which was my one true love.

"My gift of fire and his of sight, I call upon the full moon tonight. One master of time full of fiery lust, the other the harbinger of all things right and just. Both men have stolen a piece of my heart, connected to me, 'til dust do us part. Linked together, hearts beating as one. A love that burns as hot as the sun. So please Hecate, Goddess above, answer my question, are both of them my true love?"

The glass heated but did not burn or melt. Opening my eyes again, I saw both mixtures turn blue and swirl with sparkles. Through the fog of tears, I trusted my gut and poured one of the mixtures into the other. The blue turned sparkling gold, flecks popping like rays of sunshine in the morning. I covered my mouth with my uncut hand to stifle my surprised gasp.

They were both my true love. The three of us belonged together. That's why Killian could read Michael. But I knew the villain I had become. I didn't deserve either of these kind, wonderful, and loving men. Our girls needed them more than they needed me. Praying to Hecate that triangles really were the strongest shape, I tossed back the vial and steeled myself for what I had to do. But first, Ranai and I had to prepare.

Mrs. Yates stood in the kitchen doorway with her arms crossed, eyes red and rimmed with tears.

"I'm sorry. I have to. It's too risky to wait a month for another full moon. Elias and Aiden are going to come for the girls any day. My powers are the strongest right now."

"I know. I couldn't stop you if I wanted to. At least I got to see you bring these beautiful girls into the world. Go. Make sure they stay safe. I'll see you on the other side. May Hecate welcome us both home in peace."

"Make sure the nanny is prepared. Tell Killian I'm sorry. I have no other choice."

I whistled for Ranai, who reluctantly left the girls to join me. "It's time. We need energy. Only the ones on the list. Only those who deserve it."

I downed one last concoction. One meant to halt bleeding and reduce pain. Ranai nodded, I kissed William on the cheek, and we left Leighis Chateau for the last time.

Chapter Thirty-Six

An hour later, Ranai and I arrived at the gates of the enclave. We eyed each other, both covered in sweat, blood, and debris from our reaping, and took a deep breath. A metallic scent clung to the inside of my nose and refused to leave my taste buds. I picked a particularly large chunk of human tissue off my dress and scrunched my nose as I flung it to the ground. Our previous battle had been in the middle of a thunderstorm, but today, the sky was bright blue, and not a single cloud dared to ruin it. The hot sun beat down and reflected off the enclave like a sparkly crystal. A gem that I wanted to grind into dust.

My stomach had receded slightly without the extra weight of the babies, but the trek here should have been exhausting. Fortunately, our rampage had not only given me extra power but had also rapidly slimmed the residual belly growth from my pregnancy. People could say what they wanted about dark magic, but my body loved it. I pounded on the door and yelled, while the clip-clop of horseshoes and rattle of wheel carts over the street stones pulsed around us. The air was thick with the tang of horse manure baking in the heat, mixed with the yeasty scent of bread.

A loud bell sounded in the distance. Tolling the end of the Triumvirate, perhaps?

"What do you want?" a guard yelled.

"It's Astrid Leighis. I demand to speak to Elias and Aiden. Now."

Moments later, the door swung open, revealing the Triumvirate elder, heralded by a single alarmed squawk from Bas as he landed on a light post above me. "I assume it's you we have to thank for the pile of bodies in our tunnels? Every one of our older acolytes in line for the Triumvirate. Dead."

I had worried that the tunnels would be filled with young acolytes. Innocents. Those who didn't deserve it. Though they had been empty when Killian freed the children, Killian's escape had given away the location. Fortunately, we had encountered those most loyal to Elias. And it had been well-guarded. They had known who I was the moment I entered, and none of them held back. A huge grin split my face as I mentally replayed the scene.

"It's Anna! Attack her! She's here for Elias. We mustn't let her through."

"I fear you've chosen the wrong side, gentlemen." I threatened as Ranai tackled the man who had shouted and ripped out his throat.

Another charged at me. I tilted my head and watched him approach, full of pity. I didn't have much dark magic left, but I would shortly. As soon as I killed every last acolyte. This one would be the first. He lunged, but I dodged his attack and grabbed the back of his head, slamming him face first into the rock wall. Unconscious, he slid down the surface, leaving behind a giant splotch of red.

"Always underestimating me," I said. Leaning down and digging my teeth into his neck, I sucked out as much life force as I could. My shirt and face were covered in blood, and the acolytes stared at me in horror. I smiled, relishing the sharp scent of fear.

A brave one ran for me as the rush of fire and the thrumming of dark magic coursed through my veins. Flames burst from my palms and ignited him before he reached me. He dropped to the ground, rolling frantically to put out the flames.

"I'm afraid black magic witchfire doesn't work like that," I said, looking down with a pleased grin.

While Ranai tore limbs from warlock after warlock, another approached me, wielding knives.

"Don't worry boys, there's plenty of me to go around." I stalked towards him, stepping along the stone floor. Moss wove through the cracks between each rough shape. The hall reeked of mold, but before the night was through, the stench of death would overpower it.

"The door is sealed and warded. Even if you get through us, you won't get through there," the man said, holding a shaking knife in my direction.

"Oh, I know. I just need your life force. I will go through the front door."

Aiden cautiously peered out at me from behind Elias, his fingers stroking his salamander's back as if to calm it. "Did you say Astrid?" he asked with a shaky voice, pulling me from my reverie. A painfully young man joined them. He hid behind both of them, hands trembling as he clutched at his amulet. *This must be their replacement for Killian.*

"Whatever you did to your librarian wasn't fast acting enough. I got quite a trove of information out of him before his life expired. I am Astrid. I'm not surprised you're struggling with that fact. I'm equally unsurprised that Elias isn't."

"It seems we're both familiar with dark magic, my dear. In light of that, what makes you think you can stop us?"

"You took something dear from me many years ago, Elias. You may have been the youngest at the time, but you were as much a part of it as they were. Ranai watched you murder my daughter, and your Triumvirate sent the humans after me. I've spent the last forty years preparing to destroy you. I'll be damned if I'm going to fail. I just don't get why. Why do all of this? You already had power. Why did you need more?"

"It was the only way to eradicate the humans from Dracht. They're a scourge on this planet, especially that weak and pathetic constable of yours."

"I've grown fond of these humans. If that wasn't enough, I have a lot more to lose now."

"What's she talking about, Elias?"

"Oh, poor Mr. Bates. He's kept you in the dark exactly as he has Killian, I see. I had considered turning you to my side, but I'm afraid we're out of time."

The remnants of my daughters were still in me, forming one magical trio, and the swirling love potion within me formed a second triangular bond. With the heat of more dark magic than I had ever consumed in a single day, I lit flames in both palms and bared my teeth. My skin lit in rippling oranges and reds, like the surface of the sun, as I prepared my attack.

"May Hecate have mercy on you for your sins."

Chapter Thirty-Seven

KILLIAN

Strolling into the chateau with my arms and heart full and a grin on my face, I stopped in my tracks when I saw a young woman standing in the foyer with a scowling Matilda. Matilda's eyes were red and swollen as she gave instructions and sent the young woman upstairs.

"You're finally back. What in Hecate's name took you so long?"

"I went to find someone," I said, gesturing to Michael, who crept in behind me. "Thought he should get to meet his daughter. I thought you wanted that too? Go on up and see the girls, I'm sure Astrid will be thrilled."

"She's not here."

"What do you mean, she's not here?" I asked through a growl. "She just gave birth. She should be in bed, resting."

Mrs. Yates broke down in tears, and her tight hug almost forced the items from my arms. She sobbed into my shoulder for a moment before pulling back, her lips pinching as if she didn't want to tell us something.

"Out with it, Matilda."

"Astrid went to obliterate the Triumvirate. She's afraid Elias and Aiden will come for the girls. She told me to tell you she's sorry, and that it's the only way. But you can't let her. It's not about me dying; I've had a long life. But she just got the family she's always wanted. She's waited forty years for this. They need her."

"We need her too," Michael said. "I'll go stop her."

"I'm coming with you," I added, handing the supplies to Mrs. Yates.

"Just in case, I'm going to kiss the girls goodbye. Take good care of them, will you? The nanny is qualified, but it wouldn't hurt to have Michael's mother help as well," Matilda suggested.

"Don't talk like that. We'll get there in time. It will be fine," I said, giving her one last hug as we rushed outside.

Astrid's driver was nowhere to be seen, despite the carriage sitting there, but we didn't have time to waste. "Get in!" I yelled to Michael as I hopped into the driver's seat. He climbed up beside me instead as I drove the horses as fast as they could go towards the enclave. Each house had its windows open, freshly-washed laundry hanging from clothes lines, fluttering in the light summer breeze, unaware of the chaos that was about to break out. The coffee mixed with my nerves and burned my insides as I prayed for everything to go in our favor.

By the time we had broken through the crowded streets of Dracht and gotten closer to my former home, the fight had moved inside the gates of the enclave where the coach wouldn't fit. We both leapt off before the cart had slowed and ran towards the clash of magic. Witches and warlocks surrounded the entrance, held back by some invisible barrier. A number of humans gathered behind them with weapons, shouting taunts at the warlocks within.

Caltain and Flur were at the front, their magic swirling around them.

"What's going on?" Michael asked.

"Anna passed through Witch's Way with a flat belly; she and Ranai both were covered in blood and guts. We gathered as many as we could to follow her. We knew what she intended, but she locked us out with a dark magic ward. We've been trying to break it open to help her," Caltain said.

"It's starting to wane with her life force, we have to hurry," Flur added.

I joined them in trying to break it down. I had never been good with spells or hexes, though I had managed wards. The surface scorched our skin as we tried to fight through it, the scent of sizzling meat worrying me. Nevertheless, I funneled every ounce of magic from the pit of my belly and chanted along with them. My energy connected to theirs, like links in a chain, squeezing around the woven threads of Astrid's spell. My muscles cramped, and exhaustion set in, but the ward eventually fell. Flur, Caltain, Michael, and I lurched forward as the bubble of magic collapsed.

Astrid, Elias, and Aiden were engaged in battle in the open courtyard, the force of their magic levitating them yards above the ground. Roaring winds whipped around them like a cyclone, dust and leaves caught in the mayhem. Bas perched on the light post, ready to strike when the moment was right. Rex was nowhere to be seen. Likely cowering in a corner somewhere. Swirls of blue water clashed against roaring fire, bursts of flames popping over the top every so often. Flashes of light alternated with over-whelming darkness from within, like a nightmare. The smell of burning wood and sulfur permeated my nostrils.

This battle had been waging far longer than I had hoped, and even from this distance, I could see the life fading from her face, but Aiden and Elias were inches from death as well. The acolyte they had chosen to replace me was already dead below the battle. Astrid's entire body was aflame, and she and Ranai were covered in blood. The great wolf circled below, fending off any of the acolytes that tried to join the fight. She had taken down at least seven so far.

"You have to let me do this!" Astrid yelled over her shoulder at us, her voice amplified, likely by dark magic. "You need to leave and take care of our girls. They need you."

I only had to get a little closer for my water and fire to protect her, but I wasn't sure I was going to make it. Michael kept racing towards her, but there was nothing he'd be able to do either.

"Promise me you'll rebuild Dracht so that magic and humanity coexist. Set an example for Nyla and Tyra." She held a stream of fire in each hand, one aimed at Elias and one at Aiden, whose opposing magical streams were barely held at bay as their life forces dwindled. Water, flames, and tumultuous winds drowned out every noise but her voice.

We kept racing, the entire army behind us to protect Astrid, but we wouldn't make it.

She yelled, looking directly at Michael. "From the moment I met you, something inside me kept screaming you were the one. These last few months without you have been torture. And you, Killian," she said.

My heart was being crushed beneath the mountain that loomed in front of us.

"I felt a pull towards you the instant we met, and it has never dwindled. You've been my rock. I never thought it possible to love anyone, but to discover that *both* of you were my true loves. The three of us are the only reason this is working. Tell the girls I love them. Make sure they know I did this for them. They deserve to be raised by their kind, gentle, protective, and good fathers. Not their evil mother. I couldn't let the blood on my hands be their legacy."

Elias, Aiden, Ranai, and Astrid collapsed at the same moment. Michael and I skidded to a stop in horror as the roaring sounds of battling magic faded into excruciating silence.

Chapter Thirty-Eight

Michael

Dracht was a ghost town. Anna had become the heart of it, and every single person was feeling the sting of her loss two weeks later. Perhaps not as much as Killian and I or the girls, but they felt it nonetheless.

The stores of Witch's Way and the market on the human side of town had stayed closed for three days to honor her memory. Altars and memorials appeared on every street, but the town remained quiet, despite the beautiful summer weather. The usual nutty and aromatic spells from Flur and Declan's shops weren't filling the air, and neither was laughter. Nobody spoke of what the Triumvirate had done or what had happened, they only spoke of how she had saved us. Though my men had willingly stepped up to take my watch most nights, I'd taken a trip or two through town to see the desolation.

Crime had temporarily ceased. Humans, warlocks, and witches came together. The entire town had become one peaceful place, exactly like she wanted. The darkness had vanished, but so had the light.

My mother and I moved into Leighis Chateau to help Killian and the nanny raise the girls now that Mrs. Yates had passed. We had never found her body. Only a pile of dust next to the girls' crib.

Mother had never gotten the chance to meet Anna, but she took to being a nana like a dream. She loved both girls more than anything and forced Killian and I to regale them with stories of their mother, despite them being too young to understand a word we were saying. She wanted to be sure they never forgot what she had sacrificed to give them a life free of torment. Though I missed Anna more, Ranai's death left a huge pit in my heart too.

I hadn't hated Killian before, but I hadn't been very fond of him, especially when he was around Anna. But the last two weeks had proven me wrong. He was a doting father and a good man. It was a magic of its own that we had melded our lives together so smoothly to take care of Nyla and Tyra. We didn't argue, we didn't hold grudges—we just became a family. A family with a giant, gaping hole torn through the middle of it.

The deep circles under his red-rimmed eyes and his sullen mood when the girls weren't around were proof that I wasn't the only one ripped apart by our loss. He frequently eyed his guitar in the corner of the sitting room, but could never bring himself to play it. Like touching it would violate some promise he had made to her. He hadn't let it impact his care for the girls, though. He had even taught me that tinting the bottom of their feet with blueberries would protect them.

Caltain and Flur had been regular visitors since Anna's death. They brought us supplies and meals and spent time with the girls to give us breaks. It warmed my heart to know we weren't going to do this alone. All I wanted was for Anna to see what her sacrifice had accomplished. How many missed her. That she wasn't anything close to the villain she had thought she was.

Sion sat on Killian's lap while he fed Nyla. I sat in Anna's favorite chair feeding Tyla. The nanny was upstairs replacing the girls' bedding, and my mother was in the kitchen cooking us a meal while we sat in silence. The girls held our gaze as we fed them, looking around for each other every so often. They held each other's hands as they slept, like it kept them safe to be together.

"It's not fair," Killian said.

"What isn't?" I asked, knowing he could mean one of a million things.

"That we both knew her and the girls never will. They'll never get to taste her cooking. Hear her sass when she yells at us. They're going to miss out on so much. It should've been me instead."

"I have that same thought every day. But the girls are safe. I try to put that at the forefront of my mind."

My mother entered with two plates of food, smiling sadly as her eyes bounced between us. "What Astrid did was honorable. The least we can do is give her what she asked for. We raise these girls to be happy and safe, and once we have everything under control here, you boys rebuild this town in her vision. For Nyla and Tyra."

My glassy eyes met Killian's, and he nodded. "Together."

"Together," I agreed.

We were managing. But we needed her. Everyone needed her.

Chapter Thirty-Nine

KILLIAN

Michael and I had been pacing back and forth carrying the girls for what felt like hours, both screaming bloody murder. We had learned to ignore the stink the girls were capable of, but the ear-piercing squeals were too much for my eardrums.

"I don't know what's wrong. They're fed, they're changed, what more can we do?" I asked, my voice high-pitched and frantic from lack of sleep.

"Have you tried swapping? You have each other's daughter. Maybe it requires a father's touch?" the nanny suggested as she tidied up the room. "I'm happy to take one, if either of you needs a break," she added in a quiet, saccharine tone.

We handed the girls off to each other and began pacing again, their crying getting worse.

"I think the pacing is giving them motion sickness," Michael's mother suggested. "Stand still and try rocking them gently."

We complied, to no avail.

"Let us take them," the nanny offered again, gently scooping Tyra out of my hands as Michael's mother took Nyla from him.

"Go, get some rest. We'll take over for a bit," Mrs. Sheehan proposed.

"They need their mother. We can't do this without Astrid," I said.

"We don't exactly have another choice, now, do we?" Michael said, his bloodshot eyes filled with concern for his little girl. I'm sure I didn't look any better. My hair stood on end after not having been washed for days.

"That's not entirely true."

Michael's eyes met mine, his face reddening with anger. "What have you not told me?"

"Theoretically, as a timewalker, I could go back and save her."

"I thought Elias and Aiden blocked that ability?" he asked.

"They did. I don't know how they did, but it doesn't matter. That kind of magic always dies with the caster. There are rumors it's possible, but the kind of power that would require...even Astrid didn't have, and she defeated them and all the power linked to them on her own. There's no way theirs lasted."

"And why the fuck have you not done that?"

"Changing time requires black magic. Something I'm firmly against."

"If it brings back Anna, I don't care what you have to do. You do it."

I nodded. I had been pondering it over the weeks we suffered without her. It went against everything I stood for. But I didn't care. Hearing the man who firmly believed in right and wrong agreeing with me, I knew it was the right choice. We would go back in time, and I would take Astrid's place. They couldn't live without their mother, but they could certainly live without me. Michael would take care of my daughter too.

I swept out of the room to figure out how to handle the black magic part.

Michael hugged his mother and thanked the nanny, then followed me. "Where are we going?"

"I have to darken my soul with black magic. You don't want to come with me for this part." My serious tone was sinking in. It needed to be done if this was going to work.

His throat bobbed and he nodded his head. "I have an idea. Come with me."

When we got outside, he directed the driver to the constabulary.

"Why are we going there?"

"It's the only place I know full of criminals. If we're going to take lives, they may as well be the ones on death row for serious crimes that Dracht can live without." Having been part of the Triumvirate, I knew that whole wing had been questioned under truth serum. Not a single innocent soul there.

"You don't need to be involved."

"You're wrong. *We* need to save her. You're not the only one in love with her, Killian. Those girls are ours. We do this together, whether you like it or not."

Having him witness what I was about to do wasn't something I could live with, so he reluctantly agreed to wait outside as I went into the holding cells and brutally tore apart every person in there. Covered in blood, I met him back outside. "Thank you for your help. I'm ready."

He pulled a handkerchief from his pocket, handing it to me. "You got a little something..." he pointed to his cheek.

Wiping my face off, I handed the blood-soaked handkerchief back to him. He scrunched up his nose and threw it on the ground.

I swirled my hand to open the portal, reciting the incantation. Michael grabbed my other arm.

"What are you doing?"

"I'm coming with you. I told you, we do this together."

"I've never taken a human."

"First time for everything. Let's go."

Holding my breath, I dragged us through the portal. When we came out on the other side, Astrid was locked in a heated battle with Elias and Aiden, and Ranai circled the three of them. Somehow, I had not only transported us through time but landed us within the wards the others were fighting to break down. We looked at each other and ran.

Chapter Forty

Michael

Being pulled through the portal was the most bizarre feeling I had ever experienced. Like my insides were being scrambled then put back together. Every inch of my body felt cold as ice despite the intense heat we emerged into, and I was consumed by the overwhelming urge to hurl. Killian looked unperturbed by the entire experience. Unsurprising. But then reality sank in. He had done it. We were here.

Killian was fast, but I was faster. There was no way I was going to let him sacrifice himself. Dracht still needed a magical leader, and he was the right man for the job. As I got closer to Anna, I could see the light fading from her face, but Aiden and Elias were inches from death. Ranai attempted to pounce on them, but their magic was able to hold her off.

"You have to let me do this!" Anna yelled. "You all need to leave and take care of our girls. They need you."

"We already tried that. They need you more than us!" I shouted back, leaping to put myself in the path of the magic.

Killian, who was a few steps behind me, tried to do the same. She grabbed each of our hands, as Killian yanked my free one to try to pull me from the beam.

"The girls need both of you. My father was right about the

Triumvirate, it's my duty to stop them. To continue what he started." I yelled as Elias' winds howled around us. "I'm sorry I never said it, Anna, but I know you felt it. I loved you more than anything, and though I battled with it, what you had done didn't matter to me. I never stopped loving you."

"I love you too, Michael," she said, her eyes full of tears.

The roaring winds kept trying to pull the three of us apart as Elias and Aiden crept closer and closer to death. Ranai was finally able to overtake their magic, ripping a chunk out of Elias' thigh as he screamed in horror. Their faces paled, and their arms faded away into dust that got swept up in the cyclone, fading into oblivion.

"And I love you too, Killian," she said. The three of us held on to each other and pushed to take the full force of the attack away from the others. We all watched as Elias and Aiden disappeared, waiting to follow after them.

The storm died down, and the three of us collapsed onto the street, out of breath but holding each other's hands, forming a perfect triangle. Ranai ran over to me, licking my face.

"How are we alive right now?" I asked.

She burst into laughter and looked at us, eyes full of tears and joy. "Triangles are the strongest shape."

"What?" Killian asked, standing up before helping to right her.

"The Triumvirate was a triangle, a trio. It reinforced their power. They were weakened by losing Killian, and their new acolyte wasn't as strong. I killed him as soon as the fight began. But the three of us are an even stronger triangle. Parts of the girls still being inside of my body didn't hurt either. Double triangle power."

Killian and I nodded our heads as if we understood. All I knew was that all three of us were alive.

"Why are you covered in blood?" she asked Killian.

"It was the only way to change time," he answered, smiling through his exhaustion.

"Change time? I thought..."

"I told you, we tried that. We weren't fast enough to save you the first time. We couldn't go on without you. The girls couldn't go on without you," I whispered, brushing the dusty remnants of Elias and Aiden out of her hair with my fingertips.

She spun to him, eyes wide. "You used dark magic? To come back? For me?"

"Of course I did." He dusted himself off, attempting to play it cool.

"But you wouldn't even do that for your parents."

She took his hands in hers, and for the first time, I didn't feel the banging drum of jealousy against my heart. He had over-turned his entire belief system to save the woman I loved. The mother of our children.

"True love is worth darkening your soul for," he added, meeting her eyes, then mine.

"And I may have coaxed him into it," I added.

"Do you really think we were able to defeat them just because we were a trio?" She asked, eyes bouncing back and forth between us.

"You had defeated them on your own in the other timeline. But you didn't survive it," Killian said, his jovial spirit entirely depleted.

"It worked because all three of you were willing to sacrifice yourselves for the others," a velvety voice came from behind us. Caltain had spoken, and he and Flur approached, followed by the entirety of Dracht.

"I thought that light magic was stronger than dark magic, but it seems dark magic wielded with the best intentions is even stronger. I think the three of you proved that today. I can't figure out how you were next to us one instant, then in here the next," Flur added.

"It's a long story," Killian said with a charming smirk.

"Perhaps one told over drinks and treats at the Mabon festival in two weeks, after the town has had a chance to settle," I suggested.

Killian scanned the crowd within the courtyard, his leadership qualities shining through as his voice boomed among them. "Alright, everyone. Let's head inside and see what we can salvage. Remember, the acolytes and younger warlocks were likely terrified of their power. We shouldn't blame any of them for being scared or following blindly. Let's make sure everyone is safe."

Anna's lips pinched. "Stay out of the tunnels for now. Save that for Killian and myself to clean up later."

Killian snorted and led the others through the front door of the enclave, leaving Anna and I alone with Ranai. Squatting down, I ran my fingers through the fur on the top of her head, scratching behind her ears. "I'm so glad you survived, girl. I missed you so much. I still have no idea how their magic didn't kill me instantly."

Peering up at Anna, I found her crying again. The bright sun illuminating her head like a halo. She was no saint, that was certain, but she was a fucking goddess in my eyes.

"What's wrong?"

"Nothing's wrong. I just thought you should know you're petting your grandmother."

My jaw dropped as I stared up at her. "What?"

"I think that's how you were able to survive Elias and Aiden's magic, and how you prevented them from using their vision powers on you. I know you're human and have no magic of your own, but I suspect after what your grandmother went through," she pointed at Ranai, "she put a hex on the Triumvirate or a powerful protection spell on your family. The opposite of a curse, in a sense."

"What are you talking about?"

"Iona Litriu. The first victim of the Dracht purge, according to a book Mrs. Yates's familiar saved from the fire. Ranai urged me to read it. She was famous for her unmatched hexes and curses and had fallen pregnant by a human. It was a scandal for her family, who had been very close with mine. She was best friends with my mother, so when she reincarnated as a wolf, she chose to be my familiar. The alleged father was Carraig Sheehan."

"My grandfather?" I asked, meeting Ranai's gaze. The great wolf smiled at me, and at that moment, I saw it. My father's smile. And his eyes.

"It's why she loved you from the moment she saw you. She knew who you were. And it's why she pushed us together, despite what a kind-hearted person you are and what a monster I am."

"Because she knew the real you and knows you're not. You're the only one who thinks that. Your choices may not have been mine, but they weren't misguided. They came from a place of love. To protect and defend love. Just like she's done. That's why she saved me when you attacked me, too, isn't it?"

Ranai nodded and licked my face.

"I'm assuming Killian told you of our destiny as told by the seer?"

I nodded, then wrapped my arms around Ranai and buried my face in her neck.

"Killian and I are destined to be together, and it seems you and I are as well. It's something I've been struggling with, which is why I thought sacrificing myself would be the best option. Then I wouldn't have had to choose."

At that moment, the words I thought would destroy my heart didn't feel so painful. I had known true heartbreak when I lost her to Killian, but I had been more devastated when she died. I never wanted to feel that again. And so, I stood and wrapped her up in my arms and said, "You never have to choose."

Chapter Forty-One

I was alive. My girls were alive. Killian and Michael were alive. And the evil, power-hungry bastards that had been ruling Dracht were gone. The only thing left to do was fess up to my sins and prepare for the angry mob to take my life. Both men tried to convince me otherwise, but I couldn't live with lying to everyone I cared for here. Especially after they had banded together to help me fight.

The nanny and the very happy, albeit shocked-to-be-alive Matilda stayed behind to watch Tyra and Nyla, but Michael and Killian insisted on escorting me for protection. Protection I didn't need or deserve. Michael had gone to the human side to round up as many as he could to meet at Witch's Way while Killian knocked on each warlock and witch family's doors, and I knocked at each shop. By noon, almost the entirety of Dracht was gathered.

The sun shone directly down on the main intersection of Witch's Way, right on the gathered people I was proud to call friends. I flashed back to fighting Elias and Aiden in this very spot, in the middle of a torrential thunderstorm. Today, however, Hecate had blessed us with clear skies and a light breeze that fueled my energy. Just four days past the full moon, I felt strong. The men I loved made me even stronger.

I climbed up on top of my coach and used the same spell I had in the courtyard to amplify my voice. "Ladies and gentlemen, all citizens of Dracht. The Triumvirate no longer controls this town. You are free to live as you like. A tip in the balance of power does not always go the way you expect, so proceed with caution. This is not why I called you here today, though. I called you here to confess my sins."

Caltain crossed his arms before he and Flur shared a confused look.

"When I returned to Dracht, I lied to each and every one of you. My name is not Anna. It is Astrid."

Gasps sounded around me and shocked whispers filled the air. Caltain's jaw had dropped, and Flur's hand flung to cover her mouth.

"Forty years ago, the Triumvirate stole my child from me. They had convinced the humans of our beautiful town that she would be the end of the balance of magic as we know it. My newborn was ripped from my arms and brutally murdered, and then they tried to do the same to me. For years, I was on the run. For decades, I planned how I would return the favor."

Many of the townsfolk had begun crying at this admission. They had known of these horrors that had happened before their lifetimes, but many had shoved these thoughts into the backs of their minds.

"But the true horror that I must confess to you is this. I *know* that I'm the villain. Maybe I've always known it. But in light of what they did to my child—To me. To others—I didn't care. For years, I sat, and watched, and planned to make them pay. And make them pay, I did. For that, I am not sorry. But I am sorry for those of you who lost someone you loved at my hand."

My eyes met Caltain's, both glossed over with tears.

"Those whose lives I took were working for the Triumvirate. Conspiring with them, whether they knew what for or not. Elias intended to link the lives of as many powerful souls as he could with black magic, ensuring that he and Aiden lived longer and had more power than anyone else. They had already amassed a significant amount of power, and I couldn't let that happen anymore. But I am no stranger to black magic myself, as you can tell by my unaged body. I don't expect any of you to understand what losing a child can do to you. How it snaps who you are and morphs you into a monster you no longer recognize."

The entire town was silent, listening to my speech, and nobody moved.

I licked my lips, my regret like ash in my mouth, leaving me parched. My stomach soured at how they would take this. "The old Astrid would not have shared any of this with you, but since returning as Anna and getting to know every person in Dracht, I felt you deserved the truth. Learning about your families while chatting at the market, visiting my home for medical remedies, and sharing laughs over a cup of coffee. These moments are the ones I'll cherish forever. You accepted Anna for who she was, and you made me believe in humanity again. Whatever punishment you deem fit for me, I accept."

Climbing down from the stagecoach, I clasped my hands together and awaited their verdict. Michael stood on one side and Killian on the other, guarding me as if they would fight anyone who came for me to the death. Flur was the first to break her stillness. She approached me with tears in her eyes and a sad smile, clasping me in a tight hug.

"I'm so sorry for what they did to you. But I thank you for freeing us." She placed a kiss on my forehead and headed back to her shop.

Caltain was next. I had been hoping to avoid him after my revelation. He was the person whose reaction I feared the most. When he reached me, he looked deep into my eyes like he was searching for something. Remorse? A soul? He cupped my cheek in his palm and broke his terrifying silence. "I feared Alder was up to something nefarious, but I never imagined it was aiding the Triumvirate with black magic. He had so many secrets, and I was too afraid to push. It will take time to get over what you did, but I understand. There will be no punishment from me."

Hugging him tightly, I buried my face into his shoulder. I had never felt so much relief in my life. It didn't matter what anyone else said. His was the only answer I needed.

Many of the residents dispersed, heading back to their homes and businesses to ponder my words, but not a single one threatened me. None of them even seemed upset. "I can't fathom how any who lost their loved ones at my hands can be okay with this."

Killian put an arm around me and smiled. "I may have informed each legacy house of the terrible deeds their lost members had been doing with the Triumvirate. And about what that dark magic would've brought upon us."

Michael took one of my hands in his and added, "And I may have informed all the humans how you sacrificed yourself to save them. That we went back in time to stop it, but that you were willing to do whatever it took to prevent the bleak future Dracht had coming."

Nestled between the two true loves of my life, I realized they were willing to do the same. "There is hope for Dracht, especially with both of you at the helm."

"You mean the three of us. There's a far greater power in three," Killian said, smiling down at me. "And I'm willing to share if Constable Sheehan is amenable," Killian smirked wickedly at Michael over my shoulder.

Michael rolled his eyes, but his lip tipped up. "I'll settle for letting you watch."

Chapter Forty-Two

Wailing from the nursery woke me. I was reluctant to leave the comfort of being snuggled between Michael and Killian, but Tyra was a right pain in the ass if she wasn't attended to quickly, and I didn't need her riling up Nyla. I climbed over Michael since he was less likely to wake from the jostling, threw on my silk robe, and made my way to the nursery.

Ranai stood between the cribs, tail wagging as she guarded her two new charges. She had instantly adored them. I had feared she wouldn't care for Tyra as much, but she had surprised us all. She had been coming around to Killian now that his link to Elias and Aiden had been broken. She had sensed the dark magic connection they had burdened him with.

Scooping up Tyra from beneath her nest of blankets, I peeked into Nyla's crib to see her still asleep and smiled. Just like her father. Sitting down in my rocker, I fed Tyra and sang a lullaby, hoping to calm the fiery child. Hearing a creak, I saw Killian and his tousled hair leaning against the doorway with his arms crossed. His smile warmed my heart and my lower belly. "You keep smiling at me like that, and we're going to wind up with three more of these."

"I know how you get when we're snowed in. We're going to have a whole coven in no time," he said, using his fingertips to smooth out his facial hair. "What would you like for breakfast?"

"Something hearty, please. I'm exhausted from keeping both of you satisfied," I said with a wink.

"If Michael stopped being such a pigeon-livered flapdoodle, you could have us both at the same time. Half the energy spent, my love."

"You'll convince him soon enough. He's come around to sharing a bed, has he not?"

Pushing off the doorframe, he placed a kiss on my lips and another on Tyra's forehead. "I'm not as patient as Michael. I'll go cook. We have another council meeting this afternoon. Mrs. Yates, the nanny, and Mrs. Sheehan will all be here to mind the girls. We need you there this time so we can vote to elect the council members."

Silently, I stared at Tyra. I knew Michael and Killian would win, but they had also insisted I nominate myself. "What if they don't want me there?"

"Nonsense." A booming voice came from behind Killian as Michael shoved past him to peek in on Nyla. "Nobody is angry with you. They all understand why you did what you did. You never thought I'd forgive you, but here I am." He held out his arms to prove his point.

Through a smile I said, "Fine. Let me get both girls fed, and I'll get ready. But we'll bring them with us. I'm sure Caltain and Flur would love to see them." It had taken Caltain time to come around, but our relationship was almost back to normal. Flur and I had never been better.

Michael picked up Nyla and gently rocked her awake. Her eyes cracked open with a tiny grin, and she reached out to grab the finger that had been brushing her cheek. He snuggled her and paced the room as I finished feeding Tyra and then swapped with me.

Both of them had been amazing fathers these past few

months, even with each other's daughters. Hearing about how the two of them and Michael's mother had cared for them in my —and Mrs. Yates's—absence only solidified my belief that my sacrifice would've been the right choice, but I was glad to be here with my family. We were an odd group, but it worked for us, and more shockingly, nobody seemed to mind.

Approaching the enclave, now home to the human and magical council, my body tensed. I peered through the permanently open gates to the courtyard where I had sacrificed my life for those I loved in another timeline. Crossing over the threshold felt like an immense achievement. Last time I had stood here, I could *feel* the darkness. But without the magical corruption, I could breathe. The air was fresh and woven with joy, and extra crisp with the light dusting of snow covering the ground.

I had considered moving elsewhere right after it happened, but Dracht was Michael and Killian's home. It needed them. But I didn't want to pay the price of my vengeance, despite my hope for redemption. Michael was the epitome of a do-gooder, and he had understood my reasons for what I had done. He was focused on justice, and he hadn't doled out any to me. Maybe there was hope.

The vote passed so fast, I didn't fully grasp what had happened. Killian, Michael, and I were all elected, as well as Caltain and Flur. One other witch and one other warlock had also been chosen, as well as the human coroner and the human woman who was the head of the market. Three sets of three.

Standing in the courtyard after the vote, mere feet from the doors that had once held in so much evil, we looked around. Remembering. Flur and Caltain arrived shortly after and joined us in our silent recollecting while others left the enclave.

Killian's head tilted to the side. "Do you hear that? It sounds like wings."

"I've never heard a bird make that much noise. Nothing is that big," Michael added.

A shadow filled the open area as everyone searched the skies. It didn't take long for our answer, as a giant creature landed right on the precipice of the enclave, overlooking all of us.

Killian spoke first. "Is that a…"

"They went extinct centuries ago," I said, glancing back and forth between my daughters, held snugly by their fathers.

"Are either of you going to fill me in on what that is?" Michael asked.

"It's a dragon," Caltain said. "Alder was obsessed with them when we first got together. He tried to discover where they disappeared to and why. He never found an answer."

The great beast was light blue, like the Dracht Bay, and covered in scales. Its tail was spiked with white horns to match the two protruding from above, midnight blue eyes that pierced straight through me. Its wings resembled a bat's, the webbing semitransparent and glittering with shifting colors of the rainbow. It was stunning.

Tyra giggled and cooed in the direction of the dragon, drawing our eyes. As we stared, her hand lit with fire, and she launched the most massive fireball I'd ever seen at the top of the mountain. The entire cliff face was engulfed in flames as my small child clapped with glee, the rest of us looking on in horror and awe.

The dragon smiled at her before it opened its mouth wider, spewing water all over the mountain to put out her flames. Streams cascaded down the face, bouncing off the base and coating us all in a warm mist. The snow it touched melted and sizzled.

"I thought it was here for the girls, but with Elias and Aiden gone, they should be safe. And I think it protected us?" Killian's eyebrows pinched as he continued staring at the large creature.

"Give me Tyra," I said.

"What, why? I can protect her," Killian said, pulling her closer and looking hurt.

"I know you can, but I think the dragon is her familiar. Let me hold her, and everyone else step back."

He finally relented, and the rest of the crowd took a few paces backward. The dragon launched itself off the precipice and landed in front of me. It took one look at Tyra and smiled, before turning its watery gaze to me. It was crying. I held Tyra out toward it, and it nuzzled her with the tip of its nose. Holding my magical daughter in one arm, I reached out to rub its snout with the other. It let me without a fuss, Tyla giggling throughout the whole process. Its scales were cool and smooth to the touch, almost like glass. The puffs of breath that came from its nostrils were warm, just like its cheerful eyes.

I heard footsteps behind me, and turned to see Killian, Michael, and Caltain creeping towards us, careful not to spook the creature.

"Its coloring is stunning, but odd. It's got a trail of red hair down its spine, and eyebrows. Almost like..." I trailed off.

"Alder," Caltain said. The reptile offered a single nod. Caltain's face went through a gamut of expressions, and I didn't blame him. Hope, then anger, then a moment of joy, then hurt. The man he loved reincarnated as a baby's familiar. The same man who had lied to him and aided Elias in his sadistic plan. A single tear slid down his cheek before he wiped it away roughly. "I can't do this right now," he whispered as he left.

"Alright, everyone. It seems this dragon is friendly and is my daughter's familiar. We're safe, everyone can head home." Killian and Flur ushered everyone out as Michael and I stood with the dragon and our girls.

"I thought you said large familiars were rare. Ranai is the biggest I've seen," Michael wondered aloud.

"The more powerful the witch or warlock, the larger the familiar." A fact that truly worried me. "Most witches don't come into their power until their teens. Tyra shouldn't be able to do this yet. I don't even have enough power to make a fire that size or throw it that far."

"That's unsettling," he said, holding Nyla with one arm and caressing Tyra's cheek with the other. "You're going to be a good witch like your mama though, aren't you?"

Killian returned, scooping Tyra from my arms and looking at her with awe-filled eyes. "You're a powerful little thing, aren't you? With a dragon familiar. My daughter. The Triumvirate would've been right if your mama hadn't taken them down instead."

"This isn't funny, Killian."

"It's a little funny. It takes the hearts of two men to calm your fiery temper, I don't envy the poor souls that try to calm hers," he said with a laugh.

I slapped his thigh, careful to avoid hitting our daughter.

"What do you say we go home and have some fun. The three of us this time?" Killian asked, sliding one arm from under Tyla to reach for Michael's ass.

Michael slapped it away with a growl. "Don't push it, warlock."

I snorted, putting myself between them and ushering them towards our carriage.

Our big, happy family inside, Roth at the reins, and a fox, wolf, and dragon following behind, we ambled all the way back to Leighis Chateau. Fortunately, the house was located below the cliff that had been my first solace in Dracht, which would now be home to a perching dragon.

While my men took our girls inside, I looked up at the grassy bank now occupied by the scaly beast. The coating of snow did nothing to stop the tall grasses from swaying. Ranai sat down next to me as I took in the spot where I had sat each morning and plotted the demise of this town. Now I was in charge of it, the second most powerful witch in the world. Behind only my daughter. The sound of laughter from inside Leighis Chateau flooded the cold winter air along with the smell of the bread Mrs. Yates was baking. I had everything I ever wanted and then some. "We did it, girl. We made them pay."

Want More?

Read more about Anna, Killian, and Michael in book 2 of the Hearts Bound by Dust series, coming March 3rd, 2026.

Pre-order now!

Also by Catie O'Neill

Romantasy Novels

Touch of Clandestiny

Hearts Bound by Dust, A Witchy Mystery Series:

Till Dust Do Us Part

To Have and To Hex (Pre-Order Now!)

To Love and to Parish (Coming Fall 2026)

Sci-Fi Romance Novels

Love and Other Alien Concepts

Acknowledgments

For the first time in my writing career, I actually came up with this title myself. But I do have to thank my corgi Kieran for being the inspiration and for allowing me to yell bizarre things at him on a constant basis.

I really have to thank my mother for this one too. Growing up, I wished I were a witch, and it's fair to say I was obsessed with learning about them. My mother was also very fond of witches, and as a child, I believed she was one. She genuinely would joke that I must've been one in a past life because of my fear of fire (burned at the stake) and my dislike of things tight around my neck (hung for sorcery).

I'm very grateful to have found my people in the solid team that helped me through this effort. Especially my developmental editor, AJ. You've been along for the ride on all my books, and every single one of them was immensely improved by your keen eye and brilliant input. Your cheerleader comments along the way have been the fuel to my fire (see what I did there), and you've never let it burn out. It's been an honor to read your work and learn from it, and to get your feedback to improve my descriptions and plot. It's been an absolute honor to be your friend, and I'd be totally and utterly lost without you.

My dear BFF and critique partner Jude, you have such a knack for understanding my voice and catching my looming plot holes, and I'm forever grateful for that. Every brainstorming session has been so precious to me, and you've become family I never want to be without. You've been with me through it all, and I wouldn't want it any other way.

To my favorite ARC reader turned beta reader, Audrie, I'm so thrilled you asked to read this one for me. Your hilarious reactions gave me life through my first two books, and having them during the early stages of this one was thrilling. You're stuck reading for me forever now. Thank you for catching all my silly inconsistencies and for helping me improve dust so much. You're amazing.

To my lovely editors, Monica and Maria, I'm so grateful to have you on my side. Your feedback is always so educational and professional, and I'm so thankful to have found you both. I promise I'll work on not using so many adjectives, but I'm still not eating the broccoli stems.

To my author bestie Hope, thank you so much for not only proofreading and formatting all of my books, but for always being such a wealth of information and a fantastic resource. I've had so much fun attending events with you, and I'm so grateful for our friendship.

Growing up in upstate New York, I rarely saw females in STEM fields. While earning my B.S. in Mechanical Engineering from Rensselaer Polytechnic Institute, I was often the only woman in the room. Those experiences now fuel my stories, featuring fierce female protagonists who aren't afraid to prove their worth in male-dominated spaces. Because let's face it—we've all had that moment when someone assumed we were the secretary instead of the engineer in charge.

When I'm not building worlds or crunching numbers in my infamous spreadsheets (yes, I'm that kind of organized), you'll find me hiking with my beloved Corgi, Kieran (named after the

FBAA character—fellow book lovers, you know who I mean!). My other passions include experimental cooking (my crispy smashed potatoes are legendary) and tending to my vegetable garden.

Fair warning: My characters share my enthusiasm for good food and great coffee!

As an author and a STEMinist, I believe in transparency and supporting others on their journey. Whether it's demystifying sci-fi for newcomers or sharing insights about the indie publishing process, I'm here to break down barriers. My stories blend accessible sci-fi with fantasy, featuring relatable heroines who combine technical brilliance with real-world awkwardness (internal banter included!).

I currently reside in upstate New York with Kieran, who insists on proofreading all my manuscripts with his approval.

Love and Other Alien Concepts (a sci-fi romance) was my debut novel. My second book, *Touch of Clandestiny* was the first in my dip into Romantasy. This witchy murder mystery romance is my third book. I'm currently plotting and drafting the rest of the series and a secret collab project.

You can follow me on
    Instagram: @catiereadsandwrites
    Website: https://catie1024.wixsite.com/catieoneillauthor
    Goodreads/Amazon: Catie O'Neill

www.ingramcontent.com/pod-product-compliance
Lightning Source LLC
Chambersburg PA
CBHW032240310726
48973CB00008B/2224